's for your Support!

Dianna Dixon

Releasing Kaleb

By Dianna Dixon

Published by Reimann Books

Published March 2011

1st edition

ISBN 978-0-9820941-6-7

Printed in the U.S.A.

Releasing Kaleb

By: Dianna Dixon

Dedicated to: My husband for all of his support and love! To God, for blessing me with this talent and desire to write and to my son just because I love you!

Supporting scripture:

Psalms 91:11 For he will command his angels concerning you to guard you in all of your ways.

ONE

The eyes loomed above like red stars out of the darkness. They shone above Walkerton in the spirit realm announcing to all those who glanced its way, who's town this was. They blocked all light from entering while the Angels sat back and awaited a day when Walkerton would become more than a beacon of self to all its indwellers. A day when love would grow there again. A day when they would once again be allowed into its gates on the wings of the saint's praise, by the hands of the Almighty, as answers to their prayers.

//

Through the rearview she gazed one last time at the place she once called home, all she saw left was misery and regret. Her eyes gazed forward again towards the road, hoping this asphalt with painted lines and potholes would take her somewhere the memories couldn't follow. Somewhere on the map that her regret could find. Somewhere she could start a brand new life.

Her foot pressed hard against the gas pedal, the car sputtered from the sudden injection of fuel. Metros weren't meant for speed and this one particularly was lucky to run at all. The odometer sat at just over a hundred and fifty thousand and the engine sounded as if it had taken every one of those miles hard. The belt squeaked as it turned over and over and the engine clanked every few minuets, something that was a mystery to the dealer. Still she had gotten a decent deal on it and was gone before anyone in town could blink.

Kayla Holmes sat behind the wheel blaring music to drown out her own thoughts and the noise of the engine. Her shoulder length straight brown hair flung around in the wind as she drove. She had a delicate frame with hips that were bigger than she liked but who doesn't have something about them that they don't like she would always tell herself. Her face was oval shaped and her eyes took a very slight turn upwards. She always wondered who she had inherited that from. She knew the hazel eyes had been from her mother but no one in the family had the tilt of the eyes like she did. It was a trait that made her seem mysterious, a trait that made all kinds of men look her way. The nine thousand eighty two dollars next to her in a knapsack was proof of that. She despised every cent of it, her only hope was that some of it could buy her back her dignity and self respect!

The sun rose high in the sky, the peak of the noon summer heat and humidity saturated the air. Kayla had purchased the car as is and was just now figuring out the flaws it obtained. It was becoming apparent why it had sat on the dealers lot for so long. The air conditioning was what he had called two sixty. She vaguely heard him say, she was just trying to get out of there. Now she realized what he had meant. You have to have two windows down and drive sixty miles and hour to get cool. The pleather seats stuck to the back of her legs making the fabric of her jeans become wet with the sweat that built up from the lack of airflow between surfaces. She was getting a headache from the heat but she didn't want to stop now, not till the next town over. Not till she was sure she wouldn't run into anyone. Kinston was the next town, she planned to stop there and get supplies for her trip, so she drove on.

//

"Mr. Summers this is so great!" little Madison Thomas beamed at her youth pastor. Her voice echoed along the hall of glass and tile. She stared wide eyed at the floor to ceiling tank of fish, nurse sharks and shipwreck in front of her. This was the first time most of these kids had come to the aquarium. He loved sharing this experience with them.

"Yeah? What's your favorite part?" he asked

"umm … the sharks!"

"Mines the eels!" he said putting his hands together and

slithering them towards her like an eel. She giggled, her smile made his job worth the wile. He loved kids. Keith put that thought behind him, that was the last thing he needed to think about today.
"Ok, now run along with your group or you'll miss the undersea video you've been waiting for all day!"
"OH YEAH!" She exclaimed running up to the rear of her group. All of the volunteers had taken the kids to different places in groups and now he found himself alone, staring at his reflection in the glass. The day had turned out just as he had planned. The kids were learning, laughing, and excited as they did. There was only one more thing he could have asked for, but again he pushed the thought away.

Keith, when he stood up straight was just about six feet tall, he had broad shoulders and a slightly pronounced jaw. His face most of the time wore a serious frown but his eyes were full of softness and warmth. They were brown at a glance but apoun a second glance they told all of his secrets. He hated that trait. He let very few people look him in the eye for very long. He was strong but his frame was on the small side, however it fit him. He didn't look skinny or built, he was just right. About a month ago Keith had come back from his year of leave, as youth pastor of Rosewood Falls community church. He hadn't planned on being gone a year but he just couldn't face things until now. He was still having a hard time but he was determined to do a good job, the kids had gone long enough without a youth program. They needed him and it was nice to be needed again.

//

It had been hours since she had stopped in Kinston. She was fatigued, thirsty, hungry and completely lost. She was grateful to be lost. The more lost she found herself the harder it would be to get back to the place she wanted to forget. Even though the deep ache in her stomach was a constant reminder of why she was running, never the less, the harder it would be to get back to Walkerton. The harder it would be for anyone to find her. With that thought she took the next exit and found a restroom, dinner and gas for the next stretch of driving. She felt much better now that she had moved around some and the Tylenol had time to circulate. The pleather seat had dried and she hopped back in ready for it to start all over.

//

How spectacular the site would have been, could we have seen in the spirit realm. A blaze, a giant ball of fire descended, followed quickly by two others. The glorious blaze dimmed as it reached the earth to reveal the Host's, the Chosen Ones. Oren, the great warrior set his feet apoun the ground, His four beautiful white wings set to rest behind him. He had a face that spoke of warning but eyes that assured peace! His locks of blonde fell to his shoulders, a sash of purple lay across his chest over his robe of white and a double-edged sword sat at his right hip. Laurence another warrior touched down next to Oren. His eyes wore deep concern, He was sent on missions where despair was involved. His short brown hair fell just above his ears. His sash was of royal blue and just as Oren, his double-edged sword sat at his right hip. Wesley came just behind them. This warrior's hair was red as fire and his hazel eyes were fierce. His four wings unfurled at his sides, he had his right hand on his sword ready for battle. Ready to fight for the saints the Almighty had sent him to defend. "At ease!" Oren called to him and he eased his hand to his side. "She has not yet arrived!" he said. The warriors all stood at ease awaiting their assignments arrival.

//

Highway 101 was slammed with rush hour traffic. Everyone had been slowed to almost stopping by an accident. Random honking could be heard along with the squealing of tires from drivers at the back of the line who didn't expect to be stopping. Kayla's fatigued had returned somewhere between the last two exits that had slowly drudged by. She ached inside and the stress of the drive was sinking into her soul it seemed, even the metro sounded agitated. She had to get off this freeway. Had to! Kayla sat with her blinker on waiting for some kind soul to let her in, five minuets passed like that. Apparently, no one nice drove on freeways. If no one let her in soon she would miss the next exit, she reeeaaally didn't want to miss the next exit. Kayla almost caused a wreck but looking back it was worth it. She put her front end into the next lane over in front of the next car who blared his horn at her. She looked at him with a smile and shrugged her shoulders. *shoulda let me in!*, she thought. The cars ahead inched and so did she, further and further into the lane and then finally freedom. She was on the exit moving faster than she could dream. The air that was stagnant a moment before was now blowing around her whisping through her hair and cooling off her skin. She could hear one more loud honk from the driver she had cut off but she ignored it. He was still stuck in traffic and she was free!

TWO

Fallen Ones followed closely behind Kayla. They had been close to her as if part of her flesh for quite some time now. They, in appearance, looked much like the Host's. They once were Host's but they had chosen to follow Lucifer. To fall with him and fight against the Almighty! Darkness had become part of them now. Their wings that once shone brightly now were gray and blackness seeped between and underneath each feather. Their robes dulled of the glory they once were covered in and faded with the absence of the Almighty. Their eyes had become the color of tar. When they spoke darkness flowed out of their mouths like curling smoke. Still once being a Host they could mock one and the sons of man had a hard time deciphering the difference between them. Only those close to the Almighty had a chance at it. Drathon, one prized by Lucifer for his ability to deceive and confuse hovered over her like a cloud. Grafton the tormentor was directly behind him. The two together had been playing with her mind for at least a month, ever since she started fighting to change her life. Fighting to get away. Each time they played with her it got easier for them, she seemed to fight it less or not know how to fight it. They had gotten into her dreams and thoughts. Lucifer the lord of the fallen was proud of their progress. He and all his warriors knew that until the humans called apoun the Most High that they could continue to torment them.

//

Exit 12 was a scenic route through Rosewood Falls. Kayla found herself on a highway to another world. She felt like she was driving into the set of an old movie when color films had just come out. The highway was arched over with trees and the mailbox posts and houses were covered in ivy vines. *Beautiful,* she thought. She smiled a little, she couldn't help it this place was so adorable. Just ahead past a clearing of trees kids were playing soccer in a field, and others were sitting on blankets watching or reading and listening to their mp3 players. Across the street from that was a row of houses, it seemed like the perfect place to raise a family. It was a place every mother could wish to raise her children. They could look out the window wile they cooked or cleaned and know their kids were safe.

'Bbbbeeeeepppppp' The car behind Kayla was honking at her. She jolted from daydream only to realize she had slowed to a mere ten miles an hour. She pressed the gas pedal hard trying to speed up quickly. The car sputtered under the injection of fuel but did eventually accelerate. Kayla raised a hand to the car in apology. *What a place!* She thought!

A red light was all that held her back now from downtown. There had to be a hotel somewhere. She had spent the entire day driving and was exhausted. Summer was always tricky with its late sunsets, it was almost eight thirty and the sun was still barely peeking its head over the horizon not wanting to call it a day. Kayla went through a few more lights until finally a bed and breakfast came into view. The place was a quaint old three story home that someone had fixed up and turned in to an inn. The home was painted blue with white shutters and it had a hand painted vacancy sign hanging out front. The porch circled the whole house and the owner had placed white rockers out front, three on each side of the door. Small handmade tables sat next to each rocker as a holder for a drink or a book. Kayla pulled in and the gravel clinked against the bottom of the car. It crunched under her shoes as she stepped out making her unsteady for a moment. Once she was steady on the rocks, she grabbed her knapsack and suitcase and was on her way in.

The small bell on the door clinked as she went inside. The foyer was welcoming, done mostly in cherry hardwood. The whole place smelled of cinnamon or vanilla, maybe both, Kayla couldn't tell but she liked whatever it was. Directly in front of her was a large reception desk made of the same cherry colored wood as the floors, to the left were two closed French doors and directly behind the reception desk sat a flight of stairs whose steps and banisters were all made of the same beautiful cherry wood that adorned the whole foyer. The walls were white but it gave a perfect contrast of color. No one was at the desk; Kayla took a few steps in. "Hello?" She called, taking another step.

"Just a minuet!" came a stifled voice from behind the French doors.

"Ok" she called back. A few moments later a short blonde haired woman came out and greeted her. She was about five three and had light blue eyes. Her hair was long and fell to the middle of her back in straight golden strands. She was thin and graceful as she walked to the desk. "Hi, how can I help you?"

"Um… I need a room please."

"Ok, for how long?"

"Probably about a month!" Kayla said.

"Oh…. Great! It's five hundred a month; I'll need a driver's license and a credit card to get started." Kayla opened her wallet and looked inside. She knew she didn't have a credit card but she was trying to buy time so she could think of a way out of having to show one. She handed over her driver's license and the girl began typing. "Ok Mrs. Holmes I just need your credit card now." "Um… actually I don't have one but I can pay in advance in cash!" Kayla smiled a shy smile at the girl hoping it would work. Jennifer Payton the girl behind the desk and the owner of the place was always hesitant about renting without a card but being in such need of business she had come up with ways around the security of a credit card number.

" Alright, I will need an extra month in advance as a deposit, should there be no damages apaun your departure the cash will be given back to you in full."

" No problem." Kayla handed the girl one thousand dollars in hundreds and fifties.

"Ok Miss. Holmes I'll see you to your room."
"You can call me Kayla?"
"Ok Kayla, its right this way!"

//

"She is here!" Oren said aloud. In the realm they flew up gracefully alternating their sets of wings as they flew, following the calling of the Almighty that spoke to their hearts. Above the bed and breakfast they felt his urgent tug. They also sensed the presence of the Fallen ones. Under the protective shield of the Almighty they descended into the inn invisible to all but the other Hosts.

The Fallen ones stayed close to Kayla but at the moment they left her alone. They were waiting for an opportune moment, a time when she was venerable. A time when their manipulation could be put to full use. A time when they could use their skills to the fullest to possess her thoughts, dreams and on good days her actions.

//

"Here's your key and I'm Jenn if you need anything just call zero on the phone!"
"Thanks!"
"Your welcome!" Jenn walked back down the stairs and Kayla opened the door. She found the room very inviting. The walls were baby blue with white molding. The floors were cherry wood as the rest of the inn and four diamond mirrors graced the far wall. The window was decorated with two navy blue panel curtains, one pushed to each side and the bed was covered with a handmade quilt that reminded her oh so much of her Granny! Kayla closed the door behind her and sat her suitcase down on the recliner that was in the corner by a lamp. Now she lay on her back on the bed staring at the ceiling trying to ignore the pain in her abdomen and heart running her hand over the stitch work of the quilt remembering one of her favorite memories…. The sun was just above the horizon. It was bright orange and it flooded the whole sky with shades of

pink. Kayla sat on the porch swing with Granny in the cool of a spring dusk sipping lemonade covered in one of Granny's quilts. She sipped the lemonade and the ice sent chills down her spine as it touched her two front teeth. "Brrrrrrrrrr" she said. Granny laughed at her.

"I told you it was too chilly for lemonade didn't I?"

"Yeah but yours is just so good!" Granny laughed again and then covered Kayla's arms with the quilt, putting her lemonade glass on the window ledge. Polka, Granny's cat jumped up and curled in a ball on Kayla's lap wile Granny just hummed. They swung back and forth and Kayla remembered hearing the clinking of the chain but that was it. She figured she must have fallen asleep because the memory went dark after that.

THREE

The room was lit by one small lamp. Jacob Holmes sat in his tan wingback chair with his hands clasped together just staring. He was paralyzed by his thoughts, disgusted with them but he didn't fight them. He wasn't sure he wanted to, though they were thoughts a man of God should not think. '*She is such a disgrace! ....how could she have done this to me? .... To my reputation!*' His mind was racing as Diesaric whispered into his ear. He was a small demon but he was very practiced at breeding hate. The pastor had let his guard fall. He had let his circumstances get the best of him and that's how this Fallen one had slipped in. Diesaric massaged Jacob's head and spoke in waves to him. He stood up and paced in his office, the heels of his dress shoes clicked as he stepped against the hardwood. As hard as he tried he couldn't stop the thoughts. '*She degraded you! Your family!....*' The man of God had lost his will power, his fight and his prayer life. He paced just like he remembered doing the night his wife bore her. He remembered how happy he was to hear her cry and hold her in his arms, now he wasn't so sure he was glad he had brought her into this world. His heart sank with the thought, how could he have thought that? Diesaric continued speaking the thoughts at him and slowly the pastor began to allow them.

//

The airbrake spat and sputtered one last time as the bus came to its final resting spot. Keith pulled into the church parking lot. All the kids had a blast and were home safely; now at nearly midnight it was his turn. He considered only for a moment actually driving home but it was almost quicker walking since he only lived three houses down.

The night air was cool and made his cheeks cold as the wind blew his direction. He welcomed it. It made him feel something, something normal, something constant, something real. As he ascended the two cement steps that led to his front door he began to follow his normal routine. Unlock door, walk in and close door, put keys on nightstand in the dark, walk past where her picture usto be in the dark, walk past the room in the dark and go straight to bed. Doing this he could, for the most part, ignore the looming memories that hung in corners and danced around each room in hologram form illuminated by his mind when he allowed them to play out. He knew all to well however that memories, however badly you wanted to forget them, still found their way into your dreams. He hoped tonight he was too tired to dream.

//

Darkness surrounded Kayla. Where was she? Fear gripped her heart, it was racing she could feel the pound of it against her chest and hear its beats in her ears. She could see a faint light up ahead, she ascended the hill that blocked it. It was a tall street lamp that lit one corner of a vast graveyard. Kayla raised a hand to shield the light. Down the hill about ten feet away sat a small gravestone, with the light shielded she could just make out the name on it. KALEB was deeply imprinted into the stone, written in black against the gray background. " Kaleb!!!!!!" she called out as she ran quickly down the hill on her heels, trying not to fall. She fell at the grave and began digging. "Kaleb! No! Kaleb!" she called out as she dug with her hands. Finally she reached him. Opening the box that held his tiny body she reached in and cradled the infant to her chest. There on her knees she began rocking back and forth with him. "My Kaleb." she whispered repetitively, rubbing his head as she rocked him. The Fallen ones loved how easily she was manipulated when she slept!

Rinnnnnngggg…… *Riiiinnnnnnngggggg….*
Kayla jolted awake with a deep breath in. She found herself on far side of bed on her knees cradling a porcelain doll to her chest! "Not again!" She said as she wondered where the doll came from and who the heck was calling her…here? *….RRRiiiiiiinnnngggg…..* She had to answer it; she didn't

want to wake anyone. She got up from her knees and answered the phone, still holding the doll. "Hello?"

"Kayla!"

"Yes"

"It's' Jenn. What's with all the noise?"

"Uh…. Sorry! Sometimes I have nightmares and talk in my sleep!"

"There was yelling is everything ok?"

"Yeah, that was me too! I'm sorry I'll try to keep it down.

"Ok well, goodnight!"

"What are you still doing here? Kayla blurted out not thinking.

"I live here in a separated area upstairs.

"Oh! … Ok… Well, sorry again about the noise!" Kayla said.

"Alright!" They both hung up their receivers. Kayla held the doll close to her chest and lay down on her side on the bed. Her shirt was soaked with milk but she didn't care enough to change, her stomach ached so deeply she couldn't tell where the pain stopped anymore.

The Host's watched as the Fallen ones tormented her, as they manipulated her mind. To their dismay that was all they could do. Until she called out his name, the name of the Most High himself all they could do was wait and make sure the fallen ones obeyed the laws of the realm. They couldn't cross the boundaries that separated flesh from spirit. They couldn't make contact with her physically, that boundary had been set by the Most High since the days of old.

//

Drathon could not see the Host's but he could feel them. "The Most High has sent warriors!" as he spoke hatred pored out of his mouth with rolls of sulfurous smoke!

"Yes! I can feel them! Their presence is sickening!" Grafton hissed back.

"We must prevent her from calling out to him! She must not call on the Most High or utter his name from her lips!"

Drathon grabbed Grafton by the neck. "She must not!" he reiterated.

"She must not" Grafton agreed after Drathon released his neck.

//

Joshua Westbrook slowly turned the knob. He walked into the room slowly and aimed the flashlight low. In the arm that did not hold the flashlight he held a dead raccoon. He was only ten and barely stood at four foot five but he was determined to do the right thing, and a boy with determination can do anything, he told himself. It was eleven forty five and he had reach the retort oven before midnight. The room was large enough to echo should he bump anything or drop the flashlight so he stepped slowly and moved cautiously through the room. Now at the front of the oven he placed the raccoon and flashlight on the floor and pulled open the steel door. It was heavy and he had to leverage himself with his legs and pull back on it with his whole body!

The oven smelled of charcoal and formaldehyde, it made him gag as he reach in for what he came for. The small infant lay inside. Joshua pulled him out and threw in the raccoon in his place. No one would notice, for some reason they wanted to get rid of him. For some reason they wanted no one remember him or know that he ever lived, but he would do right by him if no one else would. Joshua closed the oven and snuck back out. Tomorrow in daylight he would bury her son.

//

The house was harder to deal with in the daylight. Darkness couldn't hide the memories and shield the door from view. Keith tried everyday to move on, but deep within his heart he wasn't sure he wanted to. If he remembered, if he hurt, then what he had was still real. Besides what else was there to live for? Her memory served him well when it didn't disable him, it made him feel like he was still alive. However mornings weren't the time to let those memories set up in the harbor of his heart. So instead of sitting at his kitchen table and sitting in the empty quiet house staring at the bedroom door that was in direct view, he went and had breakfast at the inn. He knew one day he would have to face it, to open the door and see what was inside, but after this long already what's another day or week or so, he told himself as he grabbed his keys and was off.

//

Kayla awoke to the smell of an array of breakfast foods. Even from her room she could smell the eggs, pancakes and sausage. The aroma's reminded her of Saturday mornings at Granny's house. She still lay in the same position as she had fallen asleep in last night and had the doll clutched to her chest. She opened her eyes and just laid still for a minuet, remembering the dream from the night before. She held the doll away from her and looked it over. '*How did you get in here?*' she wondered '*who do you belong to?*' Kayla sat up and laid the doll on the bed next to her. She could feel that her shirt was dried and stuck to her skin. She wasn't sure what to do, if she pulled it off the stimulation would awake the sleeping giant again, she had no choice, she'd have to shower with it on until the water allowed it to come off easily. She wished it would stop. Every time she dreamt of him she would wake up covered in milk. Like her body still fought for him and didn't want to let him go. The pain that engulfed her abdomen was enough and she wished these constant reminders of him would stop and just leave her memories to do the haunting.

The warm water of the shower felt wonderful as it flowed through her hair and even better down her back when she was able to take off the shirt. It was small things like this hot shower that made her feel alive again. She washed up and then just stood there in the flow of the water letting the heat surround her. She stood there till it ran cold and then stepped out into the steam filled bathroom. She was chilled now and had Goosebumps running down her spine but it was worth it. The heat had released the sleeping giant and had run it dry for now and she was grateful for that. If she had the courage, she could fill the prescription the doctor had given her but she was too embarrassed. What would people think she did? What would they assume and label her as? Instead in her wallet was a folded up prescription she was too embarrassed to fill. She had just wanted to get away from everyone and anyone that had anything to do with it.

Kayla walked down the stairs with the doll in hand. She could hear all kinds of talking and laughing from the room behind the French doors she figured that had to be the breakfast room. Her assumption was correct but she hadn't remembered seeing so many guests' cars here last night. Jenn sat at a table with a very handsome man. He was tall dark and very attractive. Kayla walked over to them, she wanted to hand over this doll and be done with it.

"Jenn?" she said from behind her. She turned around and Keith looked up.

"Oh Kayla good morning!"

"Good morning!" she replied, then she met the gaze of the man she sat with. His eyes were dark and soft. She couldn't help but blush a little. Keith could see the blush in her cheeks. She was beautiful. Really beautiful! He thought. Jenn eyed between the two, she hadn't seen Keith look at a woman that way in a long time, and the blush in Kayla's cheeks, well it was just adorable.

"Kayla this is Keith!" she said. Neither of them looked at her.

"Keith this is Kayla!" Again neither looked at her. Instead, Keith extended a hand out to her. "Hello!" he said.

"Hi" Kayla responded as she reached out the doll that had been cradled under her arm fell to the ground. Keith's trance ended with the sight of it. Flooding his memories again with her. How could this beautiful woman have sparked all of his memories alive again in just a second? "Oh! Yeah Jenn I found this in my room, I figured you might know who it belongs to!" As she spoke, she bent down to pick it up and handed it to Jenn. Keith's eyes remained on it the whole time. He felt like he was going to throw up! Like this beautiful girl had just punched him right in his gut. His stomach was twisting into knots.

"Excuse me!" Keith got up and exited the room. He paced in the foyer only for a moment. All he could think to do was run. Run away as fast as he could. He had gotten really good at that, so he bolted out the front door.

"I'm sorry! Did I do something wrong?" Kayla asked.

"No um… He's just late for a meeting." Jenn knew that she sounded like she was making it up, but truthfully she was.

"Oh"

"Hey why don't you have breakfast and I'll see if I can't find out who this belongs to."

"Alright"

"Thanks for bringing it down!"

"Sure… hey who are all these people?"

"Oh they live here in town, they come and eat here and in turn I shop at their places and we all keep eachother going! Small town ya know?"

"That's nice!"

"We think so! Now go have some breakfast!"

"I think I will, thank you!" Kayla turned to the buffet and Jenn left to find the owner of the doll.

FOUR

Alice Cartwright sat in her room in the Walkerton minimal assistance group home. She was relatively young but since the death of her husband and the loss of her sons she had decided to live there. There was company, and she didn't have to do dishes or laundry. She liked it for the most part. She had a few close friends and had gotten to know the staff by name. It was comfortable and easy to live there. The house where her and her husband made their memories she sold. Long before that, her son had moved away, she thought she was doing well by him, sending him to boarding school far away, but she had only given him wings that made him never desire to land home. He despised her for sending him away and when he received news of his fathers passing he never wanted to come home again. He finished his fancy schooling and then moved away.

She remembered the time she tried patch things up with him, the time she tried to make amends. It made her cry thinking about it, how she ruined his life once again, how she truly had no family now, thanks to herself and her husband's mistake. Today she sat knitting a tiny blue sweater. It was her way of mouring the grandson she would never have. The son of her sons that would never breathe, laugh, or call her nanna, and when she was finished she put the tiny sweater in a box in her closet and pretended her heart wasn't broken. Pretended she didn't hate herself for the things she didn't do and the other things she did.

//

Keith finally stopped running. He had made it up the street and one block further to the park. He was out of breath and nauseated. He eased himself down onto the edge of the sidewalk and placed his head in his hands. There were kids laughing and playing behind him. He was tormented by it. It felt as if they were laughing at him, at his weakness. At his

inability to deal with his memories. Jenn drove slowly along the road looking both ways hoping to find him. When she did she eased the car to the curb and ran to him. "Keith!" she called out. He didn't look up. She sat next to him on the sidewalk. "I'm so sorry! I didn't know it was up there!" there was silence for atleast a minuet. She didn't know what else she could say.
"He's never going to laugh! He's never going to smile or breathe! She's never going to again!" He began to cry and the taste of his tears got on his tounge as they ran down his cheeks and then onto his lips. He wiped his face. "Do these mom's know what a blessing they have?" he pointed behind him.
"I hope so! But Keith …. You have to know that God has them! God is holding them wile you can't and you have to let them go! She would want you to keep living! For you to laugh and smile for her! That's how she would want you to keep her memory alive! By living! By loving and by moving on!"
"I know….." He said looking her dead in her blue eyes. "But It's my fault Jenn!…it's my fault! I shouldn't have left!" Jenn hugged him and he yelled into her shoulder. "It's my fault!" It wasn't anything new she was hearing. He had said it a million times and probally would say it a million more times until his healing was at its end. Though she didn't know how that could happen if he didn't let anyone help him. If he didn't let himself grieve properly instead of having random outbursts like this, but everyone had already tried. She tried, Pastor tried, no one could get him to go into the bedroom and face it. Until he did, she knew he would constantly be haunted by them!

//

The Host's gathered in the park. "Wesley!" Oren spoke
"Yes sir?"
"I will need you to search the town for allies! I fear this will only get worse before it gets better! The Fallen ones have a hold on her and we will need more Hosts and human prayers

to defeat his stonghold on her!"
"On it sir!" he unfurled his wings. "Praise the Almighty!"
"Praise the Almighty!" they all responded to him and he was off.
"Laurence!"
"Sir?"
"We need to find out where she picked up those Fallen ones, can you find out where she came from?"
"Yes sir!"
"Show yourself only if absolutely necessary!" Laurence nodded and unfurled his wings ready to fly!
"Praise the Lord!"
"Praise the Lord!" he responded back and then Laurence was off! Oren went to Kayla's side. Where he would stay awaiting word from the Almighty, awaiting commands from the King of Kings!

//

Kayla sat at the breakfast table and watched as the people began to clear out! She sipped at her coffee and pushed the last bits of food around her plate with her fork. She wasn't sure what to do now. She hadn't had so much freedom in a long time. She could go anywhere and do whatever she felt like, not that she felt that great but the possibility was there! She stood up from the table and went into the foyer. There was a table with brochures Kayla searched them waiting for something to pop out at her. Finally one did. It was a shopping development that was built around a small lake named Brooklyn Lake. There were clothes stores, shoe stores, small retail stores and restaurants, coffee shops and even a movie theatre that all surrounded this lake. Kayla went upstairs, grabbed some cash and her keys and was on her way. A whole day all her own, excitement filled her veins as she jumped into her car, a whole day.

//

Keith and Jenn finally stood up. He had quit sobbing and the muscles in his stomach relaxed, only his ego was harmed now, though this wasn't the first time he had cried in front of her he still felt weak doing it. "I'm sorry!"
"I know! You said that the last three times!"
"Yeah" Keith agreed with her solemnly. They walked to her car slowly in short strides.
"Hey! How about you go and visit her!" Jenn looked at him. "I'll drive you back to your car!" Keith nodded.
"I think I need to! It helps to have a place to go where I can talk to her… I don't go enough…It's harder if I do…it takes me off of auto pilot and auto pilot is how I go on!" He admitted regretfully.
"I know! But hey…" she looked at him until he met her gaze. "She wouldn't want that either!" he looked away from her and at the pavement.
"I know!" She patted him on the back. She wanted to help him so desperately.

//

The lake was everything that it had promised. There was a certain magic to it. Kayla had shopped for a while and found some clothes. She treated herself to a trim and eyebrow waxing. She felt more alive today than she had in a long time. She felt like she wanted to live. Now in the park she walked the bridge that went the full length of the lake and took you to the other side where, more Benches and open grass were. The bridge was constructed of cement and then covered with white stucco. The sides were made up of gothic designs that were housed in by the top and bottom supports. It was one of thoes bridges that could be used for a romantic movie scene or a calendar picture. Halfway to the top kalya stopped by the duck feeder. She dug in her pocket and pulled out a quarter. The ducks came instantly at the clicking sound of the knob turning. She leaned slightly over the edge and threw in one piece at a time. The ducks quacked at her and their green heads shined in the sun. The water went into ripples by where they kicked their feet and the sun caught on the upside of thoes ripples. She rested her elbows on the edge of the top support rail of the bridge and bent one knee as she watched the ducks beg.

//

The sun warmed Keith's back. He sat leaned foreward with his elbows on his knees, his hands clasped and his chin resting on them. For now, he sat with his eyes closed. His first meeting of the day was over and he didn't have another for hours, so he did as his friend suggested and came to see her. The bench by the lake was his favorite place to sit. He had brought her here wile she was alive and he knew that this is were she would want to rest. Her ashes were spred over the lake and he felt like everything living in the lake was more alive because of that. He opened his eyes and scanned the length of the bridge. There she was. The beautiful girl that had awoke his emotions this morning. She was smiling looking down at group of ducks. She had her hair pulled back into a ponytail but a few strands of it fell out and rested at the frame of her cheek. He watched as she pushed them behind her ear and began to walk away down the length of the bridge. He was compelled by her, he couldn't help it. Even with his mind filled with thoughts of his late fiance he had to follow her, to talk to her. He walked quickly up the bridge catching up to her side. "Kayla? Is it?"
She looked over at the voice who called her name. The handsome man from breakfast stood by her side with an extended hand.
"Uh…yeah!" She said reaching out and shaking his hand. "Keith right?"
"Yes! Do you mind if I join you?"
"No. I was just trying to figure out what to do with the rest of my life… I mean day!"
"Well I think you had it right the first time!"

"Well what are you doing here?" She smiled at him. Her smile was amazing. He hadn't felt this way in a long time.
"Um… I just like to come here and think, and my favorite lunch bistro is just across the road."
"I see!" both were silent for a moment not knowing what to say.
"So…. What about you… What brought you to our town?" Keith asked
"Honestly… It was just a last minuet turn off of the interstate trying to avoid rush hour traffic. I liked it so much I decided to stay."
"Well I'm glad you like it! I love it here!"
"Really? Why?" she asked.
"Well everything I need is here. My favorite book store, my favorite places to eat, my church just a few paces from my home… it's just small enough to be homie and just large enough to have everything I need."
"Well then… maybe I will stay!" She said smiling and giggling a little. They had walked to the end of the bridge and stopped for a few before turning around. Kayla leaned her back on the side railing and Keith stood with his hands in his pockets. They made small talk for a few more minuets and then Kayla turned her back to him looking at the water. By her hand was a bronze two by three square plate that was bolted into the bridge. *In memory of Brooklyn! My love!"* was all it said. Even as they talked the name sparked memories in Kayla. It reminded her of her best friend. She had always called her Brooke for short. She ran her hand over the plate and smiled alittle at her memory. She missed her, wherever she was. She had left without a word when they were just about eighteen. Keith knew what she was standing by and he didn't want to see it. Not right now, not in front of her.
"So…." he said beginning to walk back "Have you had lunch?"
"No" She followed him turning away from the bronzed plate and walking back the other way next to his side.

"Want to? My treat!"
"Sure"

//

Allies, lots of them flew around Rosewood. In homes protecting saints and over the churches. Very few Fallen existed in the town. This was very good news Wesley knew that the Lord had picked this place for a reason. The saints that were close to the Almighty would sense the stirring in the realm. They would sense the need for prayer and through prayer and the power of the Almighty answering his children they could win this. Their battle was already closer to being won.

Over Rosewood community church a warrior stood at watch. He was Tall and muscular. His brown hair blew in the wind. At his side he held a gold battle-axe and a sash of red lay across his chest. His wings were unfurrled at his sides, all four of them out streached were as wide as the whole church. Wesley landed himself next to him. "Praise the Most High!" He said

"Praise the Most High!" He responded not looking away from his post!

"I am Wesley! Sent by the Most High to fight on behalf of a girl named Kayla! She is tormented by the Fallen ones and I am here to aleart all the Hosts of a possible battle." The Host took the rams horn at his side and blew it three times. Suddenly the sky around the church was filled with Host's. Then once again the angel guarding the church spoke.

"Host's..." he called out loudly. " A battle may soon fall on our town. The Fallen have atached themselves to a girl named Kayla. She is, like all humans are, a child of God! Will we stand and defend her?"

"Amen!" all the Host's called out in unison.

"Speak to the saints get them to pray! To call on the Almighty for his power so we can defeat the Fallen and win this daughter of man's soul!"

"Praise the Almighty!" they all said.
"Praise his name!" he responded and then with one more blow of the rams horn they all flew back to their posts. The large angel finally looked towards Wesley. "I am Agnosko, we will be ready!" he looked foreward again before he descended into the church where Pastor William Blake sat in his office preparing for Wednesdays service.

//

Finding the girl's place of origin was proving harder than first suspected. Laurence, at his own descretion decided to show himself. The Fallen were never far from her side and neither was Oren. With his help they would extract the information from Lucifer's agents. Drathon and Grafton were taken aback by the sudden burst of light, blinded by it. Out of requirement and for no other reason except that, they bowed at the feet of the Host's. They looked towards the ground because their eyes could no longer gaze at the splendor that they were once part of. Oren held his sword to Drathon's neck and Laurence held his to Graftons. "Speak of the girl's origin fallen one!"
"She has come out of Walkerton oh Chosen one of the Most High!" Drathon answered him in a sarcastic tone as if to mock him for staying behind with the Creator of the universe when they chose to follow Lucifer.
"Why do follow her?!"
"At the command of my lord Lucifer, Host!"
"For what reason oh lowly servant of the fallen Lucifer!" Oren pressed his sword closer to his neck as he mocked him back with both quickness to his tounge and sword.
"To torment and keep her reminded of the past!" just as suddenly as the light as appeared it dissapeared and the Fallen ones grabbed at their necks. Drathon looked at Grafton. His face twisted with his growing hatred. "We must keep control of her!"
"Yes sir! She mustn't be won over!"

"Her soul is Lucifer's! Not theirs, Not the Almighty's!!" Drathon grabbed Grafton's neck out of anger! "Never speak his name in my presence!"
"Yes master!" He agreed.

//

Inside Rosewood community church Pastor William Blake began to feel a stirring in the spirit. Above him in the realm Agnosko spoke to him. "Pray! Pray for a spiritual battle is afoot... call out to the Almighty...ask for his favor, for his guidance." Pastor's spirit felt heavy with urgency. He couldn't ignore it. He stood from his desk, walked down the hall and into the sanctuary. At the altar he paced back and forth. "Lord I don't know why, I don't know who but I feel like a battle is coming. I pray for your guidance Father...for you help. Whoever is battling against Satan, whoever is facing warfare of a spiritual kind Lord I ask that you be with them. That you strengthen them...that you comfort them. In Jesus name. The Pastor knew all to well the power of prayer and so within the minuet he was on the phone, calling the prayer team asking for their voices to call out to God.

FIVE

Joshua had gathered a measuring tape, a shovel, scraps of wood, nails and a hammer. He carried them in his book bag through the woods. He had a perfect place picked out. There was a large oak tree by the small stream that cut through the Walkerton forest behind his house. Once there he dumped out the bag and ran back home. He had a few more things to get. As he ran through the woods the leaves cracked under his feet and birds chirped. Every now and then he thought he heard the steps of another and it made him run faster. He was paranoid, scared to death that he would get caught. He couldn't fathom the things his father would do to him after what he had seen the other night. He had to hurry. It was lunchtime and that meant that only Mrs. Smith was working. She never took a lunch with the others. However Josh knew, she would, at about fifteen after, take a smoke break. Therefore, he had to get in and out during the three minuets it took her to smoke. He came out of the woods by the back of the funeral home. The back door had a keypad lock but he knew the numbers by watching his father. Two, eight, seven, six, nine. He typed and then hesitated only for about a second before he pressed enter. The knob unlocked and he was in.

The hall was quiet. Everyone was either out to lunch or in the break room down the other hall. He glanced at the clock, twelve eleven. In about three minuets she would drop her utensils, take off her gloves, wash her hands and go out the back door of the room. He stood outside the door of the room. He looked up and down the hall and listened intently. He heard no footsteps, no talking. After what seemed like an eternity, he heard her utensils drop and the snap of her gloves as they came off. As suspected the water began to run and soon after the squeak of the door opening and the slam of it closing. He turned the knob slowly and pushed the door open. Mrs. Smith was very precise he knew she would miss the formalin bottle and syringe he was taking but he also hoped she would chalk it up to old age. Quickly he grabbed the small brown glass bottle from the counter and pulled open the drawer where the syringes were kept.

"Son?" Joshua froze at the sound of his father's deep voice. "What the heck do you think you are doing?" He was silent; he searched his brain for an answer. "Well….."

"Uh…." Before he could speak the back door opened and Mrs. Smith came back in.

"What in heavens name is going on here?" She said though her old scratchy throat.

"Betty! I'll handle this!" Mr. Westbrooke put a hand out to her and then crossed both of his arms across his chest. "Now how about that answer son!"

"UH…. Well I found a dead raccoon and I wanted to bury him like you do. So I can practice for when I own the business!" Joshua's dad broke out into laughter. Betty didn't join in, she wasn't amused in the slightest.

"Mr. Westbrooke! How can you take this so lightly! He was stealing!" She fussed at him in her scratchy voice but that only made him laugh more. After a minuet or so of laughing Mr. Westbrooke composed himself.

"Betty, My son is just trying to be like his father. To do what he has seen me do! And as for you!" He pointed to his son who hadn't moved a muscle since he had been caught. "When you use that you need gloves and a mask ok!"

"Ok!" Josh finally began to breathe again. Now he grabbed a syringe and at his fathers order a pair of gloves and a facemask. "Thanks dad!" he hugged him and went out the back. Once the door shut behind him, he leaned against the side of the building and took a few deep breaths. There were so many ways that could have gone wrong.

Joshua put the supplies in his book bag that he had left by the back door and then ran to the shed. The infant lay inside a fleece blanket, he carried him in his arms and then ran out the door and back into the cover of the woods. Darting quickly around branches and over roots to get back to the oak tree. All the supplies lay where he had left them and he got to work. He put the infant in the book bag to hide him as he worked.

Joshua dug quickly flinging dirt behind him into a pile. He knew he was about three feet down at his waist so he had to go down three more. His arms ached and the muscles in his back were getting sore, but he had to go on. He had no idea how he would talk his way out of this as he did in the funeral home. He was about five feet now and the top of the hole was level with his head. *OK*, he thought, *one more foot!* He dug faster knowing he was almost there. At somewhere near six feet Joshua climbed out and began the second task on his list.

The scraps of wood didn't fit well together but he did his best nailing them into a box shape. He made a cover which he left off and then began the worst task. He opened the book bag and found the supplies. He put the mask over his nose and mouth, securing it with the elastic strap. He opened the formalin bottle and set it upright on the ground. The plastic wrapping over the syringe peeled back loudly as the glue that held the wrapper together released. He placed it in the bottle with the end sticking out and then grabbed the infant. He cried for him. He sobbed as he put the formalin inside his small body and then as he placed him in the box he made and covered it closed with the lid. Tears ran down his face and cheeks, the cotton of the mask soaked them up ad he nailed the lid closed. Finally he picked up the box and as gently as possible dropped it into the hole. Quickly now he pushed the dirt into the hole. Every few feet of dirt he would stop and jump in, compacting the dirt down. Finally the last bit of dirt went over the top and he stomped it down.

The last piece of scrap wood he carved into. He was sure his mom would have a name for him and he was also sure that any name that sounded as if it belonged to a boy would cause alarm in any passerby's, so he simply put raccoon. That's what he told his father he was burring anyway. Now he sat by the tree and watched the stream. He promised one day, no matter how long from now it was, he would find her, this infants mom and tell her what they did. He would give her back what they took away on a summer night in Walkerton's crematory and funeral home.

//

Lunch was satisfying. Juanita's, the restaurant across from the bridge always served interesting versions of the normal. They had soup and sandwiches. They customized them to your preferences. Keith had tomato/potato soup and a turkey sandwich, wile Kayla had roast beef on rye with Munster cheese. Both had pushed their plates away half full. They were full on both food and conversation. Keith told her of his ministry and the trip he had just taken to the aquarium. She admired his love for children most men seemed to be scared to death of them. Scared to have them like it would steal years from their life or something. She told him as little as possible about where she had come from but enough so she didn't seem as if she had things to hide. She told him she was in sales back home but that she hated it. In a way it was true. She told him more about what she wanted than what she was running from. She told him she wanted to settle somewhere and get a house and a big husky. Two hours passed and Keith finally glanced down at his watch. "OH NO!"

"What???"

"I got to go! I have a meeting in twenty minuets!"

"Ok! Well thanks for lunch." they stood up and he walked her out.

"Will I see you tomorrow at breakfast?" he asked her.

"Absolutely!"

"Good! I hope you stick around!" Keith smiled at her and then walked away to his car. He wasn't sure how she penetrated his shield but she had. He felt something he hadn't in a long time... he felt like everything might just be alright.

//

Laurence found Walkerton in disarray. The Almighty shielded him so he could fly under the radar Lucifer had set up there. Fallen ones of all sorts crowded the streets and hovered over the humans. Ones of each kind. Of hatred, lust, unforgiveness and many others swarmed like mosquitoes around the town. Only a few Host's were found, surrounding the saints that still remained faithful. Laurence approached one. "Praise the Holy one!" He said as a greeting.

"Praise his name!" He answered.

"I am Laurence, I am sent to find out the origin of daughter of man. Kayla is her name! Do you know of her?"

"Yes! A great evil has been done to her. She will need a brick wall of prayer to surround her so she can fight off the Fallen that are with her. They are some of Lucifer's strongest. This fight will take place in the deepest part of her soul and the daughter of man will have to call out to the Almighty for her healing."

"I see! Thank you!" Laurence said.

"Praise the Almighty!"

"Praise the Almighty! He replied and then flew off to report his findings. As he flew back he passed an old yellowing flyer. It simply read *Missing, Brookelyn, please contact her father with any information at 252-220-2825. A* picture followed, Laurence thought nothing of it and continued to fly back to Rosewood.

//

SIX

BZZZZZZZZZZ... "Keith the Thomas' are here."
"Send them in!" He answered over the intercom.
"Alright!" Mr. and Mrs. Thomas came into Keith's office. Keith stood and shook both of their hands.
"Have a seat!" he motioned to the chairs that sat in front of his oak desk. He had the deep cranberry red curtains pulled to the so light could filter in and the church could save on electricity. He liked sunlight better anyways.
"So… What's up?" Mr. Thomas asked.
Keith walked around his desk and sat. "Well…"
"Is it Maddie, was she misbehaving at the aquarium?"
"No… but Mike, Jacqueline…. she was wrapping up food from the buffet and hiding it in her knapsack. I could only assume since it was an all you could eat thing that the food was for you guys?" The couple looked at eachother. They knew she had done it but they didn't know anyone saw her. Mike put his head down into one of his hands and covered his forehead with it. Jacqueline patted his back.
"Yeah we know!" She said. "You see Mike lost his job last month and everything is running low. We kinda put her up to it!" She looked down at the tan carpet ashamed of what she had asked her child to do.
"Guys…. Why didn't you come to us? That's what were here for!" Keith said.
"We couldn't… not when there are people worse off than us!"
"Jackie! Mike! Your not leaving without a bag from the pantry! And whatever else you need to get by till we can find you a job." Jackie was still ashamed but greatful. Mike reached out and shook Keith's had tightly.
"Thank you!" He looked him in the eye. "Thank you!"
"No problem… Now listen I have a friend at the electric company he may have something for you." Keith grabbed a pen and paper. "Here, write down some skills you have so I can let him know what you're looking for!"

Bbbbzzzzzzzzzzzz "Marcy!"
"Yes Keith?" The voice called back over the intercom.
"Can you show Mrs. Thomas to the pantry please and let her get what she needs."
"I'll be right in!
"Thanks" Keith said. Just to see the look on their faces, knowing that someone was going to help, and that someone cared made his job worth it. It's what he went into ministry for. He was glad he could help.

After they left Keith sat back down at his desk. He looked down at the picture frame that was lying face down as it has been for months now. He flipped it to reaveal her beautiful smile and eyes that even in a picture could see straight through him. This was his favorite picture of her and it brought back the best of all the memories he locked away deep inside.

The sun was caught in her spirals of curls, illuminating the upsides of the twists as they fell around her face. Her brown eyes shone like the stars and her cheeks were flushed from her laughter. Keith's world fadded around him.
"This picnic was such a great idea!" She said.

The spring sun warmed them as they sipped on tea and took bites of their sandwiches. Then they walked the bridge and fed the ducks with a bag of bread crumbs Keith had brought. When the bag was empty he shoved it into his spare pocket. He played constantly with his other pocket, putting a hand in and then taking it out empty. He must have done that about ten times now. Finally he mustered up the courage as Brooke leaned her back against the bridge. He took a deep breath, pulled the box out of his pocket and went to one knee.
"Will you… be my wife?" He said opening the box as he did.

"Oh Keith! Yes…Yes…." She said when words the words would finally come. The smile on her face couldn't have gotten any bigger as he slid the ring onto her hand. He stood up and kissed her, as they kissed he picked her up and spun them around.

Keith laid the frame back down again. He wished he hadn't looked at it, but how could he move on if he didn't. For the first time since she passed he thought he might want to and as that thought came to him Kayla's face popped into his mind. He didn't know why or if it was even right for him to move on, but he was beginning to think that he wanted to, that he actually could.

//

The next morning at breakfast Jenn could see something in Keith. Something she hadn't seen in a long time. Something that concerned her. He was falling for this girl. This girl that no one knew anything about. Sure she was nice enough but Keith's heart wasn't one that needed any more breaking, she wasn't going to allow it. Not on her watch. Brooklyn's passing almost shut him down completely and she feared that any more heartbreak and he would. She needed to get to know Kayla, to find out her motives, her secrets and if their were any that could hurt her friend. Her best friend. She invited out for the day to do some shopping and maybe a manicure if their was time. Kayla agreed. It sounded like fun. Like something she and Brooke would have done had she not disappeared. Jenn had to finish some paperwork and she told Kayla she would call up when she was ready.

//

Drathon loomed above Kayla as she sat in her room.He was still livid from his encounter with the Host's. He was intent on keeping her memories alive. Intent on tormenting her with them. To keep her in a dark place where he had control over her. "He will find you here!" He whispered in her ear. Kayla couldn't figure out why but she began to think about the man she was running from, one of them atleast, Devin Copeland. The man that had promised her so much and instead stole the only gift she ever wanted to keep. The only gift she wanted to choose when to give it away. The gift she wanted to share with the one. She was remembering everything now. How honest he looked when he promised her a better life and how wrong she was to have believed him.

The sun rose high in the sky as Kayla walked home. She was coming from the library preparing in her head what to make for dinner. She knew her father had picked out a man for her and that he was coming over tonight to meet her and discuss with her father *her* future. Like it wasn't her choice. She didn't understand why he wanted something different for her than he had. He had married her mom out of love and yet he was forcing her to marry for…well, she didn't know why. She considered putting poison in the food or making it so terrible that the man wouldn't want her, but she knew better. Granny would have slapped her father across the face if she hadn't passed away but he wouldn't hear anything of the sort. His mother would have understood he said. As she walked a loud mufflered car drove up behind her. She stepped off the road further to let it pass but instead it slowed down and followed her pace as she walked. "Hello?" A man's voice called from the old orange challenger.

"Hi" She said barely looking at him.

"Do you need a ride?" He called out over the loud muffler. Kayla shook her head and looked at him. Now she wasn't sure why she had said no. He was extremely handsome.

"You sure?"

"Uh… actually maybe I could." He stopped the car and reached a hand across the seat and out the passenger window.

"I'm Devin."

"Kayla!" She shook his hand.

"Hop in, where you going?"

"Home… um Harpers drive.

"OK." As he drove they made small talk. She liked him. It was then that the idea came into her head that started her complete downward spiral. '*What if I can convince dad to let me date him?'* she thought. Jacob however was livid.

"How dare you! How dare you bring this stranger into my home Kayla... do you have any idea who he is?"
"No but... I want to!" She said in her defense. She was so embarrased that he was yelling like this right in front of him.
"Sir... My name is Devin." He extended a hand to him.
"I'm sorry what... The Devil did you say??" Jacob answered him sarcastically. "How improper of you to come home with a woman you don't know!" He said turning to Kayla and ignoring his gesture for a handshake. "Please walk him out!" He said to her sternly. By the look on his face she knew he would hear no more, begrudgingly she did as he asked.

On the porch Devin slipped his number into her palm on a small piece of folded up paper as they shook hands goodbye. "Kayla...if you ever want out, I can help. Iv'e got an extra room upstairs in my house and I might be able to get you a job." The prospect sounded welcoming, getting out, not having to marry a stranger. She nodded at him and then watched him leave and went inside.
"It's disgraceful Kayla!"
"I'm sorry I just don't understand why you won't let me marry for love like you and mom!" Jacob pursed his lips.
"Because Kayla! I want to protect you! If you lose someone you love, like I did you never recover. If you marry and never love them when they pass, you won't hurt like me. You won't be bitter like me and you will be able to live a normal life!" He yelled at her.
"Yeah but only if he dies, dad! Other than that I'll have to kiss and make love to a stranger! A man I don't love or care for." Jacob pursed his lips harder and his face got red.
"It's for your own good Kayla!" He yelled
"No it's for yours!" She screamed back. He slapped her across the face nearly toppling her over from the force and surprise of it.
"You'll never understand child!" He said using all the muscles in his diaphragm to do so.
"I won't if you have anything to do with it!" She said holding

her cheek "Because you won't let me! Now excuse me wile I make dinner for a man I don't love!" She walked away from him and into the kitchen. *Maybe she was right?* Jacob thought, but he still didn't want her to ever feel what he did the day he buried his bride. The day he buried his heart in the ground and never got it back!

At midnight that same night Kayla snuck out with a full suitcase and knapsack. She called Devin from a payphone by the seven eleven and he picked her up. His face was just as kind as it had been that day. Devin's house was huge. It looked like an old plantation house with the pilars that held up the roof. The white paint was bright even in the dark and she could barely make out that the shutters were black and that they matched the front door. Six windows went along the top foor of the house and six at the bottom, three on each side of the door on each floor. There had to be at least twelve rooms in there, Kayla thought. There were all kinds of cars parked along the sides of the long gravel driveway. She thought it odd, but said nothing. They parked out back and went inside by the screened in porch. The porch door led inside to the kitchen and from there Devin led her up the stairs that were on the far side of the room. It was dark inside and Kayla began to become uneasy. "So is it just you who lives here?" She asked nervously.

"No I have some friends here to!" He said followed by a shhh. As they neared the top stairs Kayla began to hear weird noises. Moans and some screams. She hesitated. *Maybe this was a bad idea?* She thought. "Common" He said "its ok!"

"What was that?" she questioned him as her intuition told her to run....quickly in the other direction.

"Oh that noise? Sorry! My friends are into horror films!"

"Oh" Kayla said. *It sounded plausible;* She thought and then followed him up the last step and into the third room down the hall on the left. The room that was now hers. He flicked the light on. The room was a good size, painted in a cozy off white eggshell. A bed and dresser were already there and the room

had its own bathroom. She loved that.
"Ok! Here you go!" He said shutting the door behind her. *It was ok!* She thought. He was being so nice to give this to her and help her get on her own two feet. She began to unpack, filling the drawers with her clothes. When they were full she went to the closet. Inside she found at least ten costumes. One of a french maid, one of a cowgirl and so on. She stared at them for a moment pushing each to the side so she could examine it. Behind her the door creaked open. "Like them?" Devin asked.
"What are they?"
"Your uniforms, I told you I'd get you a job!" Devin stepped in the room and shut the door behind him.
"A job where, the circus?" She said chuckling alittle to try and hide her increasing discomfort.
"No!" he said stepping closer. The look in his eyes had changed. They were no longer kind as he stepped closer and closer to her. He had a twisted smirk on his lips and a stance that spoke volumes about his intentions.
"Devin? What are they for?" She asked though she had a suspicion.
"Your clients to pick from! Of course!" He stopped by the edge of the bed and stared at her, continually keeping his evil smirk alive over his teeth.
"Wait????... You mean?" He nodded "but ive never...." Her heart was pounding in her chest and she was breathing slow deep breaths of fear filled oxygen.
"I know!" He lunged at her, grabbing her by her sholders and throwning her onto the bed.
"Noooo!" She yelled but she couldn't fight him. He was too strong. That night he stole what she was keeping sacred for the man of her dreams. He stole her hope and her chance of ever finding happiness or going home. Her father wouldn't understand this. She was defiled now and none of the men her father was finding for her to marry would want a used and defiled bride. He would never let her come home, she was

trapped. Tears streamed down her face over streams of tears that had already dried. By the time he was done her arms ached from trying to fight him off and her insides felt as if they had been ripped out and put back in out of order. Her clothes were torn and hung in pieces at her sides as she lay. Her whole body was shaking and she breathed in shaky short gasps. "Go clean up!" He said pulling up his pants and walking towards the door. "You start tomorrow!" He reached into his pocket and pulled out a little blue container. "Take these!" He said throwing a pack of birth control pills at her just before he stepped out and locked the door from the outside. Kayla couldn't clean up. She couldn't move. She just curled up in the fetal position and sobbed. She fell in and out of sleep the whole night waking to the realization that her nightmare wasn't a dream, it was real! Around three thirty she finally could stand and she got up to clean herself off. She stood in the shower for what seemed like forever but it wouldn't wash off. She couldn't get the feeling to wash off. She just felt so dirty, so wrong, so tricked and defiled. She was right though, she couldn't go home now! Even her father wouldn't want her.

The pain became tolerable with time. The clients chose her for her beauty and quickly she was making money. She found that if she pretended to enjoy it they offered her tips beyond that of Devin's fee. Tips she could hide, tips she could save! She promised herself that when she had enough she would run. Run as far away as possible. There was a spot in the woods where she and Brooke would go. She remembered the day they buried the time capsule. They had put their wishes on paper along with a few trinkets they wanted to save into an old metal fire resistant box and buried it in the woods. Three paces past the large oak tree and one step over. Kayla dug it up and put all the money she wanted to hide inside. She sat by the tree and looked through everything they had hidden inside. Brooke's handwriting was still scratchy when they buried it but Kayla had never had trouble reading it.

My Wishes..... By: Brooke
I wish to be a wife and a mommy.
I want Kayla to marry too!
Who ever has the boy can name him Kaleb and whoever has the girl will name her Rachel. Then they can get married!
I want to be the owner of the largest porcelain doll collection in the world and be in the records book.

Kayla folded the note back up and looked over the rest of the contents. She remembered putting in the string of pearls that her mother had worn, promising to wear them on her wedding day, quickly she put them down. *Who would want to marry me now?* She thought! Brooke had put in an empty locket. She said that one day she would put in it a picture of someone who truly loved her. Someone who would never hurt her! Kayla never understood what she meant. Kayla opened her note and remembered it without hesitation. It was just after her father had left for seminary.
My wishes, by Kayla...
I want my daddy to come home and I want a baby sister or brother I guess
I want to marry and have two kids
And last I want to be the best singer ever so daddy will let me sing with Granny in the choir.
Kayla laughed. Boy was that a long time ago. She put it all back and added a few hundred dollars, then buried the box again.
The next three months went by and as they did she started to feel very strange. Tired all the time, fatigued and hungry and not at all like a woman. She hadn't had a menstrual cycle since before the night Devin raped her. She had started the pills he gave but at the end of them nothing happened. At the end of the second round nothing happened. The third round she skipped, she figured they were messing up her hormones or... no... she dare not think it... could she be??? Instead she hid them in her dresser inside a folded pair of underwear. Though

the thought was right on the tip of her brain, she dared not to think it. Not to even imagine it as a possibility. What would Devin do to her then??
She counted the money before she placed it in the box. Another three hundred. If her count was correct she had two thousand one hundred and twenty dollars. That wouldn't get her very far. A car alone would about take all of it. She had to have enough to last at least a few months, enough to find a place to hide and stay off the radar for a wile.

Another month and a half passed another two packs of pills hidden and another two thousand went into the box. Once again Kayla dared not to think about the 'what if?' Devin had just this morning asked her why she looked like she was getting fat! She didn't have an answer for him so he smacked her across the face. "Quit eating so much!! Your looks are what make us money! Your beautiful face and body are my bread and butter baby!" He said in a demeaning low tone. She hated him. Now she had to think about it! If someone was growing inside her and Devin found out, she had no doubts he'd do whatever it took to kill it… so he could continue use her for his service! She had to know, and if her instincts were correct she would have to go….today!

Devin kept inside his room a stash of cash that he used for changing out large bills for the men and giving the girls their shares. Kayla waited hours till she heard him leave. It was four, five hours till the rush began. She had to be quick….in out and then gone. She packed a Knapsack full of clothes and tossed it out with the trash. Devin's room was on the bottom floor next to the living room that for now was quiet, so on she went. Using a paper clip she broke open his lock and there she went. Into the room and into the closet where the locked box was. She grabbed the whole thing. She could figure out how to open it later. Now she ran through the woods to her spot. She dug up, once again, the box her and Brooke had buried and took out a hundred. Quickly she buried both boxes and ran through the woods the other way towards town. Towards the drug store, where her answer sat on a shelf waiting for her to pee on it.

Kayla purchased the most expensive test available and now paced in the bathroom. She wore a pair of black sweat pants because her jeans were too tight and a tube top covered her recently sore chest. The test lay face down as instructed and she waited. It was the longest three minuets of her life. As she waited she looked at her figure in the mirror, only a small rounding of her stomach was noticeable. She wanted to believe that there was no way a baby could fit in that little bump but she remembered her father saying how you could barely tell when her mother was pregnant. Her hips that were the same shape as Kayla's hid it well. She only looked about four months when she gave birth. Kayla had seen pictures. As she turned over the test all of the suspicions were confirmed by two pink lines. Her heart fluttered in her chest and she felt butterflies in her stomach, she was in love. In love with the child she was determined now to protect. Kayla must have stared at the two pink lines for ten minuets, breathing in slow shallow breaths as she tried to figure out what to do now. She had to leave. She absolutely had to run, somewhere Devin and his horde of dogs couldn't find her.

Hindsight being what it is Kayla could now looking back see a million different ways to not go back and get her things. To use what she had and just high tail it, but again were talking hindsight. Her knapsack still sat inside a trash bag behind the house. She left the money where it was and went to grab her clothes. She came out of the woods at the back of the house and walked to the trash can. She lifted up the metal lid trying to avoid any clinking or clanking. The top bag as she had planned was full off garbage, she lifted it off and the second bag was as well full of trash. Something wasn't right. She had left it just under the first bag. She lifted the second, nothing. Oh noooo! She thought just as the door to the screened in porch flew open. "Looking for something??" Devin held the knapsack by one strap from his left hand. He

leaned against the door jamb and had an evil smirk on his face. Kayla looked at him wide eyed.
"Did you really think that with all these people around here looking out for me that you could pull one over on me???" Still she was silent. He began to walk down the steps towards her. Behind her about five of Devin's girls surrounded her blocking any route of escape. He was about a foot from her now. "Did you really think I didn't know what was going on in my own house??" He pulled out of his pockets the three unused packages of pills and threw them at her face!" He put his face right up next to hers and screamed. "Did you?" She flinched turning her head to the side. "I guess you had a reason to get fat… Huh??" Again she said nothing. "Answer me Whore!" He yelled.
"It's your's!" She said in a desperate tone, hoping it would make him think, make him find one bone of compassion "It's has to be I took the pills with the others! All the others! For months!" She screamed back as she put her hands on her belly.
"That thing is not mine! He yelled as he turned his back to her. "Ladies!" He said as he stepped away. On queue the girls began to attack her. They pulled her to the ground by her ponytail. Instinctively she curled into a ball covering her belly and wrapping her arms around her knees, interlocking her fingers together. They kicked at her spine punched and scratched her face trying to make her let go of her knees. She wouldn't! At all costs she would defend this life. They rolled her around and attacked the other side of her yet she still held her position. "STOP!" Devin called and on command his dogs obeyed. "Get up!" He said walking over to her. She wasn't trained and she didn't move. "GET!!!! UP!!!!!!!" He screamed as he pulled her by her ponytail. She stood to her feet wrapping her arms around her belly. He pushed her along around the side of the house and into the passenger seat of his car. He slammed the door shut making her jump with fear. He rounded the front of the car and jumped in the driver's seat.

He squealed the tires as he pulled out onto the highway, fishtailing a little from the change of gravel to pavement. Kayla could imagine all the places he might be going and what he would do to her in those places. She could see him tossing her off the bridge into the rocks by the stream. She could see him beating her to death and tossing her into the woods along highway twenty nine. Instead he drove along the main stretch of town down to Harpers drive, where she use to live with her father. He drove right up to her old driveway. "OUT!" He said. Quickly she did as commanded and he drove away with a loud blast from his muffler and a squeal of tires.

SEVEN

She stood at the end of the cement driveway staring at her father's house. *What would happen?* She wondered if she just went up and knocked? She didn't have to, the door opened and Jacob, stood in the doorway. Kayla began to sob at the sight of him. She was embarrassed by her appearance, her bruised and scratched up flesh that revealed more of her than her father had ever seen. Her scantily clad tube top revealing her shoulders and some cleavage along with her stomach. Jacob slammed the door shut.

"Daddy!!!!!!!!!!!" She yelled out! She knew it. He hated her. She was almost about to turn and walk away when the door opened again to reveal Jacob holding a blanket. He motioned her to come and she ran to him. Quickly he covered her up with the blanket and sat her down on the porch swing. She tried to meet his gaze but he wouldn't look at her.

"I'm sorry!" She said almost in tears. Again he went inside. A few minuets later he came back with a hot cup of tea.

"Thank you!" She said genuinely as he handed her the mug. Still without a word he sat in the patio chair adjacent to the swing, looking foreward, even the look in his eyes was silent. She didn't know what to say so she didn't say anything. She was just grateful for whatever he gave her. She sat silently sipping the tea letting its warmth comfort her. From a ways off she began to hear sirens. She imagined as awful as it was that Devin was in an accident was no more. The sirens got even closer and then right in front of the house. A police car and a sheriff's car pulled in. As the officers stepped out of their cars Jacob stood and walked over to his daughter. He acted as if he was going to pat her on the back. Instead he ripped the blanket off her and finally spoke. "Here! The whore's right here!" He called out. Kayla clutched the mug with both hands and pulled it in close instinctively.

"Dad?" Kayla looked up at him in shock. Still he never met her gaze. Lieutenant Colin Sherwin walked up the porch

steps. He had attended the church for years, Kayla wasn't a stranger to him, and he recognized her right off.
"Jacob!" He said in a reprimanding tone. "You can't be serious!"
"Take her away Colin! I mean it!" he took his gaze from Jacob to Kayla. She was bruised, scratched up and her eyes met his with horror.
"Did you do that to her?" He asked boldly looking back at Jacob.
"How dare you?" Jacob scolded him.
"No! How dare you Jacob…This is your child! You're only, child!" He emphasized.
"I have no children!" He said sternly, meeting his gaze with fire in his eyes. Disgusted with Jacob Colin turned his gaze back to Kayla.
"Honey who did this to you?"
"Uh…" She looked down and bit her bottom lip. She didn't want to say. She didn't want to see him again to face him or press charges; she just wanted it to be over.
"Kayla… Please?" She had always respected him. He was kind to her each and every time she saw him. He was gentle and strong. The kind of man she always imagined her husband would be like.
"Devin and his girls."
"Devin the…"
"Yeah, that one" She said before he could finish his sentence. He nodded
"Ok!" He said taking his walkie out of its holster. "Come in" He said.
"Go ahead Lieutenant" Came a woman's voice.
"I need an ambulance at 202 Harpers drive." A moment passed.
"On its way sir." She responded.
"Thank you!" He put the walkie back in its holster and sat by Kayla on the swing. "Jacob! Go inside!"
"Excuse me?" He held his hands up palms out and wore shock

on his face.
"Go inside!" Jacob hesitated only a moment and then went inside showing his disapproval with a slam of the door. "Now what happened?" Colin asked Kayla in a low tone.
"I… um... He found out about the baby and they all tried to kill it, and me I think!" She looked him in his blue eyes. They were kind as always.
"THE BABY????" He asked. She nodded. "You're pregnant?" Again she nodded. "Kayla honey! How far?"
"I think four or five months! I dont really know!"
"Ok! I'll call the hospital so they can have an ob be ready to meet you!" He looked her in the eyes. "It's gonna be ok!" He said. She hugged him. "Thank you! I protected him… I did…I did…" She repeated again and again. All he could do was hug her back and hope she was right.

The ambulance arrived and Colin carried her to it, knight in shining armor style. They met him at the back and took her out of his arms. "It'll be ok!" He told her as they closed the back doors. Colin tried for a moment to think about what it might be like for Jacob. What would happen if his little girl had made the same mistakes Kayla did and then showed back up by his front door. He just couldn't imagine acting the way Jacob did. Quickly He called the hospital and then walked back inside to finish the police report, and to try and talk Jacob out of filing charges.

Kayla recognized most of the Emit's from the church. They took her blood pressure, temp and pulse. Everything was normal. As Colin has promised an obstetrician met the ambulance at the entrance.
"Kayla?… I'm Dr. Barnes. I was informed that your pregnant, do you know how far along you are?" He asked from above her as they rolled the stretcher down the hall. She tried to focus on his face but the ceiling tiles whizzing by behind him made her nauseous. She closed her eyes and swallowed hard.
"Um… Four or five months I think.!" She opened her eyes again but it was all the same. Dizzyness and nausea. She tried

to sit up but one of the EMT's put a hand on her shoulder. She once again closed her eyes hard.
"Kayla... What's wrong?" Dr. Barnes asked.
"I feel sick!" They pulled the stretcher into a curtained off cubicle. The next thing she remembered was looking up at ceiling tiles in a dark hospital room. She buzzed the nurse who came in and told her that she had passed out in the er. That she had been extremely dehydrated and anemic. Then she went to get the doctor.
Knock Knock
"Come in!"
"Hello? Good to see you awake!" He said as he walked in pushing an ultrasound machine. "I saved the best for last!" He said. "Are you ready to see your baby?"
"YEAH!!!!"
"Your blood work was normal except for the anemia. It's very important when you're pregnant to take a prenatal vitamin." He said. "It probably would have helped your iron levels and possibly prevented the anemia." Even if she told him she just found out she knew it was her fault for waiting so long to test.
"How long exactly have you known you were pregnant?" The doctor asked as he lifted up her gown just above her belly. He covered below her belly with a bath blanket and squirted the jelly on.
"Um about seven hours" She replied.
"Oooh...k then!" He said and then sat down in a swivel chair holding the transducer to her stomach. He looked at the screen as he moved the wand around. "Did you suspect you were before today?"
"Yes but, I was afraid of what the father might do!"
"Well, we will have to make sure he get's no where near you! Ok!" he said focusing his attention to the monitor. The doctor twisted and rolled the transducer over her belly and pushed buttons on the machine. It had been only a few minuets but to Kayla it was an eternity until the doctor finally spoke again.
"It seems here we have a normal healthy five month old

fetus."
"REALLY! The baby's ok!??"
"Yes mam! Do you want to know the sex??"
"You can tell already??"
"We can tell between 16 and twenty weeks. I'd say you're probably around twenty!"
"Yes please!" She said. She wanted to be able to say him or her and not it or just the baby.
"Ok look here!" He pointed to the screen in the bottom left corner. "That is for sure a healthy… baby boy!"
"A boy?"
"Yup" She looked down at her belly remembering the note Brooke had written.
"Well then Doctor… say hi to Kaleb!"
"Hello Kaleb!" he said looking towards her stomach. He put the transducer in its holder and wiped her belly off. "You two will be just fine. I will come back and see you before they release you tomorrow."
"Ok! But Doctor Barnes?"
"Yes"
"Do you know where their taking me?"
"All I know is that Lieutenant Sherwin will be picking you up!"
"Will they let me keep him??"
"Yes! They can't force you to have an abortion just because you're in jail, and if it's any consolation they can't keep you more than forty eight hours without any proof. I hear they don't have any!" He winked at her and then pushed out the machine. Kayla caressed her stomach and sang to her baby. Like her dad had said her mother had done with her. She hummed a lullaby type tune and sang amazing grace to him. Her little Kaleb, her son, her future, who she hoped would love her back one day. Despite her failures. Despite how he was conceived. Despite who is father was. Despite it all, she hoped he would.

EIGHT

Riiinnggg……… Riiinnggg. Kayla jolted. She was back in the hotel sitting in the recliner. She must have been in some type of trace or something. How long had she been sitting here? The phone rang again. She answered it. "Hello?"

"Kayla? It's Jenn. You ready?"

"Uh… Yeah?"

"Ok common down!"

"See ya in a minuet." She hung up the phone and went to the bathroom. She hadn't done her hair or makeup she looked ridiculous. Quickly she changed clothes, threw her hair in a pony and decided to do makeup in the car.

The girls hopped into Jenn's hunter green Taurus and were off. Kayla pulled down the visor and began to do her make up.

"I'm sorry I hope you don't mind! I lost all track of time up there?"

"Really how?" Jenn questioned hoping she could gain some insight into this woman Keith had taken so kindly to.

"I sat in the recliner and must have dozed off. I woke up when you called."

"Oh! I don't mind!" She searched her mind for questions to ask. Ones that wouldn't seem threatening but ones that would also reavel some information. She couldn't let Keith get hurt again. She had to be sure that this girl wasn't trying to. That she was safe for him. "So?" She said inquisitively "Where are you from?"

"Um North Carolina."

"Did you like it there?"

"It was ok"

"What made you come here?"

"Well I wanted a change. Wanted to go somewhere new, sightsee ya know try something new."

"Oh! Ok! Did you pick us out on a map or something?"

"No!" she was starting get defensive. "Why?"

"It's just a small town, we don't get many tourists."

"Oh!...well it's like I told Keith I made a wrong turn and liked it so much I wanted to stay."
"I like it here too!" She said, trying to lighten the mood she had set. They talked a bit more and shopped some. Kayla had found a new favorite pair of earrings. They were fire topaz tear drops that dangled just an inch or so. She had never seen the stone till then. It was green but inside was dark pink and purple flames. The girls went to the mall and found a few things here and there and now they sat with their feet soaking in a bubby basin and their hands being manicured. Though Jenn remained curious she was beginning to like this girl. She seemed nice enough, she wasn't sure if she was nice enough for Keith, but she was nice. Kayla had never had a pedicure before and she laughed every time the lady went to touch her feet with the file. She managed to stay still though. Kayla finished first and she went to pay. She thought about it and she wanted to be friends with this girl. She seemed to be scoping her out or something so she paid for them both. Maybe, she thought it would lighten up the unspoken tension she felt.
"So?" she said as she sat back down. "Where next?"
"Umm… well there's this great antique store about a mile from here?"
"Sounds great!"
"Ok! Let me just go pay!" Jenn said. Kayla let her go and she came back with a huge smile on her face.
"Thank you! That was nice!" She said genuinely
"No problem! It's nice to have a friend!" Kayla said and Jenn smiled, she was still suspicious though.

//

Drathon loomed above Kayla, watching… waiting for an opportune time to strike. Oren watched him waiting to see what Lucifer's soldier had up his sleeve. Waiting for him to step beyond the realm so he could slay him. Waiting for him to go beyond the boundaries of the realm the Almighty had set way back when the nephelites were on the earth. Back when his kind had taken brides from the sons of man and conceived within them the mighty warriors of old. He knew though that the Fallen One knew of his presence, and that would affect his behavior and choices. Drathon was angry. Though he had gotten through to her this morning and affected her mind she wasn't as easy to manipulate. She had been more of a subject a few days ago when they had full control over her. When they were able to penetrate her thoughts and feelings. Here in this place with the Host's and these people she was coming out of her depression and was actually smiling. Demons don't like the children of men to smile. They want the world to be ruled by their master who despises joy for it comes from the Father. Drathon had to do something… Quickly.

//

The antique store was just that… Antique. The store was made from an old house built in the early nineteen hundreds. It had been owned by southern royalty at the time and then eventually the owner now inherited it from his parents. The upstairs had been blocked off and turned into the housing area and the bottom floor was all turned into the shop. Each room with a theme. What would have been the living room had a large old piano in the center atop a Victorian rug. Other old rugs were either rolled up in the corner or hung on the walls. Smaller pianos sat in the four corners of the room. Jenn and Kayla separated. The store went in a circle around the cashier's center in the middle. Jenn went left and Kayla right. They would circle around and meet in the middle. The next room had knick nacks of all kinds. From porcelain to china to old ivory statues made before the outlawing of tusking. Kayla looked at one. It was carved from limestone. It was an elephant and inside the elephant was a baby elephant. She had no idea how someone could sculpt like that and not break the outer shape of the mother. She was fascinated by it and decided to purchase it. She held it tightly in her hand and looked around the rest of the room unaware that Drathon

awaited her arrival in the next room over. As she passed under the archway that separated the rooms her world faded around her. The room was filled with old Victorian infant articles. Old rattles and baby blankets lavished in lace that had yellowed with the passing of time. In the corner was a old handcrafted highchair with a doll sitting in the infants seat, there were a few old rocking chairs, Next to one of them was what Kayla's gaze was fixed on. A bassinet made of oak or some other light hardwood rocked back and forth. It was lined with white lace that cascaded down the fabric. There inside wrapped in a blue blanket was a crying child. Kayla's vision blurred around the sides. Darkness filled her peripheral vision and nothing else was in focus except for him. "Kaleb!!!" She dropped everything that was in her hands, the elephant, her purse and just ran to the side of the bassinet. Dropping to her knees she reached in and picked up the infant, cradling the child to her chest. "Kaleb! My Kaleb!" She said as she rocked back and forth on her knees rubbing the back of the child's head. Drathon had succeeded. Possessing a doll wasn't something Oren could stop him from doing. He was quite proud of himself. Grafton would have loved to see it if Lucifer hadn't called him away. Oren watched distraught but it was her choice, she had to call his name out. Just call his name once and the Almighty would instantly be at her side along with the comforter the Lord had sent as promised after he ascended from the earth and took his place by the Father's side.
"KAYLA?" Jenn came into the room and saw her. Kayla opened her eyes not to reveal what she has closed them to the sights of, but reality. There she sat on her knees on the floor next to a bassinet cradling a doll to her chest and calling it Kaleb.
"Oh no!" Kayla threw the doll back inside the bassinet and ran out of the store.
"Kayla?" Jenn called after her. When that didn't work she ran after her. "Kayla wait!" She yelled. Kayla stopped by the

tree's at the back of the house. How far could she get. Eventually she'd have to face her anyway. She crossed her arms over her chest as she suspected it was wet. She kept her hands over the chest as Jenn came up behind her.
"What was that all about?" She said. "Who's Kaleb?" Kayla began to cry. She knew she was going to loose her new found friend if she told her. How could she still want to be friends with her after knowing she was such a horrible person? The owner of the shop yelled something from the edge of the porch. "Hold on!" Jenn said as she walked back up to the entrance.
"I don't know what's going on... But one of you will have to pay for this!" She held out the elephant, its trunk had broken off but the rest had miraculously stayed intact.
"How much?"
"Eighteen fifty!"
"Here! Keep the change!" Jenn handed her a twenty. The owner also handed over Kayla's purse and then Jenn was on her way back to her friend's side. That's when she realized that she hadn't gone to God yet. That's what she should have done first, before she even got in the car and began the session of twenty questions, or judged her at all. As she walked back to her side she said a quick prayer. *Lord I know everything happens for a reason, I know you sent this girl here to my inn so I can help her with something, please guide me in how to do that! In Jesus name.* " Kayla?" She said putting a hand on her back. "What's going on?" Kayla could hear sympathy in her voice now. She turned to her as the tears still ran down her face and uncovered her chest revealing the wet spots over her breasts where the milk had soaked through.
"Oh Kayla!!!!! My goodness!" She paused. "Let's go!" She motioned her on towards the car. "We'll stop on the way home and get something that might help. OK." Kayla crossed her arms over her chest again as they walked to the car. Jenn had watched her mother a few times quit breastfeeding. When her brothers and sisters had gotten their teeth in she'd wean

them off and then eventually had to stop all together for them to quit producing. She had seen all the tricks from cold cabbage leaves to tight sports bras. She could help this girl, she would help her. Jenn pulled out onto the highway. "You don't have to tell me what happened but I want you to know I'm here if you want to, and from what I saw back there honey I think you should talk to someone!" Kayla stared at the elephant in her lap. She thought that it resembled her the day she had been beaten. The baby inside was fine but her outside was pretty banged up.
"Kaleb was my son!….. I don't know what happened, only that his father has something to do with it!"
"You mean kidnapped?"
"Yeah something like that?" Kayla said in a soft voice as Jenn pulled into the drug store.
"I'm sorry!" She said not knowing what else to say.
"Thanks, it really does mean a lot!" Kayla searched her wallet. It was here… there; she pulled out a tri folded piece of paper and went inside. Jenn followed her.
"What's that?"
"Something that will stop this!"
"Oh! Ok well you get that and I'll get a few things to help you till that kicks in.! K!" She smiled at her sincerely, she knew God had sent her here and that he meant for her to react the way she did, to get her out of the house and be alone with her so she could help her without a group of onlookers. So she could be her friend and confidant.
"K!" Kayla agreed. Once again the girls separated. Kayla took the prescription to the pharmacy desk and Jenn went to gather the other things. As she collected the items she prayed for her friend. Prayed for her soul. She didn't know if she knew who God was or how he could be her healing, but she would. She would make sure of that. The Almighty heard her prayer and empowered the Hosts to step between the Fallen and the daughter of man.

NINE

Kayla had been in jail for twenty four hours now. Jacob still wasn't budging on his will to prosecute her. She knew she must have hurt him really bad when she just left the way she did, she didn't even leave a note... she just left. She wondered occasionally what he must have done the morning he woke up to find her missing. Did he care that she was gone? Was he happy to be rid of a burden or did he try and search of her. For the first time today she thought about what her decision must have really done to him. He had lost a wife and shortly after his mother and then he woke up to find his only child missing without an explanation. She hated that she sat here behind bars, but she felt sorry him. For all he had been through. He had a right to be angry with her.

The cell wasn't all that bad, it was cold and dark but it was hers. She had three square meals and no one was invading her personal space. She had her own sink and toilet in her own small cell, it was almost comforting to know that here she was protected from all the people who had objectified her for the past five months. Here she was safe from Devin and his horde of prostitutes and the men who purchased them.

Colin had been a blessing; he was fighting to get the charges dropped. There truly was no sufficient evidence that proved Jacob's charges and since that was the case they could only keep her another twenty four hours. She was comforted in knowing that she could get out of here and find a safe place to raise Kaleb.

The cell was especially cold tonight as she lay trying to sleep. She just couldn't get warm. She lay on her left side with her knees pulled up as close to her chest as Kaleb would allow and had the blankets pulled up to just under her nose. She had no idea what time it was only that it must be after midnight. From down the hall she began to hear voices. Atleast three of them from down where the guard station was. She couldn't make out what they were saying. The voices seemed to

bounce off the cement and get jumbled up. Goose bumps went down her spine and she tried to pull the covers in closer to her. She layed there listening to a serenade of snoring from the others in the cells and the jarbles of voices from down the hall. It almost became like a lullaby and her mind began to wander into sleep until the sound of jingling keys came closer and closer down the hallway of cement leading to her cell. She sat straight up and stared the guard in the face. He was very familiar. Yes he was… A client? He fumbled with the keys not meeting her gaze, he cursed in his head that she was awake. This would have been so much easier had she been asleep.
"You!" She said "You're …."
"A cell guard!" He said hoping to distract her, to keep her quiet. He could only imagine how this would go if the others woke up too. He finally found the key and unlocked her door. Its metal hinges creaked open.
"What are you doing?" She questioned.
"Quiet Whore!" He said through gritted teeth.
"Help!" She screamed as he lunged at her. He covered her mouth with one hand and picked her up effortlessly with the other. He was about six three and had massive arm muscles. Kayla remembered him definitely. He had a tattoo of a scorpion on his bicep. The night he bought her she remembered trying to focus on it and only it until he was done. He had been heartless then and apparently he brought that trait to work with him. Quickly he carried her down the hall. Though she pounded on his back with her fists and tried to kick him, he was solid. Unwavering in his attemp to carry her away. He took her down the hall to the back door and out into a van. Devin sat in the driver's seat and a man in a mask took her from the guard's arms into the back of the van. Just as quickly as she was inside he covered her face with an oxygen mask. Kayla knew she was in trouble now.

//

Kayla awoke to the view of ceiling tiles. She was groggy and confused. Her stomach ached and she felt nauseous. She could however tell that she was back in the hospital. The place smelled of bleach and cafeteria food. She had an IV in her right hand and was covered by the one of the thin white blankets hospitals use to drive their patients and nurses insane. She found the button on the side of the bed and paged the nurse. The speaker echoed loudly in the dark quiet room. "Yes! Can I help you?"
"Yeah um… I need my Doctor please."
"What's wrong mam?"
"Can I see Dr. Barnes please?" Kayla wanted to see a friendly face; someone who would tell her what was going on kindly.
"One moment please!" The woman's high pitched voice echoed in her ear and she pulled her head away from the speaker box instinctively. A few moments later a nurse came to her bedside.
"What can I help you with?" She said. She sounded kind but Kayla still wanted to see a familiar face. She was scared and cold and wanted to hear what was going on from her doctor.
"Nothing! Can I see Dr. Barnes please?"
"I'm sorry mam Dr. Barnes is off duty."
"Oh!" She took a deep breath in and sighed loudly as she let it out.
"I might be able to help you if you tell me what's wrong?" Kayla thought she sounded genuine.
"Ok! Well, I need to know what I am doing here?"
"Sure! You um had a seizure at the jailhouse and they brought you here."
"**UM NOO!**…." Kayla scrunched her face she knew that wasn't it.
"No what Mam?!"
"No I didn't have a seizure I remembe……"
"I'm sorry mam she's still a bit delusional!" A male's voice came from the corner of her room. Only then did she see the guard who kidnapped her sitting in the darkest corner of the

room in a hard hospital room guest chair.
"YOU!!" She sat up in bed and pointed at the guard. As she did she felt the deep ache in her stomach and a gush of fluid from between her legs… "Ahhh" She said putting a hand to her belly. Her mouth fell open, her breathing slowed and her heart stopped beating. He was gone. "Kaleb!" She said in a whisper. "Oh God! Kaleb!" She said louder and laid back down on her side this time with both hands to her stomach. "Kaleb!"
"Yes mam, I'm sorry!… but you did…loose the little one during your seizure. He was already gone when you arrived."
Kayla's whole body shook as she lay there on the hospital bed. She wanted to kill the guard. To kill Devin and the man in the mask, but what was the point now. Kaleb was gone and she was sure no one would believe her story about a man in a mask drugging her in the back of a van behind the jail. "We instructed the guard on duty to take the infant to the funeral home! We only needed your placenta and cord to test for abnormalities." The nurse touched Kayla's back as she rolled away from her. "Were testing your son's umbilical cord blood to see why he was discharged so early!" Kayla sat up hastily through her pain and turned towards her.
"Discharged!!! He didn't check out of my body like I'm a hotel he was stolen from me! He stole him from me!" Kayla threw an arm out in the guard's direction pointing at him as she shouted at her. She agreed that her choice of words was probably not the most compassionate but what could she say. She took a step back as Kayla stared at her with hatred and discontent written all over her face.
"I'm sorry!"
"Didn't you hear me?… He stole him from me!" Kayla's face was turning beet red as she raised her voice louder, shrieking as she yelled. She knew no one would believe her. The guard had sat quiet this whole time.
"I'll… get the doctor!" she said as she backed up out of the room.

"Yeah! Now you get the doctor!" She said with disdain. The nurse shut the door behind her and finally the guard spoke. "You will keep your mouth shut whore!" He said not moving an inch. Not blinking or bothering to get up! She got his point from where she sat. No one would believe her anyway. She held her stomach again as she laid down, remembering what it had felt like filled with life and once again she cried for it.
"Did you hear me slut?"
"Yeah!" She mumbled as she laid in her sorrow and covered her self with the blanket of shame.

Kayla awoke to Colin's smile. He sat by her bedside with one leg tucked up underneath him. He wore his street clothes and not his uniform. "Hi!" He said
"Hi" She smiled sadly at him through the cutout in the bed rail. She didn't want to move if she did all of it would become real.
"I did it!" He said with just a tinge of excitement in his voice.
"What?"
"He dropped the charges!" She propped herself up on her elbow so she could see above the rail, could it be.
"You mean.."
"You're a free woman!" She sat all the way up and almost smiled.
"Really, Oh thank you Colin."
"Your welcome!............So... What happened?" He looked at her his face becoming serious.
"Uh... I don't know?" She looked down at the tile floor, but her voice had already told the secret.
"Kayla? It's me!" She knew she could trust him, but also she knew she would have to stick around if she tried to prove the events of last night to Colin or a jury. Even though she desired revenge more than her lungs desired for breath she didn't want to be here. Around all these places and memories, she just wanted out! She looked Colin in the eye and tried her best to hide the truth that seeped out of her pupils like hot molasses. "Really!"

"Kayla the nurse told me what you said!" She bit her bottom lip wile she tried to come up with and answer. "I can't make you tell me Kayla, but I can't help you if you don't!..... The bloody sheets in the cell were not enough to prove or disprove what they said happened.
"Colin, but I... I just need to go! I don't want to be here! Near Devin or any of the men who stole little pieces of my soul one purchase at a time!... I just want it over!"
"Ok!.... But if you ever change your mind... I'm here ok!"
"Ok!"

Dr. Barnes came in half an hour later and gave Kayla her parting orders. "I will give you a prescription to stop your milk if it starts to produce. And I will give you my office number so you can set up a follow up ok! I want to see you in two weeks." Kayla nodded and took his card, knowing she wouldn't be seeing him in two weeks. "If you have any severe abdominal pain or bleeding more than your regular menstrual flow please go to an emergency room immediately!"
"Ok!" She agreed. She received the prescription slip with her checkout papers, but was just too embarrassed to fill it. With an escort of police Kayla retrieved her few clothes and things from Devins home. She went alone through the woods and dug up the two boxes of money then within the hour she had bought the used metro and was on her way, in pain but on her way never the less.

Through the rear view she gazed one last time at the place she once called home. All she saw left was misery and regret. She gazed foreward again hoping this asphalt with painted lines and potholes would lead her somewhere the memories couldn't follow. Joshua couldn't catch up. He saw her face as she pulled away, it was her. He ran after her, he had to tell her where he was. He had to tell her what happened, but he just couldn't run that fast. Out of breath he finally gave up. He hunched over and put his hands on his knees trying to catch his breath as he realized that he had failed.

//

The green Taurus pulled into the inn parking lot. Kayla had cried most of the way there from the drug store. She had as quickly as she received the pills swallowed one and put the cotton rounds inside her bra. It was three days now since she was released from the hospital but the pain still remained. Both the physical and emotional. She was so embarrassed, but she was also thankful. Thankful that Jenn hadn't turned her away. That she didn't leave her by the roadside to hitch hike or find her own way back to the inn. Both girls sat silently in the car. Neither reached for their seatbelt releases or for the car door handles. About a minuet later Jenn did turn off the engine, but still sat silently otherwise. She stared straight ahead. "You know I'm here if you want to talk. You can call me from upstairs and I'll run down, or you can come and knock on my door!" She looked over at her and met her gaze. "I really think you should talk to someone though, you can't keep him, his memory locked inside. He want's to get out and be remembered." Kayla began to cry again, she nodded as she did.

"I Know!"

"I know a great counselor if you don't want to talk to me!"

"Thanks!" She said wondering what it was about this girl that was so different. She just couldn't believe that she was still hanging around, but, she thought, she dosent know everything yet!

TEN

Inside the realm the park was lit up like the dawn. The Host's gathered there. Each took a turn as they reported their findings. "The town is full of allies, we are blessed by this, Praise the Almighty!" Wesley spoke.
"Praise the Almighty!" They all echoed.
"Agnosko the great warrior who is guarding the church has called out into the realm and the Host's here will speak to saints. He said that they would pray! That they would feel the stirring and be on their knees! They promised to be ready for any battle against the Fallen for the child of man." Wesley stepped out and Laurence spoke.
"Walkerton, the place the daughter of man has departed from is full of Lucifer's warriors. I found one Host among them, he reported that a great evil was done to this daughter of man we have been assigned to. She will need a barrier of prayer around her. The Fallen are trying to keep her sorrows deep inside her. Deep inside her soul in the places only The Almighty can go. There will be a great battle on her behalf!"
"Thank you Laurence!" Oren spoke. "We will be ready to fight! Our allies here have already prepared themselves for battle as Wesley has reported, now we must remain by her side and keep the Fallen suppressed!" Oren said. The Host's praised the Almighty with song and reported back to Kayla's side.

//

Kayla was having an effect on Keith. More than he wanted to admit. He knew if he was to move on that he would have to face up to his deamons. The memories that hung on the walls and in the corners and behind 'the door.' He stood in the hallway leaning against the doorjamb staring at it. It had been almost a year since he had shut it. The dark wood of it stood out from the white of the molding that surrounded it, yet he stared only at the bronze of the doorknob. He kept telling himself that that would be the hardest part, just turning the knob. He had lifted his hand to it probably about seven times now and then rested it at his side again. Taking deep breaths each time as he did with the anticipation that he might find enough courage to do it.

He walked to the kitchen and poured himself a glass of water. He turned his back to the room as he guzzled it quickly and put it on the counter empty. Then with a deep inhale of air and a bolt he ran to the door grabbed the knob, turned it and flung open the door open without a second thought.

The midafternoon sun shone brightly through the sheer curtains on the windows. The white blinds behind them had been left just slightly tilted open for that reason. The light filtering in made the blue of the room glow. It was a dreamy illusion Brooke had created with one of her many talents. Keith took in deep slow breaths as he stepped into yesterday. Along the far right wall was a white book shelf filled with soft covered, bright colored books. A White rocker sat in the far right corner by the window and it had a few large teddy bears sitting to each side of it. The walls were baby blue with Noah's ark wall art stickers placed intricately where she had planned them to be along the right wall. Making lines with the animals heading into the ark. In the far left corner was a white crib already graced with a mobile and covered with matching sheets, Noah's ark of course. A bear that when turned on made sounds that mimicked those infant hears in the womb also sat inside the crib. Above and just to the left of the crib were the last touches Brooke had put into the room. KALEB, was painted in dark blue on the wall. It went in an arch starting with the k and rotating up at a, l, and e and ending with b leavel with the k across from it. She had planned to put a few more things on the wall but had never gotten around to it. Keith realized how far he had let this go. Dust covered everything and a must filled the air. He hadn't mourned them, he hadn't allowed himself to. He figured if he did that it would make it real. Like if he didn't she would just come home and their lives would start again. Now here over a year later, that still hadn't happened.

He walked over to the crib and ran his hand along the top bar. He leaned over it putting both of his elbows on it as he reached in for the bear. He turned it on and listened to the sound. He wondered what the last thing his son had heard was, if it sounded like this. He rotated the dial on the back and shut it off. Then he walked over to the rocker and sat down in the warm sunlight that filtered in. She was so smart, putting this here. He imagined her rocking him to sleep as he lay on her chest in this chair warmed by the sunlight of day or dusk. Next to him on the floor laid a plush pastel yellow giraffe. He picked it up and ran his hands over the soft fabric, He looked it in the eye. "He was supposed to play with you!..... To cuddle with you at night.....To drag you around with him and get you so dirty that we'd have to steal you from him wile he was asleep just to wash you!" He shook his head and leaned back in the rocker putting the giraffe to his chest as he imagined he would have done with his son, Kaleb.

Brooke had come into his life like a whirlwind. All of a sudden this beautiful curly haired woman had just shown up at the inn. She was introduced to him by Jenn as her cousin. Jenn had told him simply that she was staying for the summer. The truth he would find out later. For weeks he found himself coming up with really ridiculous reasons to go to the inn. Like telling Jenn he was here to check on the juice machine because it was leaking apple the other day, or bringing her air filters for the furnace because he was worried about fires. Jenn saw right through it. Finally she set up a chance meeting with him. Her and jenn went to the park by the bridge and began walking. A few minuets later Keith pulled in and walked up next to them.
"Oh hi Keith." Jenn said. "What are you doing here?"
"Oh I uh was just uh getting ready to have lunch when I saw you two pull up."
"Really where?"

"Um over at Juanita's."
"Oh great I love that place." Jenn paused a second or two. "Oh yeah, Keith have you met Brooke."
"Yeah just once!... Hi!" He extended a hand to her.
"Hi" She said with a huge smile on her face and full blush in her cheeks. She was taken by him. He was handsome and she loved the way he was looking at her, like she was a diamond or a ruby that he had been searching for and finally found.
"Are you hungry Brooke?" Jenn asked.
"Sure"
"Keith you ok if we join you?" Keith was staring at Brooke.
"Keith!"
"Huh?" He said finally looking at her.
"I said is it ok if we join you?"
"OH! YEAH!" He said trying with fail not to sound so excited. As they walked back to the restaurant Jenn's watch beeped at her.
"Oh no!" She exclaimed.
"What" Both Keith and Brooke said in echo?
"Ive got to go, the juice company is meeting me to fix the machine." Jenn winked at Keith. "Brooke honey would you be ok if I go? I'm sure Keith can bring you home!"
"Yeah, I guess!"
"That fine Keith?" Jenn asked.
"Yeah it's great!"
"Super! Thanks, I have to go!" Jenn jogged off ahead laughing as soon as she was far enough away from earshot. It worked, she thought.

Keith and Brooke began the conversation slowly. Each was so nervous. Brooke constantly looked down at her plate and bit her bottom lip, and Keith kept fiddling with his nails or silverware. Eventually they did strike up a good flow and were able to look each other in the eye. Her brown eyes radiated him to his core and her smile made him weak at the knees. He was so glad they were sitting. They talked till the entire lunch crowd had left and the dinner crowd was filtering

in. Finally after about fifteen offers for coffee and dessert they got the hint, paid the bill and left. They walked the park for another fourty minuets or so. They fed the ducks and paced the bridge. Keith like a true gentleman, drove her home and walked her to the front door of the inn. He so longed for this to work out. She was amazing. He didn't know what to do. Should he shake her hand? Hug her?   He scratched the back of his head. "Well uh, Thanks! I had a great time!" He said dropping his arm to his side.
"Me too!" She smiled up at him, he was about six inches taller than her so she had to tilt her head up some to look into his eyes. As he met her gaze she blushed again. He was so perfect, she thought. My mom would love him. He saw the flush of red come into her cheeks as she smiled up at him. He melted. Maybe she did feel the same way he did.
"Will I see you again?" He asked boldly.
"Well, I would say that is up to you kind sir!" She said jokingly with a little chuckle.
"Well then my lady…till morrow?!" He said. They had talked about her love of reading and Shakespeare and they were playing off of that.
"Till morrow!" She held out her hand to him and he kissed it gently. Brooke walked inside and shut the door. She didn't take a step she simply leaned against the door with her back and took a deep breath. She caressed the hand he had kissed and held it close to her. One day she hoped to kiss those lips. Those soft kind lips.
"Sooo???" Jenn said from the reception desk. "How did it go?"
"Great!" She said getting giddy and skipping to the desk. "He's um….. He's mmmhhhh."
"Ok!" Jenn said laughing hysterically. "I'm glad….. He's a great guy!"
"mmmhhhmmmm!"

Keith and Brooke had gone out every night for a month now. They took moonlit walks along the lake. They went to the movies and very quickly they became inseparable. If you needed to find one of them you started looking where the other was. Brooke was so grateful to finally know what true love, real unchanging unconditional love from a man was like. She hadn't told Keith yet why she was here but she knew the time was coming when she would have to. The end of the summer was nearing and Keith was becoming nervous about her departure. "I don't want to lose you!" He would say. "Why can't you stay?" He would ask. The truth was she didn't know if she was going home. If it was safe to go home, atleast until today. She walked into the inn after a picnic lunch with Keith to find boxes stacked at the reception desk and Jenn holding out a letter to her.

"Hey?" She said inquisitively "What's going on?"

"This was addressed to me but it's really for you! Here… read it!" Jenn's tone spoke volumes. It was solomn and full of sadness. She pushed the letter to her across the top of the cherry reception desk. Brooke pulled the letter out of the already opened envelope and unfolded it.

Dear Brooke, My precious daughter.

I am sending you this letter along with most of your things because I do not…. I CAN NOT let you come home!!!!!

Brooke put a hand over her mouth and paced back in forth in a one foot line as she read.

…. Your father has threatened to kill me and you if he finds out where you are. I had to sneak out for weeks and get your things one by one out of the house. I'm still not sure how I got as much as I did. He has seen your room, how empty it is and has beaten me for it. I was only hospitalized for a few days this time, but I fear it will only gat worse with my continued silence. I can't let him hurt you again. If I can I will meet you down there and we can start a new life together. But do not, DO NOT contact me. No letters or phone calls honey I cant risk your life too. I will write occasionally if I can, look for letters that are post marked from different addresses and with different names on them. I don't know if I will see you again

on this side of heaven, but I will see you again. Promise me that you will make it to heaven so I can see you again. Know that I love you very very much and that I am praying for you every moment to be able to find happiness where you are. To be able to heal the wounds your father left on you both physical and emotional. Know that I am so so sorry for all that he did, all that he stole from you. I love you so so very much my baby Brooke, Sincerely Mama!

Brooke held the letter to her chest and let out a cry from the deepest part of her soul. She knew that her father would not hesitate to kill her mother for hiding her from him. She knew that she may already be dead and that her mother had truly saved her life by sending her away. She hunched over and then fell to her knees. Jenn ran around the desk and met her on the floor. Holding her as she sobbed. As she sobbed Keith came in the door, Brooke had left her hair tie in his car. He was silenced by what he saw.

Frozen for a moment. What in the world… He thought.

"Brooke… Baby?" He said as he walked over to her side and dropped to his knees. Jenn met his gaze with a look that informed him not to speak. Not to question but just to be there. She took the letter from Brooke and handed it to him. He stopped breathing as he read it. It angered him that a man had hurt her, had laid a finger on one of the hairs on her head with ill intentions. He wanted her to stay but not like this. He put the letter down next to him and put his arms around the both of them. All three sat there in that hold for atleast ten minutes. Finally when Brooke's sobs quieted both Jenn and Keith released her and they stood. Brooke looked into Keith's eyes.

"I'm sorry!" She mouthed without sound.

"No baby.. No! You have nothing to be sorry for!" He engulfed her into his arms and pulled her into his chest.

//

The next day Brooke unpacked her things into a room that Jenn had given to her. Room three. She folded her clothes and unpacked her porcelain dolls. Her mom had remembered them. She was going grateful. She loved them, they reminded her of happy times. She had received them mostly on her birthdays or at Christmas. On days when her father acted normal and kind. She liked to remember those days. To pretend for a moment that her life was normal and that she lived in this bed and breakfast just because she wanted to. Jenn let her paint the room any color she wanted and furnished it with all the extra's like a mini fridge and a bookshelf for her to set up her dolls. Brooke, Keith and Jenn all painted together. It made for a fun day surprisingly. Brooke had never painted walls before and she was getting paint everywhere. She would put to much paint on the brush and the blue paint ran down her arm. Another time she tried to wipe off some sweat from her upper lip and got paint all over her nose. Keith had never seen something so beautiful. He just wanted to fix it for her. To make all the bad disappear and implant something wonderful in it's place.

As the weeks passed each day became a step in healing. She started to smile again. She was settled in her room and for the first time in a long time she felt safe. She wasn't worried about going to sleep, about who might jump out from behind closed doors and attack her in the middle of the night. No finally she was safe. She was so grateful for what her mother had done, she was right by sending her away, but she missed her desperately.

Keith and Brooke grew closer by the day. He was in love, he was sure of it. Never before had he felt this way. She could look at him and butterflies flew inside his stomach. He never before was able to reach his arm out and touch the stars in the heavens but now he felt like one of those stars was here with him, in Brooke. His shining star. His angel. As a few more months passed Keith kept putting aside money. He had plans for it. Each week he went down to the corner jeweler and put down as much as he could on a carat marquise white gold diamond ring. He had made Jenn sneak up to her room and get her ring size off of her rings in her jewelry box. Then he picked out the perfect ring for her perfect hand. He also had started an account he called the Brooke fund. For their honeymoon if she would have him.

The day was perfect. Sunny about seventy two degree's and a cool breeze that blew at about sixty eight degree's. The park was quiet and there was minimal humidity in the air. Keith had planned a picnic and brought Brooke here. They set the green blanket down just to the left of the bridge in the clearing on the far side of the lake. They had eaten sandwiches and sipped on sweet tea. Keith had brought a bag of bread crumbs and now they walked the bridge occasionally stopping to toss some crumbs over the side. He had reached in his pocket and brought it out empty about ten times now. He was so nervous. Finally the bag was empty and Keith pushed it into his other pocket. Brooke leaned her back against the side of the bridge. "This was such a great idea!" She said. "I've had a great day!"

"Really?"

"Really!" She smiled at him. OK, he told himself now or never. Quickly he pulled the box out of his pocket and went to one knee.

"Will you…" He hesitated as he opened the box to reveal the ring. "Be my wife?" Brooke's mouth fell open as she looked from the ring to Keith and then back again.

" Yes! Yes!" She exclaimed finally when words would come. He took the ring out of the box and slid it onto her perfect finger. He stood up and kissed her picking her up as he did and spun around. He put her down and she kissed him deeply. "I love you" He said pulling away from her lips only a moment to look into her eyes.

"I love you!" She agreed.

Back at Brooke's old house her mother shoved an envelope into her purse. It was midnight and she could hear snoring from the bedroom. Good, she thought. He's asleep. She quickly snuck out the back door went to the car. She threw in her purse and put the gear into neutral. She dared not to start the car yet. She just pushed it down the driveway using all her might. She felt a sharp pain in the back of her head and fell to the ground. The car rolled just a bit more and stopped. The silencer on the gun smoked and Mr. Easton blew the smoke away. He stood tall, a good six to six one in his brown leather jacket and flannel pajama pants. Quickly he pulled his wife's body into the garage and poured bleach onto the spot where she had laid in the driveway. He pushed the car back up to its proper spot and retrieved her purse. He took out the envelope and read the address. Between the information Alice had given him and this….. Finally! He thought, I have found her.

//

The weeks passed and the plans were underway. They had agreed on a quick engagement and small wedding. They had picked out the wedding cake and decided on the song for the first dance but now as all the small details were starting to be planned, once again sorrow filled Brooke's heart. Since she could remember she had always imagined doing these things with her mom by her side. She had always imagined, as terrible of a man as he was, her father walking her down the isle. As she wrote out the guest list she realized just how hard the day would be. None of her family could know where she was besides Jenn. Her heart ached. Jenn's father, Brooke's mom's brother agreed to walk her down the isle but no one could take the place of her mom. She tried to hide her saddness but Keith could see it in her eyes. They had been going all day, stopping at the flower shop and arranging the caterer's menu. They had planned the ceremony with pastor and now it was time to slow down.
"Hey baby? Do you want to go to get some coffee and walk the bridge?"
"Yeah sure!" She said, hoping that the sadness she felt didn't reek from her pores into his senses. They stopped quickly at

the coffee shop and Keith got their favorite coffees. For Brooke it was a vanilla latte and for him it was a mocha. Her's however had to be iced. Brooke loved it that he knew the small things like that. Things she liked and didn't. It was nice, it showed his care for her. They hardly spoke a word as they drove and now as they walked the bridge it was the same. Brooke held her coffee with both hands and sipped it slowly never taking it more than a few inches from her lips. Keith watched her as she tried to hide her sadness. He didn't understand what she was feeling. He wanted her to be happy, they were getting married. He had forgotten about her mom. As they neared the end of the bridge Keith walked ahead and found a bench.

"Come here baby!" He said as he patted the spot of the bench next to him. She sat down and he took her coffee from her placing it down on the ground next to him and making her look into his eyes. "What's wrong?"

"I just … never imagined having to do this without my mom!"

"Oh honey!" He said exasperated. "I didn't even think of that, I'm so so sorry!"

"It's ok!"

"No it's not I souldh've been more thoughtful!"

"No Keith you are everything I want, everything I need!"

"What can I do?"

"Hide me! Make me invisible for awhile"

"I love you but I can't make you invisible." He said.

"I love you too!" The sun was fading further and further behind the horizon and was filling the park with darkness so they decided to leave. From behind a bush in the darkness a man stared at them. Watching their every move wile he plotted his next. They walked the length of the bridge and got into the car. The man noted in his head the license plate number. Keith and Brooke took off and the man went on his way.

After a quick bite to eat Keith drove Brooke back to her car that was in his driveway. She had every intention of

going home before Jenn began to worry but as she got out of the car the sudden urge to use the ladies room fell on her. "Um Keith?"
"Yeah?"
"Can I use your bathroom real quick?"
"Sure!" He let her in and suddenly a great idea washed over him. Quickly he lit a candle and turned on a slow jazz soundtrack. As she came out of the restroom she heard the music. As she turned the corner into the living room she saw the candlelight and Keith standing with his arms outstretched. " Dance with me?" He said. "We need to practice for the big day ya know?" Even in the candlelight she could see his quirky smile. How could she refuse?
"Ok!" She smiled and walked over to him. He bowed like an old gentleman and she curtsied. They took one hand of the other and she put one hand on his shoulder, he put one hand just above her waistline. They waltzed in his living room for a wile like that and then the stance relaxed and she put both arms around his neck and he put both hands at her waist. They rocked back and forth slowly like that. Enjoying just being together. Just breathing the same air together, grateful that they had found each other. She took her hands from around his neck and put her arms around his back embracing him and leaning into his chest. He rested his head on hers lightly as they swayed and spun. He whispered to her in the candlelight about how wonderful their lives were gonna be together. About his love for her and how he would protect her. About how all he wanted to do was keep her safe and happy, forever in his arms. He brushed his hands over her curls and rubbed her back. "What can I do to take away your sadness?" He asked in a quiet whisper.
"Stay!" She said desperately clinging to him tightly. "Just stay!" she repeated a little louder this time.
" I'm right here!" He said embracing her just as tightly as she did him.
"Promise me I won't have to fear you! Promise I won't have

to be afraid forever!"
"I promise!" He made her look into his eyes. "You will never have to be afraid of me, our children will never have to be afraid of me and I will protect you with my life if I have to! That was all she needed to hear. A well of tears sprang up from the innermost part of her soul and she just let them come. Keith walked her over to the couch and they sat. She leaned into him and his arm strung around her back. "Look at me!" He said after a wile had passed. She did and he wiped the remaining tears from her cheeks with the back of his hand. The ones that would not dry he kissed away gently. "I love you so much… I never want you to have to be afraid! I know your father hurt you but I won't and as long as I can help it no other man will." She believed him. He was the man her mother had told her stories about when she was growing up. He was her knight and she let herself be swept away by him. Deeply they kissed and Keith hoped that he was enough. Enough to take away her pain enough to bring her happiness. That night, though they had made vows to one another and God they couldn't fight it. They had gotten themselves into a situation where they were alone, where they both needed the other desperately and they couldn't fight it anymore. Brooke had never felt a love like this she wanted to never let it go and Keith just wanted to make her feel like she really truly was loved. Each took a turn thinking about stopping but then quickly worried about the other and if they wanted to. Keith felt like their closeness right now was the only thing taking away her sadness and he didn't want to steal that from her too. Brooke felt like she was giving Keith the only gift she had left. The rest of her was damaged and this one thing she could give him. Even if it wasn't completely whole it was his.

Brooke never made it home that night. The next morning Brooke woke up next Keith in his bed. She was embarrassed and ashamed, she never should have let it go that far. It wasn't how she had always dreamed it to be. The man was but everything else was wrong. He hadn't hurt her or made her afraid by his caresses but she had broke a promise she had made, to herself to her future husband who still laid asleep next to her and most importantly to God! Quickly she wrapped herself in the sheet and went to find her clothes. As soon as she dressed she woke up Keith. He confessed that he felt like she did. Within the hour they were on their way to pastors to let him know what happened. Before they did they both got on their knees beside Keith's bed and said a prayer together.

"*Jesus, we come to you now in need of your forgivness. We took what was sacred and gave it away before it was time. We are in need of your cleansing blood and gracious forgiveness. Please Lord grant us this in your holy name we pray .... Amen!*"

"*Amen*" Brooke agreed! She fell even more in love with him in that moment. She was so happy that he loved the Lord. So grateful to find a man who was also in love with the Almighty and quick to admit his faults.

Keith stood up from the rocker and let the giraffe fall to the floor. He walked out of the room and shut the door behind him. It turned out that turning the knob hadn't been the hardest part after all.

ELEVEN

Pastor Blake continued to feel the stirring in the spirit. He prayed each and everyday for the Almighty's favor to rest on the one's in battle. He posted the prayer request in the bulletin and made sure that the prayer warriors in the church didn't let up calling out to the Father about this battle he sensed was going on in the realm. As they continued to pray Host's began to appear. They took up residence in all the places where God knew the daughter of man would go. Warriors from the south, north, west and east appeared. Ones of of great stealth and skill arrived and by that Oren knew the fight was about to begin. Drathon sensed the increasing power of the Host's and descended himself into the earth, far below the surface to where Lucifer dwelled.

"Sire!" He bowed before who was once the most beautiful Host.

"Speak!" He said letting the darkness billow out of his mouth.

"We need more troops to battle, the Almighty has sent warriors! The saints are praying master!" Lucifer cringed at the sound of the name he once worshiped! At the thought of the Host's army he was once part of. At the thought of the saints and their prayers.

"It will be done! Now remain by her side! I will assign Grafton to see to the saints and their prayers!"

"As commanded Sire!" He bowed again and ascended back to the earth leaving a streak of darkness behind him as he flew.

//

Peace! Kayla felt peace. She sat in her room at the hotel and for the first time in awhile she was beginning to have faith in people again. Jenn could have turned up her nose and go about her own business but she hadn't. She took the time to help someone she hardly knew it gave Kayla courage and challenged her once again to believe that above all people are generally good and someone does really exist that lives out what they believe. She smiled. The prayers of the children of men were empowering the Host's to ward off the Fallen and Kayla felt like some degree of her sadness was being lifted away. She still ached inside from her body trying to return to normal but her milk had dried up and she was beginning to feel like herself. The Host's couldn't make the Fallen completely abandon their mission till she herself called apaun the Almighty but they could push them further away from her. She felt absolutely sure now that she would stay and as she counted the money left in her knapsack she was sure that she would need a job too.

//

Rrrrrrrrriiiiiiiiinnnnnnnngggggg……Rrrrrriiiiinnnnnggg ggg…
"Hello?"
"Pastor?"
"Yeah?"
"It's Keith… can you come over?!"
"Sure"
" Can you hurry!"
"Right over. I'm at the church so give me five!"
"K" Keith and Pastor hung up the receivers. Pastor hurriedly paced the few houses between the church and Keith's home. Keith paced as he waited. Pastor rang the bell and Keith ran to the door, he had a tool box in hand. "Ready?" Keith said with impatience in his voice. He feared if they waited much longer he would talk himself out of doing it. Talk himself out of facing it once again.
"Ready for?….."
"To take down Kaleb's room!" He said turning on his heels and heading to the room.
"Wait!" Pastor said. He had to remain level headed here. Keith wans't going to. He knew how he was. He would get an idea and just run like lightning with it. It was one of his endearing qualities but also one that got him into a lot of

trouble. His motivation's were strong but sometimes too much so.
"What?" He said not turning to face him.
"Can't we talk a sec?...... How about you tell me why now?"
"I.... can't we just get it over with?"
"No!... You need to take it piece by piece and let yourself feel. Mourn over them! That can't be rushed."
"I can't do it Pastor, I can't...." He fought the shaking in his middle that was trying to make him cry. "I can't fear my own house, I can't be afraid to sleep for fear that she will be in my dreams............ not anymore!" Pastor walked up behind him and put a hand on his shoulder. Suddenly Keith could no longer fight it, he dropped the tool box and fell to his knees. He let hiself succumb to the sobs his stomach was shaking to try and ward off. "I wanted him! I didn't care he came from a mistake!"
"I know! He wasn't a mistake Keith! He might have been conceived from one but God ordained him to you and Brooke!" Pastor went to one knee beside him.
"It's my fault!"
"No, it's the fault of the human condition. The fault of a man who didn't allow right and wrong into his vocabulary!"
"I wasn't there! I couldn't stop him!"
"You did everything you could!" Pastor wished Keith hadn't waited so long to face all this. It was now an ocean of emotion raging inside his soul. An ocean he knew only tears and time could heal.
"Keith why don't you go for a walk and I'll wait for you ok." He nodded. "Better yet why don't you go get some coffee? Put it on my tab at the shop ok!"
"Ok, the boxes are in the hall."
"I might start, we'll see! Like I said I think you should face them."
"Alright!...I'll be back."

//

Jacob searched thru the attendance records, he didn't understand why they were down so much. He knew a lot of the congregation knew of his accusation's and enprisioning of his daughter, but in the bible days girls like her would have been stoned, she needed reprimanding and not sympathy. He knew he had been harsh with her but he didn't understand why no one believed in tough love anymore. She needed a wake up call, He thought to himself as he wondered how the church bills would be paid by such low tithes. He was still battling the thoughts he had toward her. He battled against hating her, something he knew he shouldn't think or feel because he was a man of God, yet still his flesh wanted to. His flesh battled against Diesaric the Fallen One as he lingered outside the church, waiting for him to leave the house of the Most High, a place he wasn't welcome nor that he wanted to enter.

//

"Two coffee's please, one large black and one large with cream and sugar."
"Sure! That's three twenty five Keith."
"Pastor said to put it on the church's tab!"
"Ok!" Keith stepped to the side and let the next person order. He tapped his stubby nails against the counter, not out of impatience but habit. Something he had picked up from his father from before he was sent to boarding school. It seemed to help him think.
"Next!" The girl behind the counter called.
"Um. Can I get a venti vanilla latte please?"
"Sure would you like to try our cheesecake, it's half price with your espresso drink." Keith heard the order. It was Brooke's favorite, only she had to have it iced.
"Um no thanks, however I would like to get the latte iced please?!" Keith looked over, almost expecting to see his Brooke, but instead it was the beautiful girl who had sent all of his emotions on this train headed into 'Feeling-Ville' in the first place. It was Kayla.

"Ok mam, that's four seventy five please."
"Here, keep the change!" She handed over a five.
"Thank you!" They smiled at each other and she stepped to the side.
"Hello?" Keith said.
"Oh… Hi?" Kayla said in a surprised tone. "Are you everywhere or are you just following me?" She said jokingly.
"I'm just everywhere!" He played back.
"Ok!" She giggled.
"What are you doing?"
"Um well I was hoping to get a job here. There a now hiring sign outside."
"Oh.. Well maybe I can help, I know the owner!"
"You'd do that for me?"
"Well only because I think you will look cute in the uniform!"
"Shut up!" She said as she blushed from his tease.
"No really I'll talk to him….. But you have to have to promise to stick around for awhile." It was amazing how she seemed to settle all the raging emotions inside of him, even though it was her who had brought them up to begin with by dropping the doll.
"I promise!"
"AAAHHHH!!" Keith yelled as he sipped his coffee.
"What?"
"I burnt my tounge!" He said.
"That's why you get iced!" She said sipping her's through the straw and smiling up at him with a sly half smile and then a giggle as she finished her sip.
"Maybe next time!"
"Ok"
"I got to get this back to pastor but I promise I'll call later and talk to Sam the owner!"
"Ok thanks, but remember, iced next time!" She smiled at him.
"Alright… See ya!"
"See ya!" Kayla picked up an application and sat down with

her coffee. This time she would do things right. There in a café half a mile away from her home at the inn she would begin. Begin to make money the right way. Begin to live and maybe… love. Maybe she would even see the counselor Jenn had mentioned. She felt like she had a million possibilites in front of her, all of them finally good.

//

Keith walked into a mess. The crib was in pieces on the floor, the Noah's ark stickers were pulled off the walls and the book's that were in the bookshelf were in a box on the floor next to it. All of the stuffed animals were in a box and in the corner was a box labeled memories.

"I don't know what you want to do with all this but… The Odonnel's are expecting … it sure would be a blessing?" Pastor said as he took his black coffee from Keith.

"Sure! But…" He walked over to the stuffed animals and picked out the giraffe. "I want him!"

"Ok! This one box is going with me. One day when I know you are ready I will find a way to get it back to you!"

"What is it?"

"Trust me??"

"Fine!" Keith looked around. He couldn't believe it all was going. The crib where he was supposed to sleep, the rocker where he was supposed to be fed and comforted, the books, everything but the giraffe. He just couldn't let him go for some reason. Maybe it was because Brooke had bought it or maybe because when he dreamed about Kaleb he imagined him growing up playing with it. He wasn't sure why but it wasn't going anywhere.

"I'll go call the Odonnel's wile you let all this sink in!" Pastor walked out and patted Keith on the back as he passed him. Within the hour the couple came and took everything. Piece by piece Keith watched his dream walk out the door and become someone else's and then suddenly he was standing alone in an empty baby blue room that had Kaleb left on the walls painted in dark blue as the last resemblance of it's former glory. He remembered the day she painted. He had argued with her that it wasn't safe for her to be around the paint and that he would do it for her when he came home from work, but instead when he walked in the door, the room was already painted and she was on a step stool painting his name. She had her hair pulled back in a red bandanna and paint on her face and arms. She was amazing; he remembered thinking, stubborn and amazing.

"Uh Huh!" He had said loudly from the doorway. She turned around and shrugged her shoulders at him as she smiled coyly. "I uh… couldn't help myself?" She had said. The memory still lived as if in the present in his mind, so vividly he could see every detail.

TWELVE

Kayla stood in front of the mirror in her work uniform. Keith was terribly wrong, she didn't look cute in this thing she looked foolish. She laughed at her reflection. The bright red visor and apron made her look like a large pimple, oh well, she thought, here's to honest living!

The job itself wasn't hard. She took orders for coffee and served it to the customers at the pickup window. When it was slow sam promised to teach her how to make the different coffee's and along with that knowledge would come a raise. The hardest thing she found to be so far four days into it was trying to understand what some of the customers were talking about. Latte's she got. Venti, grande and tall she understood but whatever a triple nonfat sugar free, extra hot, caramel mocha macchiato filled seventy percent of the way was she had no clue. Luckily she didn't have to actually make that yet.
"Next" She called out as the patron stepped to the side.
"What can we make for you today?" She said looking at the order screen in front of her making sure she was ready to punch the buttons as fast as some of the people talked.
"Um… How about dinner?"
"Sir we…." She looked up at him "Don't serve dinner here!"
"I know… that's why I'll have to take you to dinner!" Keith said. She was embarrassed for him to see her like this.
"Well maybe if you give me time to change!"
"Why, I told you that you would look cute in the uniform and I think I was right!" She shook her head.
"Uh No! I look like a giant zit!"
"Well would the giant zit like to have dinner with me?"
"Sure!"
"What time do you get off?"
"Six"
"I'll be here!"
"You gonna order or not kid!" An older gentleman behind Keith piped up.

"Oh.. Yes sir, I'm sorry!, could I have an ICED coffee please, medium, with cream and sugar!"
"Coming right up!" She said flirtatiously with a smile. " Two forty three please."
"Ok little miss, here's a five. Keep the change!"
"Thank you!"
"I'll see you at six!" He said as he stepped to the side.
"See ya!" She said as the old man quickly jummed up to the counter. "Yes sir?"
"Can I have a tall caramel latte please?"
"Yes sir, on its way. That'll be three o five please." She was self conscious as she felt Keith watching her.
"Here!" He tossed the exact change on the counter and grumbled on his way to the pickup line.
"Have a nice day!" She called after him.

//

Kayla ran her hands thru her hair trying to get the lines from her ponytail to disappear. She folded her apron in half and hung it over her arm and she held the visor on the ends of her pointer and middle finger. She looked in the mirror again. Much better, she thought. She walked out of the shop to drop her things off in her car. As she did she saw him. Keith was waiting for her. He was parked by the curb. He leaned his back against his silver Camry. He had one leg crossed over the other resting on the toe of his shoe and his hands in his pockets. He wore a button up and a dressy pair of jeans. He looked like a male model trying to sell a car in a magazine ad.
"Well now that's the way to pick up a lady for dinner!" She said putting a hand on her hip and holding the café door open with the other.
"Your chariot await's!" He took his hands out of his pockets, spun on his heels and opened the door to the car.
"Oooh, that's even better!" She said jokingly trying not to show all of her feelings like a giddy teenager. She walked over and got in gracefully. She was so glad her clutz side

hadn't chosen to show itself. Keith had thought really hard about where to take her and his only conclusion was the boardwalk.
"So where are we going?"
"Nope, my secret!" Kayla for the first time thought about the what if's. What if was only posing as a nice guy. What if he… no she thought she had to give him a chance.
"So how did you like iced coffee?"
"Well it was strange you see… it was cold!"
"No kidding! I bet it was the ice!" They played back and forth with sarcasm.
"You know I'd give it a fifty fifty chance." They both laughed. She was glad someone else shared her sence of humor. Keith was washed over by his roller coaster ride of emotions. As much as he still and always would love Brooke he was just as much falling for Kayla. He hadn't talked it over with Brooke about the what if's but he would imagine that he would've wanted her to move on and that Brooke would have felt the same.

The boardwalk was built to overlook a small waterfall and stream that ran underneath it. Shops were built along the walkway and in the center of it all was a restaurant. It was a casual lover's lane or a place for the family to come and play games at the arcade. In the middle directly in front of the restaurant the boardwalk went into a tee. The long extended area was used as an outdoor dining room. There were five square tables turned sideways in a row down each side leaving a center aisle. Each table was covered with a white table cloth and each also had a battery powered tea light lit in the center of it. Along the sides of the railing were white rope lights strung in u shapes every four inches or so. "Here we are!" Keith said.
"Wow! This is nice! Are you… Sure I look ok?"
"Positive!….. Do you want to eat inside or out?"
"Outside!"
"Ok, Pick a table and I'll let the hostess know we're here."

Keith went inside and Kayla picked the table at the far end. It was closest to the waterfall. The rope light's reflected in the stream below and the tealights finished off the atmosphere with a glow. Keith came and sat down. He handed her the menu "madam?"
"Not fancy huh?"
"Well not really!" He said. They both looked over their menus and sipped on their drinks silently. After they had ordered Keith broke up the silence. "So…. Tell me more about you."
"Like?"
"Um what is your favorite food and your most hated!"
"Alright… I would say the hate would be sardines and my favorite that's hard because I love fettechini alfredo and I love mint chip ice cream! It's really a toss up between them."
"Well I… hate spinach!" Kayla began to laugh.
"What?" He said.
"I had a best friend who hated spinach. It was really childish how she acted when found out it was in something!"
"Well mine is just as childish I promise! You see my mom made this awful spinach soufflé when I was a kid and she made me eat every bite. I haven't felt the same about the plant since. The only reason I even ate it all is so that I could get my brownie witch is my favorite food by the way!
"Ooh good choice, why didn't I think of that?"
"Nope! It's mine!" He said "No take backs!"
"Hey!" Kayla took her cloth napkin crumpled it up in a ball and threw it at him!
"Ok… Ok maybe I can share!"
"Fine!" They both laughed.

After the meal and a chocolate brownie for dessert they walked the boardwalk, passing by all kinds of unique shops and stands. Suddenly Keith got excited. "Ooh" He said.
"What??"
"An arcade!"
"Oh, I've never been to one!"
"Really?"

"Yeah my friends never wanted my dad to tag along and he never let me go without him as a chaperone." She shrugged her shoulders with the explanation.
"Well, I guess I'll have to be your chaperone today!" Keith opened the door and motioned for her to step inside. The smell of nacho's, popcorn and plastic filled the air. Bleeps and buzzes came from all around her in a non rhythmic fashion. Kids and Adults alike were cheering and 'aw manning' as they won or lost.
"Wow"
"Go look around, find a game you want to play and I'll get the coins!"
"K" She walked around. She saw games with guns games where you had to ride a motorcycle, literally, and games where you just pushed buttons as quickly as humanly possible. She stopped by a pinball machine. It looked safe, non invasive and inoffensive. She stood by it and waited for Keith.
"Hey, I found one!"
"What about this?"
"Pinball? No you'll like this better!" She followed his lead to a game that was making another person look really foolish.
"What is it?"
"Dance off!"
"ooooh noooo!"
"It's fun!"
"Not for that guy!" The teenager on the game was missing every few steps and his buddies were booing him each time.
"Looks like a humiliation center."
"Common one time, I'll be on the one next to you, I'll miss on purpose!"
"Alright!" she agreed. The teenager and his friend stepped off. And Kayla hesitantly took his spot. Keith took the other and he inserted the coins. "Ready!"
"No!"
Da da dance off the voice called out from the game's

speaker. *Ready... start.* Kayla followed along with the steps. She had great hand eye or in this case leg eye coordination. Quickly she caught on and had a crowd building behind her. *Winner... Winner* her screen proclaimed in bright red flashing letters. Keith stepped off as he was proclaimed *loser* Kayla almost did but another girl wanted to challenge her. She played again and then one more time winning each. Finally she stepped off. She hadn't had that much fun in a long time.
"Wow! That was great!"
"Told you!" They played a few more games and then headed back to the car. Keith walked around the car opened the door for her and then walked her to the door of the inn like a gentleman. "I had a great time!"
"Me too!" She agreed."
"Maybe… we ca…."
"Keith? Kayla?" Do you have any idea what time it is!" The door flew open and Jenn stood in the doorway.
"Uh No!"
"I have been worried sick. Kayla was supposed to get off at six and it's eleven!" Jenn's mind raced with thoughts of the last time one of her friends went missing for a night. The night Brooke and Keith conceived their son and she just couldn't stand the thought that it might happen again.
"Sorry mom!" Keith said.
"Very funny! Can't I worry about my two best friends?"
"Sure, were fine! Now if you don't mind I would like to say goodnight my date!" Jenn looked at him with spite. A week ago he wasn't ready to open the door to Kaleb's room and now he was on a date? She didn't understand how Kayla could help him but she couldn't. She slammed the door shut.
"Well then, I was gonna say maybe we can go out again but maybe we should ask mom next time!"
"I'll make sure and do that!" She said. Keith took her hand and kissed the back of it gently. He leaned in and hugged her. She fit in his arms completely and she felt like she was wrapped in a warm blanket that was just taken out of the

dryer.
"Goodnight!"
"Goodnight!" Kayla watched as Keith drove away. She was amazed that he hadn't even tried to kiss her. It was nice to be wanted for more than her body for once, and by a man like him.

The weeks went by and Kayla settled into her job. Keith worked around her schedule and they either met and had breakfast together or he picked her up for dinner. Eveyday was something new for Kayla, Something special. Sometimes at night they would walk the bridge in the park and lie on the grass on the other side and count the stars. Still Keith had not tried to kiss her. She didn't know weather to be offended or flattered. If he revered her and respected her this much to not even try and kiss her than she was amazed by his will power, By his standards.

Keith continued to work on his grieving. Wile Kayla was at work he went to the bridge and talked with Brooke. He ran his hand over the plate and remembered the day he had dedicated this place to her. He knew she wasn't in the bridge or even on the earth, he knew her soul had gone to be with God the moment she passed but somehow just talking to her like she was here helped, and then he'd call out to God. He prayed constantly, *Lord send me your healing grace for my heart and help me to accept what happened. Help me to move on to another stage of my life through your mercy!* He prayed that same prayer over and over and it felt like the Lord was answering it. He kept her picture now in a drawer in his desk face up and looking at it didn't change the course of his entire day. The door to Kaleb's nursery remained open now and he embraced the fleeting memories that came. They came and he cried and he wiped the tears away to start again. Start again on a road that was passing him by now, the road of grief that was no longer at a stand still. Every time was easier, every night came to new dawn and he began to live again. His dreams still were haunted by her but less and less were they a haunt but a remembrance of her life and their love. He began to accept the dreams as a gift, a way to see her again, and then one night it wasn't Brooke, it was Kayla.

Jenn was growing on the fact of Keith and Kayla's romance and didn't impose too much, she hoped Kayla had told him about her past, about her son that was stolen, her son that was strangely named the same thing as Keith's was going to be. Though she wanted to know why it took a stranger to help Keith she tried to just let that go and move with the flow of his progress. She loved Brooke as he did, she was her cousin and she too missed her dearly. She knew in her heart that Brooke wouldn't have wanted Keith to stay in sorrow always, or for him to live in the past so Jenn just went with it. She took Kayla on as her new found friend and helped Keith as much as she could. Keith had decided that it wasn't time yet to tell Kayla about Brooke, he wasn't sure how she would take it. He wasn't sure what she would think about a man who's been engaged and already lost a child, maybe that would be just too much baggage, he thought. Kayla Also hadn't told Keith about Her son or Devin or what she had done in Walkerton. She didn't know how he would feel about dating someone so 'experienced' or someone who couldn't give him her all should they marry. A few times she almost said something but her fear got the best of her. She didn't want to loose what she had with him and she hoped Jenn would remain quiet, though she only knew alittle she knew enough to ruin a good thing if the comment was placed just right! Each held their secrets on the tips of their tongues, embracing secrecy like an old friend. Each wondering how long they could keep the truth from the other!

THIRTEEN

Life as it tends to got hectic. Pastor was busy getting ready for revival Sunday and the board was busy arranging the seating and what the coir would sing and what meal would be served afterwards. Prayer was easily put to the side as the saints did the work of the church. Somehow in their daily lives it just got pushed back to let the business of daily life keep moving. No one meant to let it happen but each were human. As always there were the quick prayers at meals or bedtime but somehow they all seemed to forget about the spiritual warefare at hand. The Host's could feel it. They weren't empowered as much as they had been. Their strength was still the same as it had been but with the Holy Spirit answering the prayers of the saints they were energized and full of the Almighty's will.

The Fallen felt it too. They heard less and less utterances from the saints to the Almighty. They were grateful, this meant they could try once again try to remind her. To make her remember every moment of pain and anguish. Make her fall deep again into the pit of despair.

Kayla laid on her bed in the dark wishing for sleep but none would come. She tossed this way and that and no comfort could be found. She rolled over now facing the wall with the four diamond mirrors. They were reflecting something! *How odd?* She thought since the room was completely dark and the blinds were closed. She looked around the room and fear gripped her as she realized there was nothing in the room that could be making the reflection in the mirrors. Quickly she sat up and lightly patted her cheeks hoping to awake herself if this was a dream but nothing changed. Shadows and lights still reflected in the mirrors. She stood up and walked in the darkness to the wall. The reflection was of a crib and mobile projecting a prism light show. She could hear it now, the baby, he was laughing as it played its show of dancing light. Kayla looked behind her desperate for it to be true but there was nothing; again she faced the mirrors and called out for her son. "Kaleb" She cried out as she tried to reach through the mirror and become part of the illusion. Again and again she tried managing only to break one of the mirrors and wake up Jenn who was now pounding at her door. Once again the Fallen had found a way to seep into her mind and torment her.

Regardless of Jenn's recommendation to stay home Kayla went to work in the morning trying to just forget the night before. She had Band-Aid's over her cuts and began her shift right on time. Kayla stood at her post pressing buttons and calling out orders for coffee and pastries. She tried but she just couldn't focus. She was fatigued and specie. There was a man who stood in front of her ordering she couldn't focus on him. She was suddenly filled with fear. "He is here!" Drathon whispered in her ear as her stood behind her. "Kayla…he is here!" Kayla looked around franticly she didn't see anyone that resembled him. So she tried to focus on what the man at the counter was ordering and press the right keys on the screen so she could charge him correctly.
"Mocha… Grande!" She called out to her coworker who was doing the brewing. "Three twenty five sir!" She said. He paid and then stepped to the side. For a moment her line was empty, it was the lull of the afternoon and as usual there would be about a twenty minuet gap between customers. Kayla turned her back to the counter and tried to focus. *What is wrong with me?* She thought. *Where are these thoughts coming from? He couldn't find me?…. Could he???…* As she thought about him and what he might do if he found her she began to get really nervous. Her palms began to sweat and she was breathing franticly. She put her hand to her forehead and tried to clear her thoughts.
"Mam…." A man's voice came from behind her. Kayla turned to take his order. She stepped to the screen and then she looked up at him. All she saw was Devin. His face his eyes staring right at her! She steeped back out of fear. "May I order

please?" The man said trying to be polite. Kayla didn't hear him she heard Devin. Drathon stood in front of the man and made him appear to be the man she was afraid of, the man who stole her child and so so much more. Oren's orders from the Almighty allowed this. This was in his plan. She had to fall before he could pick her back up and give her reason to run into him. To want him once again as she had when she was a child.

"NO!" She said in a loud voice.

"No I can't order?" He said still polite, because he could see that she was afraid.

"No you can't hurt me! You won't hurt me again!" She screamed.

"Beg your pardon?" He said.

"No! Ho.. H..how did you find me?" Kayla still saw Devin. He spoke to her in harsh tones, she never heard a word the customer was saying. She heard things like your coming with me and I should have killed you. Drathon was skilled at the mockery of the children of men and was proud that once again he was pulling it off. "You can't talk to me like that!" She screamed. By now all of the employees and patrons were looking at her trying to figure out what was going on. Her boss Sam was questioning her from across the room.

"KAYLA?!" He yelled trying to get her attention. To get her to look anywhere but at the man in front of her. She didn't hear a word he said. Sam walked over to the counter quickly. Kayla had a look in her eye and he didn't know what she might do. She turned away from the guy and grabbed a cup of coffee. Sam caught her arm just before she released the cup into the air at the man. She looked into Sam's eyes but there he was again. Devin. He was hurting her again holding her arm and keeping her from running away. Sam took her other arm and made her face him. "Kayla!" He said.

"No Devin NOOO! Please don't hurt me! Please!" She begged.

"Kayla!" He said sternly. "It's Sam, I'm Sam!" Oren had told

Laurence to find Agnosko and to have him urge the saints to pray again. "It was time now. Time to bring her out and into the light of the Almighty."

Agnosko got right on the task. He descended into the church and spoke to the Pastor. He was preparing the sermon for Sunday. He felt immediately the stirring in the spirit and he realized that he had forgotten to pray today. He closed his word and pushed himself away from the desk. He was sorrowful that he had forgotten to pray for the people he was trying to help. He got to his knees and threw his hand up to heaven. "Father I ask for your presence to be with the one facing this spiritual battle. I ask for your power to bind the powers of darkness and its leader Satan. Bind him and cast him into the pit where he belongs, and Lord I ask that you give comfort to all of your children facing battles and warfare with the Devil. In Jesus name amen!"

Oren revealed himself in the realm to Drathon and blinded him. The Fallen One dropped to his knees and was now out of the way of Kayla being able to see Sam's face.
"I'm not Devin! Kayla!" Sam had her by the shoulders and shook her lightly to try and jolt her out of this trance.
"I know your not!" She said. She looked at him like he was crazy. "Why would I think that?"
"Kayla! Do you know what just happened?"
"No!" She looked around the coffee shop and saw everyone staring at her.
"You were calling me and that man at the counter Devin. You almost threw hot coffee in his face!"
"Oh my Lord!" She put her hand to her mouth that fell open with shock. "What have I done!.... Oh God!" She ran past Sam and into the employee bathroom down the hall. Sam ran after her and continued to knock on the door until she opened it.
"Kayla! You need to tell me what's going on! Who's Devin?"
"Um.... He's..." She stood in the doorway of the bathroom and stared at her boss wondering if there was anything she

could say that would save her job and her reputation. "Common… Let's go to my office!" He led and she followed him down the hall. His office was nice. It was painted a light yellow and was well furnished. There was his mahogany desk in the middle and a tan suede couch pressed up against the wall by the door. In the other corner was a bright green bean bag next to a book shelf. She had only been in here one other time when she was being interviewed. Quickly she sat on the couch and folded her arms around her middle. How could he ever …How could he understand. Sam took a seat behind his desk. Silence filled the room wile both thought about how to proceed. Sam interlaced his fingers together and rested his clasped hands on the desk in front of him. "Kayla…. I really like you." He started "You do a great job and you're here on time… but you really need to give me a reason here why I should let you back behind the counter! You nearly gave a man a third degree burn on his whole face! I'm… fearful for my customers and my employees!" Still silence filled the space in-between the two. She didn't know what to say or where to start so she just looked at the floor. Sam put his clasped hands to his forehead and rested his head on them. He shook his head back and forth. Suddenly he stood up and walked out of his office, slamming the door behind him, leaving Kayla alone. She cried as if on cue as the door slammed shut. She didn't know how it happened. She hadn't had an episode like this in over a month now! She had before today, been feeling better. She wasn't sore anymore and her body felt almost like it did before pregnancy, even before Devin. She knew now that she would have to go see a counselor or a therapist, someone. Kayla continued to sort through her thoughts on the couch, about ten minuets later the door swung open and in the opening stood Keith. He came running when Sam called him. He figured she would talk to him more honestly and more easily than him and then Keith might be able to explain what happened to him and he could then explain it to the customer he now owed a lifetime of free

coffee!
"NO!" Kayla yelled as she stood and ran past Keith out the door and across the street!
"Wait! Baby!" He called after her, running just behind her trying to catch up. When she stopped he came up behind her and put his arms around her. He wasn't letting her go. "What is going on?"
"No!" She fought him trying to get out of his hold.
"Kayla! Who's Devin?" He asked as he struggled to hold her.
"He.... He.... I can't! You won't want me anymore!" Keith turned her around and made her look into his eyes.
"I'm right here! I'm not going anywhere!" He said. She looked into his deep eyes that told all of his secrets and she saw truth in what he had said. She threw her arms around his neck and he held her tightly. She still needed him to want her. She talked into his chest. "I'm damaged!"
"You're not making any sense!" He continued to hug her.
"He stole my son! He raped me!" Keith hugged her tightly and his face was overcome with shock. How could she have kept such a secret? Such pain inside hidden from him. How could she have not told him? It was no wonder she was tormented by it, by him and his memory! He was almost angry with her for only a moment until he realized that he had kept just as much from her.
"Oh baby!" He whispered.
"I don't know what happened! It's all ruined!"
"No...No, we can fix it!" Keith released his death grip o her and looked her in the eye. "We can fix it! But I have to tell you some things to!" She just looked at him concerned. Was this it? Was he breaking it off? She thought. "Walk with me?" She nodded and they began to walk slowly down the sidewalk. Keith didn't know where to start so he just started where ever his mind would let him. "I have a reason for not kissing you!" He realized how dumb that sounded outside of his head. "I have kept something from you too!" They continued to walk, he couldn't look at her, he just stared ahead and talked. "I

haven't told many people about this, but I need you to know! I need you to understand my past so we can have a future together!....Ok"
"Ok"
"About fifteen months ago I lost my fiancé" There it was out, why didn't he feel any better? "We were careless and one night we just couldn't stop! She carried my son inside her because of that night! She.... Came here to be safe and I..... I.... didn't protect her!" Kayla stopped at a bench and sat down. Keith sat next to her and put his elbows on his knees and his face in his hands. Kayla let it sink in that he was hurting maybe even more than she was. He lost his love and his child.

//

The state youth conference was only two days away now. Keith packed his bags and made sure the house was stocked with everything Brooke might need. He filled the fridge and pantry with groceries and put a wad of cash in the cookie jar just in case she wanted take out or a pizza. She wanted to go with him but he didn't want to leave her alone in a hotel all day and if she was to have any problems she would have to go to a different doctor and trust someone she didn't know to deliver Kaleb. He hated that thought! He just couldn't let her go! He had given Jenn strict instructions to check on her and call him if the slightest little thing was wrong! Brooke was about eight months now. She was all baby up front and felt like a house. She was Kind of grateful that Keith wouldn't let her go. She didn't want to be stuck in a hotel room all day or go into labor in a strange town and have a strange doctor deliver her son Keith was right about that.

Keith Kissed the mother of his child good bye and shut the door behind him not knowing it would be the last time he would see her alive. He pulled out of the driveway and saw her wave from the window, not knowing it would be the last time this side of heaven he would see her with life still running through her veins.

Mr. Easton was a cunning and evil man. For sometime now he had hung around Rosewood and staked out the situation his daughter was in. He had been patient up until now. Watching from a distance and plotting her last moments. If she didn't want to share her life with him, if she wasn't going to include him in her child's life than the life he gave her he would take away! Just as he had her mothers for sending her here! Today from across the street in a small compact car that had very dark tinted windows he watched as his only obstacle drove away with his suitcases.

That night he found an unlocked window and snuck inside. He looked around the nursery and Saw the Name painted across the wall. Slowly he crept down the hall to the room she slept in. He stood over her bed and watched her breathe. She looked like her mother, He thought. He also thought of all the wicked things he could do to her right now. He could kill her and then subsequently kill the child. He could kill the child and then watch her die. He could take her body once again and please himself first before he took her life. Brooke rolled over in bed and was now facing him. She opened her eyes and shut them again. The sight went in through her optical nerve and then finally registered in her brain. She opened her eyes again quickly sitting up as she did, but the sight was gone. Her father wasn't standing above her. It was just a dream! A dream that really disturbed her. Quickly she called Jenn to come over and then called Keith. She kept him on the phone until Jenn got there and then Jenn helped her lock up the whole house. Only one window was unlocked in the place but neither could see evidence of someone having suck in so they just chalked it up to a nightmare. Jenn stayed the night and waited till the light of day filled every corner and cranny of the house before she went back to the inn.

That afternoon Brooke was beginning to feel cabin fever, she had to get out and do something. She decided to take a bag of crumbs from the counter and go feed the ducks at the park, and then she would go to the ice cream shoppe and get a sundae. She figured she was safer around a crowd of people than all alone at the house. As she pulled out of the drive the small compact car pulled out behind her staying far enough back so he wouldn't send off any alarms in her head. He didn't want her to know she was being followed or to even suspect it.

The park was quiet today! Brooke thought as she tossed the crumbs over the side of the bridge. There was a group of about ten ducks calling to her for more. She smiled at them and in her happiness Kaleb kicked. "Oh! Hi there!" She said patting her stomach. Suddenly she began to feel the same fear wash over her that she had felt the night before. Like she was being watched or she was in danger somehow.

"So… My child, we meet again!" He said from behind her. Quickly she spun on her heels and faced him.

"YOU!….How did yo……"

"Your clumsy mother, her letters and her friend Alice tipped me off to where you where! I just didn't know you were whorring around!

"I am marrying him! And let me just say he is ten times the man you could ever wish to be!" He slowly took steps towards her and she stepped backwards.

"So you'll give yourself to him and not me!" Anger rose inside him and his face became beet red.

"Yes!" She said boldly as she looked around trying to find a way and the courage to protect herself and Kaleb.

"You are mine! She had no right to take you from me!"

"You were hurting me!"

"I was preparing you for the world! Showing you what real men want!"

"NO! No you weren't!" She yelled. She continued to take steps backwards and she was nearing the end of the bridge. She begged heaven for someone to pass, for someone to be in the field or jogging past, but there was no one! "Please Daddy! Please don't hurt me again!" She changed her tone in her desperation.

"I won't hurt you! I'll only do to you what I did to your traitorous mother!" She was silent. She didn't know what he did to her mother. "What? I didn't tell you!... I'm sorry" He was speaking with pure evil sarcasm in his voice. " .. I shot her right in the back of the head.... Her blood poured all over the driveway"
"Mom!" She cried out, putting a hand over her mouth.
"She deserved it for hiding you from me, you are mine!" Suddenly he lunged at her. She tumbled to the ground underneath him and curled in a ball. She had to protect Kaleb. To keep Keith's son safe. As Mr. Easton pounded on her face a jogger camme running by.
"Hey!...HEY! STOP!" He yelled. Mr. Easton saw his window of opportunity closing so he stood to his feet and picked her up by her ponytail. He slammed her forehead into the side of the bridge and then tossed her over into the lake!
"Nooooooooooo!" The jogger called out to him as Mr. Easton ran the other way down the bridge. He jogged after him and caught him on the other side where a group of walkers stood in the way of his escape. The jogger caught up to Mr. Easton and jumped on him. He fell to ground and another man helped him keep the villain down, they sat on him wile someone called 911. Another one of the walkers went into the lake and pulled Brooke out, but it was too late, she was gone. Her forehead and face were fractured and the back of her head had landed on a large rock in the lake. Blood poured out of her ears and from the gash in the back of her skull. The only hope was that maybe the paramedics could take the baby out and save him. The man who pulled her out desperately performed CPR hoping to keep oxygen flowing to the fetus. He fought hard and kept going with breaths and compressions till the ambulance arrived but despite all his hard work when they arrived there was no fetal heartbeat. There wasn't anything anyone could do.

//

….. "By the time I got home she was already in the morge and I had to make funeral arrangements." Keith said.
"So the plate on the bridge is for her!" Kayla said.
"Yeah, they let me dedicate the place to her that's why it's called Brooklyn park."
"Oh Keith I'm sorry!" He turned on the bench and hugged her. Ok now tell me about your son.
"Keith this is really strange."
"Ok, go on!"
"His name was Kaleb!"
"Kaleb?"…Really??? With a K??" His face twisted from the oddity of it.
"Yes! You see Devin raped me and then he made me…. He made me be his…." She hesitated. She hated calling herself that, it wasn't something she was proud of or even something she chose. "His prostitute!" She closed her eyes and scrunched her face as she said it. She stayed that way for a second waiting for Keith to freak out. She opened her eyes and looked at him.
"Go on!"
"You don't hate me?"
"No!" He said genuinely "We all have a past and there is nothing any of us can do to change what's in it… so go on!"
"Oh thank you!" she hugged him as she sighed with relief. He hugged her in response and patted her back. "Um so… I found out I was pregnant for sure when I was almost twenty weeks. Devin and his group of girls beat me and then I was dropped off at my dad's house. He turned me in for prostitution. So I spent forty eight hours in jail. The last night Devin was able to manipulate the system through a dirty guard who took me from my cell threw me in the back of a truck and then someone put an oxygen mask over my face. The next thing I remember is being in the hospital and not having Kaleb inside me anymore!"
"Kayla? Are they investigating?" Keith asked. She shook her head.

“Honey you can’t just let them get away with it!”
“Yes I can!”
“No! Kayla no! You have to find out what they did to him!”
“I thought that too but since I met you I am getting better and everyday is easier than the last.” Keith was so angry. He hated hearing about someone treating her that way, hating hearing about the slaughter of a baby. “It’s fine really! I don’t want to ever have to go back! Ever!” She emphasized
“Alright but if you ever want to I’m going with you!”
“Fine!” Kayla smiled at him she loved how protective he had become over her. She loved that he cared. Keith took both her hands in his and looked into her eyes.
“Together we can help each other heal!”
“Together!” She agreed and for the first time he leaned into her and kissed her lips gently.

FOURTEEN

Keith stood in the middle of the Bedroom amazed at how far he had come in the last three weeks. He had faced this room and told Kayla about Brooke and Kaleb. Keith stood in the room with a can of paint in hand ready to cover up the memories and begin again. Suddenly an idea sprung up in his head.

Rrrriiiiinnnnggggg………rrrrrrrrriiiiinnnnnnnngggggg…

"Hello?" Kayla answered.

"Baby! Can you come over?"

"Sure what's up?"

"It's a surprize!"

"Ok be there soon!" Keith hung up with Kayla and opened up the can of paint. With a three inch paint brush he began to paint all the names she had mentioned. All the names of the people who had hurt her and then he painted all the names of thoes who hurt him. It was an idea he had gotten from one of the youth conferences on counseling. It was called paint therapy. Kayla arrived and he walked her into the room. She saw all the names painted in red over the baby blue of the wall. Above them she saw the large dark blue letters that spelled out the name of her and Keith's sons. Suddenly she realized how odd it really was that both of them were going to name their son's Kaleb with a K. She stared at the name for a moment.

"I thought this could be a way of therapy for us we can paint over all the names that haunted our past!" She wasn't listening to him she was thinking about the names Brooke, Brooklyn, Kaleb and Mr. Easton. Brooklyn Easton……."

"Hey honey?"

"Yeah?"

"What made you choose the name Kaleb?"

"Oh um Brooke had a friend back home.. Um .. Kay kay I think she called her, anyways she had promised her that she would name her son Kaleb." Kayla's head was whirling. It

couldn't be!?
"I need to see a picture!" She said franticly.
"Whoa! Why?"
"Please Keith! Please just let me see her!"
"Ok but my only picture of her is at work in my desk."
"Could you please go get it?"
"Why?"
"Please??" Keith left and Kayla stood in the middle of the room. She felt dizzy so she sat cross legged on the floor. It couldn't be her Brooke. Her best friend could be dead and she never even got to say goodbye. Keith returned quickly from the church a few houses up and handed her the picture in the oak frame. Her curls and that smile. It was her. It was her best friend and she was gone. She ran her hands over the frame and glass.
"Now will you tell me what is going on?"
"I'm kay kay!" She said in a low tone.
"Huh?"
"I'm her friend! We both promised to name our son's Kaleb and our girls Rachel when we were kids!" She looked at him and paused a second. "I'm kay kay!….. She wrote it in a letter that we buried when we were younger, I read it again just before I found out that I was carrying a boy!"
"Whoa!" Keith said. He was shocked. How could they have both found their way here?… To him?
"I guess my wrong turn on the interstate led me exactly where I needed to be!" She smiled at him softly.
"Your Kay kay!…" He sat on the floor in front of her. "You know… she missed you!"
"Really!"
"Yeah!….she did! She told me that she felt horrible leaving without saying goodbye but she couldn't tell anyone that she was leaving or where she was going!"
"I guess so, but her secrecy just wasn't enough! He found her anyway!" Keith shook his head in agreement.
"Her mom sent her here to be with Jenn, her cousin and…"

“Jenn’s her cousin??”
“Uh huh! On her mom’s side!”
“Oh.”
“You know, she was great! She made Brooke feel so welcome. The room your in must have been hers because you found her doll.”
“It was her porcelain doll?”
“Yeah. That’s why I had to get up and leave when I saw it!”
“I get it now!”
“It was maybe two weeks before I left for the conference, we were up there and Brooke was trying to show me how to hold a baby, how to change a baby and how rock a baby! I was so nervous, see I never had a baby brother or sister so I havent to this day actually held a baby! I remember her telling me to support the head and that the larger side of the diaper goes underneath!…… she would have been a really great mom!”
He was going back down memory lane right here in front of Kayla. To his awe she didn’t seem to care.
“I know she would have!
“Hey….. You would have been too!” He said reaching out and brushing her cheek with the back of his pointer and middle finger. She looked down at the floor.
“Maybe!”
“I know you would have!…. And I know that God is holding onto our sons!
“Keith please… don’t get religious on me!”
“But Kayla I am. I am in a relationship with my creator and when that happens he is just as much a part of life as breathing.”
“Well then maybe you’re the only Christian I know, my father was a fake he never believed in forgiveness...only rules. Only should and shouldn’t and I said so!”
“Kayla… maybe he tried… maybe he just didn‘t want to do anything wrong and he ended up doing it all wrong!”
“I know that he made it impossible to believe!”
“Well I hope I can help you with that!”

"Keith ...I just..."
"Ok we don't have to talk about it right now... but I do want to talk about it!" Keith stood up and helped Kayla up.
"Ok....."
"Let's go get some lunch... We can paint another day!"

//

Remorse is one of those things that can find its way deep into the crevices of your soul. It can find its way so deep that only God can see where it ends. Alice was there. She couldn't tell anymore if her soul still existed inside of her or if ramose had taken it's place altogether. If her son was the man he claimed he was. If he was the Christian he claimed he was then maybe by now just an ounce of forgiveness might be flowing through his veins and maybe, just maybe, he would allow her near him. She was tired of waiting to find out! She packed her bags, checked out for a few days and was on her way. On her way to find out if salvation could truly be found on the road.

//

Keith hadn't thought about Mr. Easton in a wile. About six months ago he almost went to go visit him. Maybe, he thought, it would help. Maybe if he learned to forgive him then maybe he could learn to accept things and move on? He never went. Forgiveness is something that is more of a gift for the one giving it than it is for the one who receives it! Keith knew that. He had just never found the strength or will to want to forgive him. He knew that when you forgive someone you're telling them that what they did to you won't rein over you. That they no longer have the power and that you have given them back all that they had given to you. All that they had tried to oppress you with. All that they had wronged you with you hand back to them and say, no thank you. Keith ran all this through his head as he drove. Now as he sat in his car in the parking lot of the state penitentiary he wasn't sure he could go through with it. Could he go and see the man who intentionally killed his fiancé and son! Could he forgive him and if he couldn't how could he speak about forgiveness to his kids and to Kayla. How could he claim to be a Christ like or even saved if he didn't even attempt it?

The sun warmed his back as he paced the parking lot. It felt like God was reassuring him in his decision to walk inside, in his decision to atleast try and face him. Inside the concrete guard station with faded white tiled floors and blue painted walls that were chipping severly Keith signed in. A few minuets later a guard checked him in. He had to show identification and verify that he never had a criminal record. He had to take off his shoes to prove that he didn't have any knives or weapons hidden in his socks and he also had to endure a pat down. About halfway through this process he wondered if he should just leave but he took a deep breath and endured the humiliation. He felt like this was another step in his healing and he had to go on, for his sake not Mr. Easton's. His clergy affiliation made the process a little easier even though he wasn't on the visitor's list. About twenty minuets later Keith was sat in a cubicle with a phone and a thick payne of tempered glass separating him and the criminal.

The man sat on his side of the Payne and looked trough at Keith. He recognized him as the man who had been with his daughter those few months that he watched her and plotted against her life. His bright orange suit reflected against the glass and he looked deep into the man's eyes who had put life inside his daughter, who had kept her from him. They stared at each other for atleast a minuet. Keith's heart pounded in his throat, he could feel it just behind his adam's apple where it had moved from his chest. Mr. Easton was curious. What did this man want over a year later? Finally Keith picked up the receiver and Mr. Easton followed his action.

"Hello!"

"What do you want?" Mr. Easton said trying to portray his coldness and heartlessness through the line. His eyes were dark and full of hate.

"I'm Keith, I loved your daughter sir and our son! I just wanted to tell you that I am here to forgive you!"
"For what?"
"For taking them away from me! For murdering them!" Keith was trying to be calm and as steady in his words as Mr. Easton was with his.
"It was my right!"
"YOUR RIGHT?!" Keith was getting angry.
"YES!" Mr. Easton smiled visiously at him. "I brought her into this life, she wouldn't share her life with me so I took what I gave back!" Keith was flabbergasted! How could any man truly believe that mudering his child was his right? He took a few deep breaths with his eyes closed. Once again he wasn't sure if he could do this but from somewhere way beyond himself he found the strength. Wesley went with him today as instructed by the Most High and he spoke power and courage directly into his soul. He grasped onto Keith's adrenal glands and made them produce less adrenaline. Keith stood up still holding the receiver.
"Life isn't and never will be your's to give or take, only the true God has that power… and I choose to follow him ……
…I choose to forgive you and take this burden you've given me and place it once again on your head!" Silence fell over the line as the two men stared fiercely at one another.
"Tell your mother thank you again for me!" Mr. Easton said with a devious smile over his teeth. Keith hung up the phone and walked away! Wesley released his adrenal glands and they began to produce again. Keith couldn't understand how he made it through without jumping through the glass and punching Mr. Eastons face in but he had. He had accomplished what he came for and now with a deep breath he walked away from his past.

//

Alice gave no concern to the hour or that her bladder was full, she just drove. She was adamant on getting across the state line before she stopped for the day. Then tomorrow only an hour separated her and her son! Her and her redemption...hopefully!"

//

Kayla was realizing a little everyday that love can reach beyond the bounds of the past and pull you out into a better place! She was realizing that the truth can set you free and that forgiveness is a gift not only for the recipient but for the giver!

Keith had spoken with the pastor and Kayla and Keith were both set up for counseling on Sunday. Pastor felt a breakthrough on its way, he knew Keith was really going to go forward with this and he had anticipations about meeting Kayla and helping her. He also had a suspicion about her being the one who was facing such spiritual warfare, but as usual only time would tell. He couldn't believe Keith had finally opened up to someone and he was amazed by the Lord when Keith told him that Kayla was Brooke's friend. No coincidence could be found in this situation at all he thought.

//

Alice awoke to the site of a brownish orange carpet and a brown leather chair in the corner. She jolted awake and it took her a few minuets to figure out where she was. She rubbed her eyes and looked around again. The old motel she was in looked like it hadn't been refurbished since the seventies but she was almost to her son. The night had been filled with dreams of the day he had disowned her. The dreams were silent, something she thought strange because her memory of the day was in full audio. He was handsome standing in his suit until he began to yell at her. His screams made his face contort but still the whole dream was like an old silent movie. She wondered if that was truly how she felt about that day because she had never gotten to explain, it never would have helped anyway! She had come to see him a wile back and she had run into that missing girl. She had to go back and tell that man where she was! To get her revenge, she never knew it would end up the way it did. That by getting her revenge she would harm the soul of her only living relative. The day he disowned her was the day of that girls funeral, the day her son buried his hopes and dreams at her expense. The day she realized what she had done. What kind of consequences she had brought apaun herself. She truly couldn't blame him now that she knew, but she still needed his forgiveness. She needed to know that he could forgive her, because if he couldn't how could God? If her son couldn't find it in his heart than how could the creator of the universe.

Alice held multiple shirts up to herself in the mirror, she couldn't decide what to wear. As she sorted through her clothes she tossed them onto the bed. Funny, she thought, those shirts had been just fine a few days ago. She did eventually decide on an outfit, put some gell into her short curls to define them and then she was off. Fifty nine minuets to Rosewood, fifty nine minuets to her son, Keith!

//

Rrrrrrriiiiiinnnnnnnngggggg.... *Rrrriiiiiiii*..... "Hello?" Kayla answered the phone. She was dressed but otherwise barely put together, her hair needed work and her face needed some touching up.

"Hello beautiful!"

"Hi" Kayla was blushing, how could he do that to her even over the phone , she thought.

"Look out your window!"

"What?"

"Look out your window!" He said. She put down the phone and walked over to the window. She pushed aside the drapes and there he was. Parked by the curb leaning against the car holding two coffees. He lifted one of the coffee's as a waive. Kayla ran back to the phone. "What are you doing?"

"Come down!"

"I'm not ready!"

"You looked great to me!"
"Alright give me five!"
"Four and a half?"
"Ok!" Kayla threw her hair into a ponytail and tossed on some blush and eyeliner. She went down the stairs and out the door.
"Coffee for my queen?"
"Thank you!" She said taking the cup of iced coffee from him.
"Just the way I like it!"
"Yup… now hop in!"
"Where are we going?"
"Well I thought we could start today instead of tomorrow!"
"Start??"
"Therapy! There's someone I think you need to meet!"
"Uh……Ok!" Keith drove until he was directly in front of his house!
"Here we go!"
"So who's here?
"Nope, not yet!" He said. Kayla stepped out of the car and clung to her latte. She held it tightly with both hands and sipped it often as they walked up the drive!
"Keith I… if it's someone important then I need to fix myself up more!"
"You look great! Now stop!" He ascended the few steps to his door and opened it before she could object any further. She stepped into the house and the smell of paint caught her nostrils. A man stepped out from behind the door and extended his hand.
"Hi…. I'm Pastor Blake!"
"Kayla!" She shook his hand and they went inside. She saw two white painting uniforms flung over the back of a chair and could smell the paint coming from the old nursery.
"Keith was impatient to start… sorry!"
"Paint therapy?" She asked
"Yeah!" Pastor agreed and picked up the uniforms handing one to each. "These should just pull over your clothes and then we can get started."

The room was to become an office or library Keith had decided so he picked a deep red color to cover the walls. A primer tinted to the same color was the first coat to go on, over the names they had painted the other day.

As they rolled the paint over each name pastor had them explain why the person should be put into the past. He explained that they weren't forgetting the memories or the good times. They weren't forgetting the bad times either they were simply asserting their will to keep the past where it belongs so the future could start. They had finished every name except for Kaleb. Kayla and Keith finished his name together. Each took one end and painted inward.

Every wall now was covered with the primer and they stepped back to look around. It was a different room. It looked bigger and forever their past would lie underneath this paint. Their reasons for regret covered up forever. It was really good therapy, Kayla thought!

"You see!" Pastor said. "It's like the blood of Jesus has covered up your past. Great color choice Keith!"

"Yeah!" Keith agreed Kayla didn't know what to say. She hadn't ever thought about Blood as a cover up, she didn't understand that phrase.

"You see Kayla; Before Christ came we had to offer sacrifices to have our sins forgiven. We had to offer spotless lambs and now Jesus became the Lamb of God, he is our sacrifice and his blood our passage into the kingdom!"

"I've never had it explained that way!"

"Well maybe we can talk about it, if you want; I promise I won't pressure you."

"Ok"

//

Alice stopped in Jackson the town before Rosewood. Now she sat in a diner sipping coffee and poking her food around her plate with her fork. She had been hungry when she stopped but the more she thought about seeing her son the less

appetite she seemed to have. She still didn't know what to say to him or how he would act, if he would even let her say a word before he turned her away.
"Is everything ok mam?" The waitress asked.
"Oh... Yeah!"
"Ok well you just haven't touched your food is it too cold or do you want something else?" Alice could tell the girl was sincere, or atleast sincere in trying to get a good tip.
"No honey I'm fine I'm just not as hungry as I thought I was."
"Ok well how about a to go box?"
"Oh no, but a to go coffee would be good."
"Sure!" The waitress scurried to answer her request. Alice held her cup to her lips and sipped slow quick sips of coffee as she gazed out the window. A woman walked in with her son. He couldn't have been more than two. He couldn't step up onto the sidewalk, his legs were too short still so his mom swooped him up and carried him in. She watched as they sat down. Oh how she wished Keith was still that small. Still trusting her and looking to her for his needs and happiness.
"Here you go mam!" I left room for creamer and sugar in the cup, do you need anything else?"
"Just my check!"
"Here you are!" The lady pulled the bill off of her pocket order slip book and laid it on the table. Alice paid and was off with one more glance at the little boy. The little boy she hoped was still inside her son somewhere. The boy who once loved her that could maybe make the grown one forgive her.

//

"Ok... how about lunch before we put on the top coat!"
"Sounds great!" Keith and Kayla agreed in unison, the coffee had worn off atleast an hour ago. Quickly they pulled off the paint uniforms and were ready to go!
"So what will it be?"
"Pizza?... Burgers?"
"Burgers!" Kayla quickly responded. It was one of her

weaknesses. A good burger with a few red onions and cheddar cheese was gonna hit the spot.
"Ok!" Pastor said.
"I'll drive" Keith piped in.

//

Alice was just crossing over into town. She figured she would try all of the places he would typically be and just look for his car! Hopefully he had the same one? She was about ten minuets from the inn. However if he was there she would wait till he left, she didn't want to face Jenn. She knew she was the one who started the whole downhill spiral that led to Brooke's death with her big mouth and she didn't want to face her cousin. Facing her son was enough! As she drove she tapped her fingers on her gear shifter. It was a habit she had picked up from her late husband as had Keith before she sent him away to boarding school. She watched him pick it up as he grew, whenever he would get impatient he would tap his fingers. Keith's car wasn't at the inn so she kept on. She remembered the last time she saw him tap his fingers it was the day he had found out she was the one who who revealed Brooke's whereabouts to her father. The day he disowned her and swore to forget she ever existed! She was disgusted with herself, if she had just… left it alone she would have a son a grandson and a daughter in law! This whole situation was all her fault. She couldn't blame Keith if he didn't forgive her but she hoped he would.

Keith's house had a car parked in the drive but it wasn't his. She pulled against the curb on the far side of the street. She had rented this car and it had deep tinting on the windows. Keith wouldn't recognize it or be able to see in so she just sat and awaited his arrival.

//

Alice was followed by a Fallen One and Drathon saw him. He flew to him. "I am Drathon servant of Lucifer"

"Apollyon!"
"From where do you come?"
"Walkerton!"
"I as well, what is your assignment?"
"To keep this woman in her regret!"
"My assignment is being guarded by the sevents of …"
"HIM! I can feel their presence!"
"We must not loose her for Lucifer!"
"Agreed! I will help if I can without sacrificing my assignment!"
"Thank you!"
"Lucifer reigns!" He pointed his sword to the ground! Drathon responded with praise to Lucifer as well and pointed his sword towards where the Lord of the Fallen dwells. The Fallen hovered over Alice's car and waited. Apollyon's sword floating trough the antena.

//

Alice fidgeted with her radio dial. She couldn't get anything to come in. Eventually she just turned it off and listened to the quiet. Silence was better than static. It had been nearly an hour when she saw Keith's car in the rear view heading her way. Alice watched as the man she knew as her son stepped out of the car along with another man. She wasn't prepared for what she saw next! Keith walked around the car and opened the door. She saw it all in slow motion as the girl stepped out of the car and kissed her son's lips. As she turned her head her brain recognized her. The daughter of her Pastor who had become a prostitute! A girl who didn't belong with her son! "Oh No!" She said out loud. She thought about her first mistake with Brooke only for a moment before she decided that she was right this time! Her son deserved something better. Something that wasn't used up. Her son deserved her to fight for him! One day he would thank her! She thought as she peeled out and went back home. Back to Walkerton to find the one the whore belonged to. Prostitutes needed their pimp and she would reunite them. Everyone looked towards the road as they heard the tires sqeel. No one realizing that one more time Alice would try to ruin her son's happiness. That in that very moment the war between the realm's for Kayla and all she was meant to be would be beginning!

FIFTEEN

The last time Kayla had seen this many dresses was at her mother's funeral. A day she remembered mostly in black and white. Being only five at the time and the mix of black dresses against the light colored skin of her grandmother and relatives made her memory seem like an old back and white movie. Mostly she remembered this day as the last full day she would spend with Granny.

On the front row under a black tent and on a folded seat Kayla sat dangling her feet, she was still too short to touch the ground when she sat in a chair. She wore a black hat that looked like someone from the fifties would have adorned and a calf length black dress made of velvet. She had on white tights that were printed with flowers. She was still unsure of what was going on. People who all wore black were walking past a long box and placing flowers on it. She remembered the flowers in color for some reason, and then the people would file in behind her and sit down. Strangers kept trying to hug her and say they were sorry. She didn't get it. Granny had told her that they were all going to get together today and wish mommy goodbye as she went on her trip to heaven, but she hadn't seen her mommy yet! Nothing made sense to her. The next part of her memory began to come into color with flashes. Flashes of full color and then back to black and white! A man she hardly knew was walking across the lawn. She knew he was her dad and that he was away at school except on holidays. He came and sat next to her, emotionless in his black suit and tie. Full color filled her memory now as the man went up by the box and began to read out of a large black book she now knew was the bible.

"What's in the box?" She asked Granny

"That's mommy's box, she's going to travel to heaven in it!"

"Mommy's in there?" Kayla said exasperated. Granny shook her head sadly as they began to lower the box into the ground. Kayla's memory was nothing but red now, everything was

red. She jumped up from her seat and ran to the casket. She jumped onto the box and began to yell!
"NO! NO! You're going the wrong way! Hell's down there Noooooooo!" It was the consequences of that moment that killed Granny. The fight that caused her heart to break enough that it quit altogether. To this day she still wasn't sure if she blamed her father or herself for her death. If her father hadn't fussed at Granny so harshly maybe she wouldn't have had the heart attack, but if she hadn't ran to her mothers casket and made a fool of herself than her father wouldn't have had to fuss at her.

Kayla brushed the memories away, she had to focus, she had to get this lump out of her throat and her stomach to untwist itself so she could walk inside this place. This place that if it wasn't for Keith she wouldn't be going to at all. "Here it goes!" She said stepping out of the car. Her feet felt heavy as she ascended the steps to Rosewood Community Church just as the bells were tolling.

//

Oren, Laurence, and Wesley followed Kayla in, each calling aloud to the Lord. Praising him for guiding the girl here and praising him for his existence. Kayla felt chills down her spine, she had never felt like this before when she walked into a church, maybe it was nerves, she thought. "Holy spirit… Comforter, come to her!" Oren called out to the Lord.
"Call to her heart Almighty God!" Laurence called out.
"Draw her heart you Father!" Wesley called out!

//

Kayla felt strange today. She picked out a seat in the back and crossed her arms to try and ward off the chills. She looked around at all these strangers and wondered what they must be thinking of her. Keith saw her come in from his seat next to the Pastor. She was so beautiful, he thought, he so wanted her to feel what it was like to have the hand of the creator inside her soul pouring out love into the places she could never reach. She was so uncomfortable, he could see it in her face. He tried to wave at her but she was staring down at her feet. Jenn was going to take kids church today so he could sit with Kayla after worship and opening prayer which he usually led wile pastor prayed for the morning service from his office down the hall. "Lord!" Keith prayed silently. "Please ease her discomfort and come to her Father, let her feel the true you so she can understand how full her heart can be with you in it!" Keith opened his eyes and finally met her gaze she waved and for some reason she was beging to feel less uncomfortable.

//

Pastor Blake was pacing in his office. Today was important, he could feel it in his spirit. About two weeks ago God had given him a sermon and then never directed him in using it, today he felt like it was time. He heard the choir singing the last song on the pamphlet and he knew he had to run with what he felt led to do, the Lord wouldn't lead him wrong.

Keith was just finishing up the prayer as pastor walked into the sanctuary from the side door leading to his study. Jenn took the kids as Keith announced that children were dismissed for their service. He knew Kayla would need him today. She had this false idea of what a true Christian is and he needed to be there to make sure she knew it wasn't that way. It was his mission no matter how long it took to show her the true God.

"Good morning" Pastor said as he took his place on the pulpit.

"Good morning!" The congregation responded. Keith walked down the aisle towards Kayla and then slipped in next to her.

"And good morning to you beautiful!" He whispered.

"Good morning!" She said with a fake smile. She was still somewhat uncomfortable but it was fading slowly especially as Keith slipped his arm around her shoulders and she leaned

back.
She settled into his arm and prepared for the sermon.
"Today, I want to talk to you about choices." Pastor said. "Now I know what you must be thinking, No it's not your choices I'm talking about, it's the ones Jesus made for us." Pastor was overwhelmed by the Holy Spirit, the words were flowing out of him so easily and he felt energized by God presence. "When we think about choices we usually think of a right and a wrong, but when Jesus came here to die for us it wasn't either. It was a choice of love. He loved us enough to come from his heavenly home that is filled with eternal light and splendor. With mansions and heavenly Hosts calling Holy Holy Holy, to come here and be born into a humble life. Into the human body that is made up of dust and that is venerable to the elements of emotions and the world. He loved us enough to come here and suffer the weight of the temptation without fail. To live in his human body for fourty days and nights without food or water and he was tempted by the same Satan that made man fall in the beginning. All without fail because he wanted to show us that with the Fathers help nothing is impossible for us." Pastor walked to the edge of the stage. "Could you imagine even two days without food or water?" Then if you had a way out would you not take it??? He didn't because he wanted to show us that the word of God is as important to our souls as bread is to the flesh." He walked to the other side of the pulpit and stopped at the edge of the stage. "Satan knew that the son of God could pick up a stone, change its molecular structure into bread and eat it but he refused. Because man cannot live by bread alone but by every word that procedeth out of the mouth of God!" He was silent for a moment letting the powerful words sink into the hearts sitting in the congregation. "Do you know what some of those words say ladies and gentleman?... Psalms 103:10-12 says that He does not treat us as our sins deserve or repay us according to our iniquities, for as high as the heavens are above the earth so great is His love for those who fear Him. As

far as the east is from the west…" Pastor raised his arms and outstretched them as far as they would go. "As far as the east is from the west so far has He removed our transgressions from us!" Pastor breathed in deeply with his arms still stretched out.

In the realm Oren, Wesley and Laurence could see the Holy Spirit all over the man on in the pulpit. They bowed in reverence to the Comforter. Then suddenly the Spirit that was all over the Pastor doubled and half went to Kayla but every bit of the spirit that had been around the Pastor still remained with him as if the Holy Spirit had performed some type of mitosis so he could be everywhere at once. Even the Host's watched in in awe every time, how amazing is the Lord, they would call as they did now again watching him work inside the children of men.

Kayla felt weird again, but at peace. Comforted almost and warm. What Pastor was speaking of her father never portrayed. He was all about right and wrong and consequences. Was this God he speaks of different than the one her father serves or was her father just missing the point? She wondered.

Pastor looked around at the faces in the crowd. "This is what he provided for us on the cross, a way for our sins to be erased, for our sins to be as far away from us as the east is from the west!" Pastor put his arms down at his side. "Do you have any idea how far that must be? The Bible doesn't say as far as our planet is from east to west, it just says in general as far as the east is from the west. A distance only the Lord knows beyond the reaches of space, of the universe he created, think about how far that must be for a moment?" Pastor paced the stage for thirty seconds or so and Kayla really thought about it, billions, trillion of miles, light years away. Could it be that all she had done wrong could be that far from her? Could all her sins be cast that far away? "Millions, billions and trillions of miles away people! Light years from you, the Lord who created you said that he would

cast your transgressions that far away. You know what else the word says? In Micah 7:19 it tells us he will turn again he will have compassion on us, he will subdue our iniquities and cast them to the depths….
Of the sea, yet another place that we have no idea of the depth of. How amazing is his love for us? I know what some of you are thinking now. These scriptures could only be pertaining to the small sins, the white lies, the gossiping but let me tell you something church in the eyes of God there is no gray. Sin is black and good is white. God sees all sin the same way…. You know David was a man said to be after Gods own heart and yet he was an adulterer and a murderer. Yet his heart sought God for forgiveness and the Lord gave it." He walked out from behind the pulpit and met Kayla's gaze he hadn't seen her yet today, he felt like the power of God was flowing through him into her. "I don't know who needed this today but God wants you to know he loves you and that nothing you could ever do is unforgivable. No sin is in the way of you and him because of what Jesus chose to do on the cross." He looked away from Kayla and across the congregation. He met different gazes. "Adultery, lust, greed, gossip, prostitution! He wants to forgive all of that and be your God!" Kayla hadn't told him about that, how did he know? She wondered. "If there is anything big or small you need to confess before him please come, the altar is open… if you need to ask God to come into your life as your savior, please know that he wants you and is waiting!" The Holy Spirit filled Kayla with peace, with assurance that what Pastor was saying was genuine and that God really did want her. Kayla jumped up from her seat before she had the chance to talk herself out of it and she ran to the altar. She fell to her knees on the only open spot. "I want you too! Jesus I want you too!" She called out not caring that she was loud or that half the church was probably looking at her, she only cared that the God that created the universe wanted her. "Come to me please God, I want you!" Keith came up behind her and began to pray silently. Pastor walked

to her. “Kayla?”
“Pastor?” She opened her eyes and looked at him. “I want my sins that far away!”
“We all do!” He pulled her up from her knees and took both of her hands in his. “Pray with me!.....Jesus!”
“Jesus!”
“Please come into my life as my savior. Please forgive me for all my sins, I accept what you did for me on the cross” Kayla continued to echo Pastors words genuinely and the Holy Spirit did as she asked. “Cast my sins as far as the east is from the west wash me clean and adopt me into your family as your child, in Jesus name, amen!” The Holy Spirit was at work consuming all her sins and throwing them beyond the reaches of space and time where they never would be remembered by Him again. All the Angels within ten miles were lifted up by the power of the Almighty and began to sing for a soul had found its way home, one more soul was now God’s and Satan had lost once again! The Fallen ones knew well what the singing of the Angels meant and they slunk underground to drown out the praise of the Host’s.

Kayla didn’t understand but she felt clean, light as air and free! “Wow!” She said “This is what you have been talking about isn’t it!”
“Well do you feel free?”
“Yes! Finally!”
“That’s it, you know Kayla I’ve had that sermon for weeks now and God told me today was the day to preach it, He knew you’d be here, He loves you!” Kayla felt so special, God had been preparing things for her all along. From where she would end up to the sermon she would hear today, He had it all planned.

//

Walkerton was buzz in the realm. Fallen Ones of hate surrounded Alice , A deamon of power and greed clung to Devin tightly. As Alice told him of what she had found he started plotting to get her back. She had been his top seller and he wanted all that money to return into his house. The money she stole and even more she could bring in within a week if he made her work double time! She would, he told himself, he would find her and make her. The Fallen One clung to his soul squeezing all decency out of it.

Alice was simply filled with anger, her son couldn't forgive her but he could cling to, kiss and who knows what else with a prostitute? Did he even know? She thought. Did that whore even tell him? Alice had made a few calls already. Jacob was one of them. He had this hold on his life because of her, he didn't want to see her yet, he just needed prayer that he could as a Pastor learn to forgive her. He lost the last part of his heart when she disappeared and then when he found out where she went that empty space filled with anger, hatred and remorse for what he had tried to make her do! He souldn't have tried to take her chance of true love away, all this was his fault! He thought!

Alice felt strange conversing with the prostitute king, the pimp of Walkerton. Never before had she had a reason to look in his direction and when he fixed this situation for her never would she again, but today they sat close plotting and planning her removal from a diner outside of town. Devin didn't know Keith but he knew that in the past few months he had reeled over Kayla, he had desired her and he didn't want any other man but him to have her. She was the prize he had picked up on the side of the road. If he let himself feel he could almost say that he missed her and their son.The son he tried to erase from his memory. He had seen the horror the night he helped steal him from inside her. The Doctor had told him that the baby was just a blob of flesh inside her but as he pulled the head out of her he realized it was a lie. The Doctor had pierced his brain and the boy, his son, jerked in his hand. When he pulled out the limp infant and he saw his face, he knew it was nothing like what the Doctor had said. He had features and his face wore pain as its last expression. Devin could see a personality in it, a human inside the lifeless child. He had eyelashes and fingernails and tiny little feet, he wanted to scream "Put him back I… don't want this anymore!" but it was too late, he was already dead and in the arms of the mortition who was to cremate him and make it so the child never was. Just like that he was never a father. No one would ever see his son or know his name, no one would realize that he was the one who let his son die in the arms of a Doctor who swore to *first do no harm!* Then he had gazed apaun the mother that son who laid bruised and bloody before him, he watched as she convulsed from the amount of medicine running through her veins and he watched as the Doctor quickly made them stop and saved her life. For the first time he was sorry for what he had done to her, he almost cared for her he thought, but that wasn't him and he pushed his feelings aside. He had a business to run, a coldhearted dirty business that needed him to be emotionless!

"So…" Alice said. "We can drive down and stake out for a few days. We can watch them and their habits then once we know what to expect we can get her alone and snatch her up before Keith even has an inkling!"

"Huh?" Devin shook his head and closed his eyes trying to shake his memories away.

"Devin pay attention!"

"Oh sorry!" he rubbed his eyes. "Ok say that again!" Alice repeated her plan and he agreed that it could work.

"Let's plan… to go down there and plan the rest then!"

"Fine!" Alice replied.

"So go pack and I'll meet you just before sunrise at the gas station on the corner of main and third."

"O dark thirty it is!"

//

Criton massaged the part of Devins brain where memories were held, making him remember only that night. Making him feel only what he felt that night and making him desire to get her back at all cost's! Devin threw some clothes into a duffle bag and then from the bathroom he tossed his toothpaste, deodorant a razor and his other necessities onto the bed where the duffle bag sat. He put them inside after pacing the few steps from the bathroom to the bed and zipped it up. He let himself fall backwards onto the bed. His legs hung over the side and dangled just above the carpet, he fell asleep that way his mind filled with dreams of his son. The son who never cried or took his first breath by the works of his hands.

//

Dr. Steele was performing a routine sonogram when the call came. Jacob was so frustrated, he wanted his daughter to be the girl she was and not the disgrace she had become. Jacob had found a friend in Dr. Steele years ago when Kayla had to begin her internal physical's. The Doctor had assured him and Kayla that everything would be fine. He had a nurse stand by her side in her mother's absence and Kayla found him very gentle. The exam didn't hurt like she expected it to. Today once again Jacob looked to his friend for assurance. He had no idea he wasn't the man everyone thought him to be, by day, yes, he was a respectable Doctor, but by night he was a last resort murderer! Under the table girls came with cash and he got rid of their problems no matter how far along they were!

The first time he had done this was supposed to be the last time. The girl was being abused and the fetus was dead inside her already, Dr. Steele could justify that one, but when her friend came too with cash and threats of revealing his secret he did it for her too, this time however the infant still moved and lived inside her. To this day he could vomit at his reflection but he was trapped by his secret and then one day Devin the prostitute king brought a few girls to him for his 'extraction' services and they made the same threats the others did. If he refused they would turn him in or kill him. He was trapped by his mistake and everyday he feared the old saying that the truth shall find you out, for now atleast he worked on borrowed time!

"Who's on the phone?" He asked, not blinking away from his work.

"Jacob Holmes sir!"

"Tell him I'll call him back.

"Ok!" the Doctor hadn't heard from Jacob in months.

"mmmm" he thought wonder what's up? He brushed the thoughts away and focused once again at the monitor. He moved the transducer around on the woman's jellied belly and looked at the healthy fetus on the screen in front of him. "Ok do you want to know the sex?"

"Yes!" The woman piped up and the husband nodded in agreement.

"On look here on the screen" He pointed with his left index finger

"Right here you can see two curved lines, you have a very healthy baby girl!"

"Really?... you sure!"

"Yes!" the couple kissed and awed at the screen a few moments as the Doctor wiped off her belly with a towel. I'll make you a copy of these pictures and I'll see you back in about three weeks!

"Ok!" The Doctor removed his gloves and pushed the machine out of the room. This is what he went into medicine for. Making couples happy and keeping babies and their mom's healthy! Quickly he printed a copy of the sonogram for the happy parents and then was just as quickly on the line with his old friend.

"Jacob! What's up?"

"They found her Robert, Alice found Kayla!"

"OH!"

"Yeah, what should I do?"

"How about go see her?"

"No I ... I ... there's no way!"

"Why?"
"She hates me and I can't find it in me to forgive her even though it's my fault! All of it!
"Jacob!"
"Robert!"
" I bet she blames herself!" Silence fell over the line as Jacob pondered that. He didn't know if he was more afraid that she blamed him or herself. If she blamed him than how could there be any reconciliation? If she blamed herself well….
"I thought you'd understand!" Jacob said. The truth was that he did! He wasn't sure if she had heard him that night, if she recognized his voice or if she knew who he was as he drugged her. The truth was if she did and she told his life was over, so he too didn't want to see her. He didn't truly want Jacob to see her. To mend it all up and bring her home where she would see him and maybe recall his voice or his hands that were the last thing she saw wile her son was inside her. If only Jacob knew what he had done to her, if only he knew he had a grandson, if only a lot of things. The Doctor thought.
"I got to go Rob!"
"Jac…." beeeeeeeeeeeeeeeppppppppp. The line was dead. Dr. Steele quickly dialed another number. "Pickup! Pickup!" the Doctor said as it rang.
"Hello?"
"Westbrooke?"
"Steele?"
"Yeah listen, they found her!"
"Who?"
"Who?… Who do you think?"
"Kayla?" Westbrooke whispered covering his mouth with his hand. On the other line Joshua listened in quietly blocking the receiver with his hand to cover his breaths. He was extactic at what he heard; finally he could tell her where her son was.
"Yes!" The Doctor said through gritted teeth.
"Who told you?"
"Jacob and Alice told him!"

"Alice?"
"Yeah I don't know how she is involved!" Suddenly after two clicks he heard dead space again. He had been hung up on a second time but wait... Did he hear two clicks?

//

Ring.. Ring.. Devin opened his eyes he still laid on the bed next to his duffle. He sat up with a groan thanks to his stomach muscles lack of use. The phone sat on the dresser about ten feet from him, he could see the buttons glowing blue but he wasn't exactly motivated to get up yet so he just listened to his ringer. Then silence. He knew in about nine point five seconds if the person left a message the phone would beep loudly and obnoxiously. He would get up if it did. Instead it began to ring again and Devin figured it might be important so he paced the few steps and answered. "Hello?"
"Devin?"
"Yeah!"
"Westbrooke!" Mr. Westbrooke for some reason always referred to himself by his last name, he wasn't sure if it was because of his years in the military of if he just thought it sounded more like he meant business.
"Can I help you?"
"They found her!"
"I know!"
"You do?"
"Yeah listen I'm taking care of it!"
"Devin you just can't..."
"I've got this...ok were going to get her!"
"Who?"
"Me and Alice, it seems she's got a thing for her son!"
"Please let me go!"
"We have to be discrete and quick!"
"YES SIR!" He said as if he was a grunt responding to his c.o.
"Tomorrow morning at o dark thirty we meet at the corner gas station on main and third"

"Thank you, I just can't let her ruin my business and my family!"
"Yeah whatever Westbrooke just be there!"
"Affirmative!"

//

The boardwalk was even more stunning now. Kayla felt like she was walking around with a brand new set of senses. Everything looked new, somehow everything had a sweet smell to it. Her mind was clear and her thoughts were all her own. God really was real; he really was her creator for only he could change her truly, only he knew all of her soul and how to fix it!
"May I take your order mam?"
"Oh yes… I'll have the chicken marsala with broccoli and we want to go ahead and order a brownie, al a mode to be brought out after our meals."
"And you sir?"
"Sirloin, rare with mashed potatoes."
"Thank you!"
"It's nice inside too, isn't it?" Keith said
"mmmm!" She agreed. "A little warmer too!"
"Kayla I have to tell you something!"
"Ok?" She looked at him with concern.
"I went to see Mr. Easton."
"What?"
"Yeah!" He leaned foreward and put his elbows on the table. "I had to, I had to let her go and I had to forgive him!"
"How did it go?"
"Well he basically told me that he didn't need forgiveness because he was just taking a life he had brought into this world. That it was his right!"
"That's sick!"
"Yeah! So I told him it didn't matter if he thought he needed it or not, that he was getting my forgiveness anyway!"
"Wow! I… don't think I will ever be able to do that! She said solemnly.

“Yeah you will. Forgivness is a funny thing to our flesh, it wants to hold onto those feelings of hurt so we can remember and protect ourselves.”
“I suppose!”
“But hey it only hurts us more because we end up building walls and not letting in the ones we really love.”
“I’m just not that strong I can’t imagine looking Devin the face and telling him that I forgive him.
“Well it’s like me, I wanted God for along time to let me hate her father but it’s like Pastor said, sin is black. Evil is dark in the eyes of the Lord, all of it! The hate I would have had for Mr. Easton qualified as just that, black. But the good is white! It’s not some scale of colors rating one sin worse than the others! He gave us all free will and unfortunately the freewill of the bad cross the paths of good people…. And it’s what we asked for, we want to do whatever we want, live however we want and then when bad things happen we blame God!”
“I guess, I just never thought of it that way!
“People want their freewill to do whatever they want, but they want God to take the freewill of others that get in their way but God is loving and he set us free because he wants us to come to him by choice, by our freewill he wants us to love him!”

//

SIXTEEN

Joshua hung up just as his father did, he had to go too. Somehow sneak in the trunk or a suitcase, she just had to know and he had promised himself he would tell her! Frantically he waited for his father to fall asleep. He laid in his bedroom in the dark listening. He knew the louder his fathers snoring became the more deep of a sleep he was in. when it was loud enough he knew a bomb couldn't wake him and so he began to pack. One small bag with a change of clothes and a toothbrush.

At five after midnight he snuck into his parent's room and gently kissed his mothers forehead. "Love you!" He whispered in his head. His bedroom window was a great way out all he had to do was step over onto the pump house and then make the three foot jump to the ground. Also his bedroom faced the woods at the back of the house and all he had to do was quickly disappear into them. The trip to the gas station wasn't far, just a quick dash through the woods and then about a half mile walk on the highway. The trick would be not to alarm any of the passerby's. For some reason adult's didn't think a child could take care of himself after dark so he would just have to jump into the ditch should anyone drive by. A small price to pay for doing the right thing, he thought.

The trip through the woods was proving to be harder than he thought. The leaves crunched under his feet and the owl's hooted. He thought once already he had heard a wolf or that he heard someone following him. Though the moon was full and rose high in the sky the light it gave only made the woods creepier by casting ominous shadows wherever it may. About ten minuets later Joshua emerged from the dark and creepy woods to the freedom of the open road. His heart beet slowed as he exited the brush and began to walk in the open. The distance was short now so he decided to run. Six minuets later he came up on the station. To his surprise Alice and Devin were already there, tossing their luggage into the backseat as he rounded the corner. He slunk back and watched from afar. Devin took his car across the street and Alice went inside, this was it his only chance. He bolted to the car and quickly opened the back door which was thankfully unlocked. From there he pulled up on the locks that held the seats in place over the opening to the trunk. He crawled inside and pulled up one side of the seat locking it into place. The smaller side he left just barely cracked so he could escape if he needed to.

//

At o dark thirty Westbrooke pulled into the gas station. To his dismay there was no one else there. He waited for two hours and no one ever came, he could see the sun peeking his head over the horizon and it finally sunk in, he had been left! Anger bubbled in his veins and ran to his heart where it was pumped once again through his whole body. He hated lies, he hated even more that he now had to leave his problem in the hands of Devin and some old woman. He always believed that if you want things done right you had to do them yourself, and now he couldn't.

Ring …ring… Westbrooke looked at his phone, home was calling.

"Westbrooke?"

"Tom!" His wife said frantically. "Joshua's gone!"

"What do you mean gone?"

" His window's open and his bed was never slept in!"

"Marge! Don't call the police I'm on my way!"

"What, Tom, Why?"

"I'll find him!" He shouted into the small cell phone! "Please let me find him!" He calmed his tone to try and calm his wife.

"Tom why!"

"Honey just give me some time ok!" He lowered his voice; he needed her to trust him. He could at least do this himself and the last thing he needed was Colin coming and snooping around. He had been looking for clues to solve Kayla's case for months and though he was sure there was no evidence left he was still paranoid that the perfect cop would find something. Plus if he slipped up, if he said something, if Colin found out someone knew where Kayla was and he talked to her, if she remembered anything at all, his life could be over. All he wanted to do was make that night disappear. The only other child he had seen born was his son, Joshua. That day was joyous. That day had almost brought this strong marine to tears, to see how hard his wife had worked for their family. To hear their family start with a strong cry from his son. He was gut wrenched to have stolen that from someone else. He wasn't sure now why the money had persuaded him. That night as he watched the lifeless child come out of an almost lifeless mother he just wanted to scream. Cry, common baby cry, and then when they placed him in his arms it took all of his training to not weep hysterically. He didn't show any feeling at all till his back was turned and he was down the hall. He imagined Joshua and saw his face on this child's. This stolen murdered child. "I'll find him Marge!" He said through the lump in his throat.

"Soon!" He could hear the desperation in her voice and he felt the same, his son was a blessing, a gift, and he was missing.

"Ok!"

"Ok!" They both hung up. Tom suddenly remembered that last night he thought he heard someone breathing on the other end. What if… He had actually heard someone, what of it was Josh? What if he snuck out to meet him here…no he hadn't done that since he was atleast five when he had hid in the backseat floor for hours covered with a jacket, as he drove away for a business trip. He just wanted to be with his daddy back then, now they were drifting apart. He couldn't make it add up though, Josh didn't know who Kayla was, why would he want to go on this trip? Westbrooke searched his trunk and backseat only to find everything he didn't want. No Joshua, just junk filled the car.

//

The Host's could feel a stirring in the dark side of the realm. The Fallen Ones buzzed underground plotting against the girl, against her future. The Almighty spoke to Oren's heart. " This is about more than just Kayla. Her salvation is my will because I love her, but she is one of the keys to Walkerton!" Oren heard everyting the Lord spoke to him. He wondered if the Fallen knew of her destiny? Regardless, Oren knew their would be a great battle over her. He knew she would have to return to Walkerton before this was all over, and he knew that when she did, an army of Fallen Ones would be waiting for them. For now atleast the realm was thick with Host's, each ready to battle for Kayla, for the Almighty!

//

Joshua felt as if he had been riding for days. He stared at the crack between the the seat and car that let in just a faint line of light. He had stared at it for so long now that he feared he would see that line forever, that it was going to be burned into his cornea's memory and he would never be rid of that line in his sight wherever he looked from now on. About an hour ago Alice had slammed on the breaks and he had gone rolling into the back of the trunk. He had banged his head against the inside of the lock and yelped a little out of the shock of the pain. He could hear Alice and Devin questioning the strange sound from the front seat. "What was that?" She said.
"Sounded close?... Did you hit something?"
"No!" Alice said as she released her foot from the gas pedal letting the car slow some. Joshua held his breath as he listened to them talk. What if they stopped? What if they looked back here? Joshua heard the engine roar from the gas Alice had just pushed into it and the car accelerated.
"Maybe it was the tires?" Devin said. Josh let out his breath slowly as he slinked back up to the deep part of the trunk by where the seat split and he could escape. He secured himself

in the corner and braced his sneakers against the edge of the trunk lining. If they slammed on the breaks again he could hold himself in place with his sneakers. He looked once again at the line of light, it was larger now. The car stopping so suddenly must have opened it some just by force. He had to do this delicately. He had to find the handle and pull the seat further in where only that small line of light was visible. He was afraid that the line of light being as large as it was meant the seat wasn't secure and that if she slammed on the breaks again it would fly open and this whole mission would be ruined, if not his life too. He used the tips of his fingers and ran it across the upholstery feeling for the loop of harder fabric. He found it and slipped his fingers inside, pulling slowly he watched the line of light get smaller, smaller and then perfect. He held himself in the corner with the soles of his sneakers against the side of the trunk hoping he would be strong enough to keep himself there if she slammed on the breaks again, but right now every muscle in his toes, feet and legs were shaking, and ached from his positioning. He only wished to get there.

//

Oren needed to get her away. She needed to be at the right place at the right time. It had been revealed to him by the Most High what was to happen and now he needed to get her to where it would all begin.

//

Keith stood above the glass case, he had been staring at all the shiny items for atleast twenty minuets now. He wanted to buy her something special, something that would make her feel special.

"whatcha think Keith?"

"I don't know, I can't remember specifically if I saw her wearing earings or a necklace? I thought this would be a bit of an easier decision. I don't know if she even likes jewelry?"

"Keith?... A woman not like jewelry?"
"True!... but let me think about it! Maybe next time I see her she'll be wearing something that will give me clue!"
"Ok! See ya soon!"
"See ya!" Laurence was brushing his wing against Keith's shoulder nudging him along. Keith didn't understand why all of a sudden he felt such an urgency to leave but he listened, the bell to the door clinking as he steeped out of the shop.
"Take Kayla out Keith!" Laurence whispered "Somewhere you've never taken her!"
"mmmm!" Keith said to himself as he pulled out his cell phone. Beep, beep, beep, beep, beep, beep, beep. The keys sounded as he dialed. After three rings she picked up and her beautiful voice came through the speaker at him.
"Hey babe!"
"Hey! You uh, wanna just get out of town for a wile?"
"Sure,... you ok?"
"Yeah! I just want to get away for the day!"
"Ok come get me!"
"On my way!"

//

Alice and Devin were arguing with each other. Fatigue and hunger were getting the best of them. Devin wanted to push on but Alice was getting dizzy from the lack of food they had consumed today. She hadn't had anything since this morning and it was almost five now. "We can stop just out of town!" Devin insisted.
"Well I have the wheel and therefore I'll decide!" Alice interjected.
"We need to get closer!"
"Well we won't get anywhere if I pass out behind this wheel!" Alice and Devin went back and forth, Joshua resisted the urge to yell out at them from the trunk. He considered only for a second yelling SHUT UP! From where he layed scrunched up in the trunk. He thought about how funny it might be if they

thought it was God or an Angel calling out to them, but then he realized that if they didn't they'd search the trunk and he'd be dead! Eventually Alice did pull off onto an exit and just ignored Devin as he fussed at her!

Jackson was the largest major city just before Rosewood, so in a way Devin had gotten what he wanted. The main stretch of town was filled all kinds of chain restaurants and clothes stores. There was a two story mall and gas stations of every kind on each corner. Alice stopped at her favorite chain restaurant and informed Devin that if he wanted something other than this he could walk! Joshua loosened his muscles and snuck up to the crack. He opened it up an inch more so he could see and he watched until they were inside the restaurant. Now he had to hurry! He had to get out and stretch, pee and maybe grab a snack from the gas station across the street with the change he had in his pocket then quickly get back in the trunk and close the seat behind him.

He pushed down the third of the seat that separated him from the inside of the car and crawled out into the backseat. He pushed the seat almost closed again. His left calf began to spasm "Ahhhhh!" He yelled pushing through the pain. He knew that this car, like most, probably had a child lock on the back doors and that the alarm would go off no matter what door he tried to open, so he decided that he would have a better chance getting out of the front door. He hit the unlock button and to his luck the alarm did not sound as he opened the door. Him unlocking the door must have turned off the system. He shut the door and slunk along the car below the windows until he had to run. He was in the open and he had to bolt across the street and hope Alice or Devin didn't have a window seat.

//

Kayla and Keith had been driving for about fourty minuets now.

"Where are we going?" Kayla asked.

"Jackson!"
"What's that?"
"It's a big city with tons of cool places to shop and eat!"
"Oooh! Fancy!"
"Yeah just wanted to do something special with you!"
"Oh! Thanks baby!"

//

Joshua held his breath as he used the very… no, extremely unclean bathroom. Apparently by the looks of the cleaning chart that was crinkled and stained and yellowed from time, the gas station had just given up on cleaning all together. Reguardless Joshua felt much better.

//

Alice and Devin followed the waiter to their seat. Along the way they passed the salad bar. Alice was so hungry and she eyeballed the different toppings, lettuce and dressings laid out along the bar. Suddenly she shrieked. The waiter Devin and a few other customers looked at her.
"Are you ok mam?" The waiter asked.
"There's…a….roach!" Alice pointed to the bar and the three watched as the bug ran across the lettuce leaves and over the side of the bar! The waiter had no words as Devin and Alice walked out!

Joshua watched from across the street as they got into the car and pulled away somewhere down the road out of sight. He froze as he watched, as it hit him that his ride just drove away and he was in the middle of nowhere, alone and his book bag was still in their trunk with his initials written on the tag.

Keith and Kayla crossed over the border of town and into Jackson. The streets were crowded and it wasn't long before Kayla could see why. Every restaurant and shopping center you could hear about on TV was present along the main stretch of town along with a two story mall that had many

more stores and offerings.
“Where do you want to go?” Keith asked, but Kayla just looked wide eyed.
“Oh, um, I’d never be able to choose! Tell me what’s good?”
“Nope! You decide!” Kayla looked around as they stopped at a red light. Her vision seemed to become superhuman as her eyes caught the sight of a little boy. Oren sat behind her and touched her shoulders. “Lord give her sight!” He prayed to the Almighty. She could see. She knew this boy. He was very familiar, but why? She thought as she searched her brain for the answer.
“Joshua!” Oren spoke into her ear!
“Josh?”Kayla said.
“What?” Keith looked at her strangely.
“Pull in over there!” She pointed to the gas station. As the light changed Keith pulled into the turning lane and waited for the lane to clear.
“What are we doing?”
“I… I know him!” She said.
“The kid!”
“Yeah! He’s from home!” The lane cleared and Keith pulled into the station right next to the boy. Kayla quickly got out and called his name.
“Joshua!” He looked up. Could it be! His heart leaped, the person he came to find.
“Kayla!”
“Yeah!” She walked over to him. “What are you doing here?”
“I came to find you!”
“Me?”
“Yeah I have something to tell you!”
“Really! Well how about where are your mom and dad, or how did you get here?” Josh just looked down at the ground.
“Ok!…. how about we get some dinner and then you can tell me what’s going on!…u hungry?”
“Yes!” Joshua perked right up. He was starving! Only ninety percent of the trip here had he dreamt about food.

//

Oren blew the ram's horn and all around the realm Host's prepared for battle. They could sense that it was about to begin. The powers of darkness were swirling and plotting against the girl, something was coming. Something flesh and something led by the power of the Fallen. They had to separate this son of man from the Fallen Spirits attached to it. Soon the powers of darkness and the powers of the Almighty would battle. They would clash in the sky above the children of men and fight for Kayla, fight for all that she was and all that she would be by the power of the Most High!

//

The restaurant was full of wonderful aroma's that tickled and teased Joshua's nose. His tummy spoke volumes to him as they were seated. He was so grateful this was one of those places that served rolls before you even ordered! He snatched one up and bit into it wildly. As they ordered Joshua envisioned his plate before him. He could never remember being this hungry and he hoped that he would never be again!
"Ok little man how about that story!"
"Oh yeah!"
"Slowly!" Kayla insisted. She knew how kids mumbled and rushed through things. She imagined what it would be like raising Kaleb, if she would have had a conversation like this with him.
"Ok!" Josh agreed and Keith watched as Kayla handled him, keeping him calm. She would be such a great mom! He thought.
"Well, I needed to find you, so when I heard that Devin and Alice were…"
"Devin!"
"Yeah Devin and Alice and my dad were supposed to come here and take you!"
"Take me where?" Kayla looked at Keith with fear in her eyes

and then quickly looked back at Josh.
"I don't know! All I heard is that Alice doesn't want you with her son!" The statement hit Keith like a ton of bricks. It couldn't be his mother they were talking about! He hadn't seen her since…
How did she know Kayla?…or know she was here, with him?
"Josh wait! What's Alice's last name?" Keith interjected.
"Um…. Cartwright!" Keith put his hand to his mouth as he gasped. It was his mother. She was trying to ruin his life again.
"What's wrong Keith?" Kayla asked.
"Not again!…No no no not again!" He said wondering why she hated him so badly and always wanted to ruin his happiness.
"Not again what babe?"
"It's my mom!"
"Alice Cartwright is your mother!?"
"Yeah! How do you know her" Keith and Kayla were looking at each other intently.
"She goes to my dad's church."
"Walkerton!… I get it, that's how you knew Brooke!"
"Yeah I told you!"
" I know but it just never sunk in before! I never thought you'd know my mom!"
"I never knew she was! I never knew you were from Walkerton!"
"I'm not, she sent me away to boarding school!" Joshua looked back and forth between the two.
"Oh!"
"It just never added up in my head! I didn't know what church she went to or that she even went to church!"
"She does! I can't believe she's your mom!" suddenly they remembered that Joshua wasn't done with his story and they both looked at him. "Go on!" they said in unison.
" Well I just know that after Dr. Steele called my dad everything got crazy!"
"Dr. Steele? What does he have to do with it?" Kayla

interjected again.
"He's the Doctor who stole your baby!" Kayla froze. Did she just hear what she thought she heard? She took slow deep breaths trying to prevent herself from passing out. She had so much she wanted to ask but she couldn't speak. Keith seemed to be reading her mind though. He asked the questions she was thinking.
"How do you know that?"
"I watched him steal the baby!"
"How!"
"I was playing hide and go seek in the funeral home with my hamster late one night when I shoulda been sleeping and I hid in the cabinet when I heard voices coming down the hall." He said it so matter of factly it took Keith by surprise. Kayla felt like she could speak now, like she had to.
"So your dad has something to do with this!"
"Yeah!" he said solemnly. "He was supposed to cremate the baby!"
"Supposed to?" Keith said.
"Yeah I stole him and hid him! I wanted to tell you that I gave him a funeral Kayla!" Tears welled in her eyes and began to fall down her cheeks without effort. Her baby! Her son! Someone knew where he was, someone cared enough to give him a funeral!
"Thank you!" She said through her tears.
"Thank you!" Keith agreed.
"It wasn't right what my Daddy, Devin and that Doctor did!, I'm sorry!" Joshua turned towards Kayla and looked her in the eyes. "I never thought my Daddy could hurt someone!" He said sadly as he looked down at the floor! He remembered that night with horror, as he watched from the cabinet and saw the Doctor hand the tiny baby to his father. He still wondered if he would have put the baby back if he had jumped put of the cabinet and insisted he do so! "I didn't have a name to put on the grave!"
"That's ok! You want to know what his name is?"

“Yeah!”
“Kaleb!”
“I like it!” Josh said. “I wanted to find you this whole time and tell you!”
“You did good! You’re a good boy!”
“Thanks!” Kayla hugged him and then took her seat again. The waiter served their food a few minuets later, Kayla couldn’t eat and Keith barely touched his plate. Both knew now that returning to Walkerton was the only choice. They had to take Josh home, they had to face their deamons and put them to rest, for good this time!

SEVENTEEN

Kayla and Keith quickly scurried back to Rosewood. Discussing plans as they went. They had to leave tonight! Keith couldn't risk losing her, he couldn't do this again. His heart could only break and heal so many times. Only once would he allow himself to be the reason his love was stolen. Only once would he let his guard down long enough to let the enemy slip in and steal the very things that made his heart beat. Only once!

//

Along the highway a woman's coffee spilled over the side of the lid and down her white silk blouse. It took her eyes off the road just long enough for her not to see the light change and the car in front of her stop! Alice and Devin jerked in their seats. Their head's flew foreward and then back simultaneously hitting their headrests. After a few seconds of initial shock they looked at each other and then behind them at the woman who was still more concerned about her blouse than the fact that she hit someone.

//

"Keith?.... Can we just drive halfway tonight?"

"I guess. It's not like Walkerton has any good hotels anyway!"

"And also none where we wouldn't be recognized, me and Josh I mean!"

"mmm, good point!"

"I need some time to let this sink in too!"

"Yeah it has been quite a night!

"Ok it's settled then! Next hotel we stop and then go get ice cream!"

" Is that ok Josh?" Kayla looked in the backseat at Josh who sat quietly next to the suitcases.

"Ok!" he had been so quiet since his initial burst of information Kayla was worried about him. She knew it took a lot for him to tell on his father, it would take a lot for any boy to do what he did. To decide what was right and regardless of what his fathers example was, to do it. To keep a secret that big for that long, she was amazed by him. Once again she wondered if Kaleb would have been that kind of child. If she could have been the mom she wanted to be. To teach him virtues, would he live them out!

//

Alice received an accident report from the officer to give to the rental car company and they were on their way. Now they sat across the street from Keith's house…watching…waiting. To their dismay only one light was on in the whole house and no motion had been seen. No shadows cast through the shades or any other lights turned on or off and most importantly no car sat in the driveway.
"Maybe he just forgot to turn that light off."
"Doubtful!" Alice chimed in without missing a beat or blinking. "Besides where is his car!"
"I don't know it was just an idea!"
"No… an idea would be that something fishy is going on around here!" Alice put the car in drive and spun tires as she jerked out of park.

//

Joshua slipped under the covers of the hotel bed and flicked through the channels on the TV. Keith sat next to him and Kayla tucked one leg underneath her as she half sat on the other bed bracing herself with her left leg that pressed against the floor.
"Kayla? How much did you tell Jenn?" Keith asked
"Not much, we rushed out of there so quickly!"
"mmmm I think we should call her and fill her in, if I know my mom she'll look there too!"
"Alright!" Kayla took out her cell and began to dial.
"I just know her or Devin, more than likely since she doesn't

know him will try something!"
"Ok and you call the police. Have an officer patrol the inn, Devin can be violent." She hated that her past once again was threatening her future and now the people she loved!
"Ok! I'll call them you call Jenn!" Kayla hit send and it rang once! Jenn was on edge, worried about her friend's.
"Kayla?" She said in an exasperated tone.
"Yeah, Jenn listen! Devin is in town! He's with Keith's mom! I think he's gonna stop by there and try to find me!"
"What?"
"Yeah apparently his mom knows me and they both want me away from Keith!"
"Oh no! Alice is doing it again!!!"
"Yes and Devin is worse than her so just be alert! He's evil! Were calling the police and having them send over an officer!"
"Is he that dangerous?"
"I don't know what he's he capable of Jenn so just be careful!"
"Ok, you too! Tell Keith I love him!"
"I will!"
"Ok love you girl!"
"Luv ya!" Kayla hung up and looked over at the boys. Josh was fighting sleep so hard. He would close his eyes for a few seconds and then shake his head to wake himself up! This boy had risked his life to tell her about her son and the wrong that was done to him. Maybe, that's what the Bible meant by we must come to Christ as a child. We must risk everything to make things right! She loved this boy for all he had done for her. She walked over to him and took the control. She helped him lay down and kissed his forehead. "Goodnight!" She whispered. Keith was on the phone still with the police so she stepped outside. She leaned on the handrails of the second floor walkway and just let her mind go. Go to the memories again. To thoughts of her son. She cried a quiet cry for him. For the pain she now knew he suffered. For the lack of power

she remembered feeling as the man with the scorpion tattoo carried her away to the place her son would be killed. Her heart ached for him. She loved him and only wanted to hold him. To keep him safe and she had failed.
"Hey!" Keith stepped out. Kayla turned to him and pushed her face into his chest. "Tough day huh!"
"Mmmmmm!" She mumbled into his chest. They stood like that a few minutes as Kayla calmed her tears.
"I love you!"
" I love you too!... Thank you!"
"Shhhh!" Keith put a finger to her mouth and kissed her. He kissed her lips softly and then her cheeks to catch the tears.
"You have nothing to thank me for!"
"But I ..."
"Shhh!" he said again.
"I love you!"
"I love you!" He pulled her in close again and hugged her surrounding her in his arms. She so desperately hoped that one day this man would be her husband. Her one and only.

//

About ten minuets after Jenn and Kayla had hung up Keith's assumptions came into reality. A strange man walked into the inn and paced ever so calmly over to the reception desk. "Hello Miss!" He said casually with a sly smile.
"Can I help you?" She said trying to hold back her fear.
"Um... well I'm looking for a friend who might have stopped here!"
"I'm sorry sir our guest list is confidential!"
"Oh really!"
"Yes sir I'm sorry I am unable to provide that information!" Devin stood as close to the desk as his body would let him trying to intimidate her but Jenn held her ground.
"Well maybe I'll just have to look for myself!" He reached over the counter and grabbed the log book. Jenn let him not

moving a muscle or stepping back. He flipped through it.
"It's empty!" He exclaimed.
"I know! It's been a slow week, wanna rent a room?" She said without missing a beat!
"No….how about last week's log!"
"Like I said sir, it's confidential!"
"Please! Or just tell me if a girl named Kayla has been here!"
"Who?"
"Kayla… k,a,y,l,a!"
"Name doesn't ring a bell." She was steady in her voice and stance though her heart was in her throat and her stomach was on the floor. "Why don't you try the the motel downtown, It's a common stop for people who are just passing through!" She smiled at him. He hated her for her wit.
"Thanks, maybe I will!" He turned to walk out.
"Have a good night!" She said.
"You too!" He gritted his teeth and resisted the urge to turn around and lunge at her. To jump over the counter and pound her smart alick face in. She held steady as he exited, got in the car and pulled out of the driveway.
"Ok Jim!" She called out. From behind the breakfast room doorway a police officer stepped out. "I think were safe!"
"You think they suspected anything?"
"I don't know!"
"Well I'm gonna stick around all night anyway, just incase the bozo tries anything else!"
"Thanks! I'll put some coffee going." Jenn said.
"Sounds great!"

//

"She was here!" Devin said.
"Did she tell you?"
"No, she flinched just a little when I said her name!"
"Oh!…. So what next!"
"Sleep!"

"Where?"
"The cheap motel the girl recommended!"
"Fine, But I'm not sharing a room with you!"
"Good! Just don't leave me in the middle of the night ok!"

//

Keith slept with Josh and Kayla slept alone. The room was dark but the streetlamp cast a line of light through the curtains that wouldn't shut completely. Kayla could see Keith as she lay on her side sleepless. She wondered if he was dreaming and if she was in those dreams. If he truly felt for her what she did for him. The light cast a shadow across the pillow of his face it made his nose look elongated, even still he was handsome. Kayla lay there with her mind wandering through the past few months. She couldn't believe that after telling Keith the truth he still wanted her, after all the trouble she was causing him she couldn't believe that he would still care. He never placed a hand out of bounds, never tried to get more from her than what was right. She was in awe at him. He was from a fairy tale she was sure. Her prince charming and she was Cinderella, she even had the wicked step mother or future mother in law. Either way she was evil… One day maybe she would be related to her. As long as she got Keith she didn't care how evil her mother in law would be. She tossed and turned for a wile. Apprehensive about tomorrow and everything it would bring. Walkerton was a place she thought was behind her. Just yesterday, just a few hours ago she planned on never returning. Colin, A picture of him flashed in her mind. She knew he would help, she had to call him! Kayla recalled the faces and voices she heard the night Kaleb was murdered and now she knew who they were. Dr. Steele, a man she trusted. Mr. Westbrooke and of corse Devin. Each man's face ran through her mind. She had to call Colin, someone had to make this right! Someone had to put to justice these men who valued life so little, who stole and Killed her son! She fell asleep on that thought only to be woken up a few

hours later by the alarm. She gasped and sat straight up in bed scared by the sudden noise. Keith sat at the small hotel table in the corner crunched over with his head in his hands.
"Looks like you slept the same way I did!"
"Yeah if you mean not at all!" He said
"Exactly!" She agreed!
"Mr. sneaky pants over here seams to be sleeping just fine though!" She said looking at Josh who still lay snoring on the bed.
"Kids! They can sleep through anything!"
"Let's get him!" She said standing up and sneaking to his side with her hands ready to tickle. Keith came to the other side and waited for her cue. "1, 2, 3" They both began to tickle him and he woke up laughing.
"Hey!" He said. "Stop!"
"Wake up sleepy head!" Kayla said.
"Ok!.... Ok!" He said. A moment passed. "Hey Kayla can I have a hug?"
"Sure!" She leaned down to hug him and he pulled her onto the bed where both he and Keith tickled her. She laughed and she loved it. Maybe one day her and Keith could have a family like this or even bigger! She lay between the boys until they quit tickling her. She looked into Keith's eyes. "That wasn't fair!" She said smiling up at him. Keith met her gaze, he could see his future in her eyes, he could see himself being happy. The Lord had truly blessed him with her. She was like a vine that grew back after a devastating fire. A sweet fragrance in the air after a storm, he loved her so much more than he ever believed he could love again.
"I love you!" He said leaning into her for a kiss. This was him, she knew it. He was the one. She only wished she was able to give her all to him. That it wasn't stolen from her and she could share that gift only with him.
"eeeeeewwwww!" Josh yelled! "Gross!"
"Gross!" Keith said!
"Yeah!"

"Yeah well mister you need to go get ready!"
"Ok! As long as I don't have to see you kiss! Gross!"
"Go!" Keith laughed.

//

Oren was preparing an army of Host's around Walkerton. They floated above above the town invisible to the realm and the shroud of Demons that swarmed below. They could sense the stirring however, and were on edge awaiting the Host's revelation of themselves. The battle that would occur as they did! Each side was anxious about the next few hours when the battle of darkness and light would be fought over a girl who was awaited by both sides.

//

Alice and Devin once again sat outside Keith's home. It was ten a.m. and there was still no movement to be seen. The same light that had been on last night remained on now and they could see they dull yellow hue it cast over the sheer white curtains, even in the daylight. "Something's not right!" Alice said. "He would have had to leave for work by now!"
"Maybe…. Or!"
"Or what?"
"Maybe we made an enemy back home. Maybe they snitched and the love birds took off!"
"Like who?"
"Westbrooke!" Devin knew the man was intent on doing things himself and because they left him behind he might have tried something sneaky. They still hadn't been in the trunk so they hadn't found Joshua's bag yet but even without that information Devin knew Westbrooke and his deep internal need to do absolutely everything himself.
"The morgue owner!"
"Yup!"
"Why would he know or care about Kayla Devin?"
"He's involved!"

"Involved in what!" Alice said forcefully.
"Nevermind!"
"OOOH NOOO! All this were doing is compromised because of something you failed to tell me! Spill it!"
"No I can't!"
"Tell me now Devin! Why is the morgue owner involved in this?" Devin was surprised by her tone. His anger was rising inside him and he turned in his seat facing her.
"WOMAN! I don't have to tell you anything!" he pointed in her face and raised his own tone to meet her's. "The less you know the better! Trust me!"
"OOOH! I outa….!"
"What!" he challenged her.
"Drop you on the side of the road and let your secret's bring you home!" silence fell between them as they shot hateful stares at each other. Devin broke the stare and turned foreward in his seat.
"Please Alice just head back to Walkerton!" Devin knew she was right. He did compromise this mission with his secrets. He did ruin this by leaving Westbrooke behind but he was trying to avoid this very situation. Trying to avoid admitting to the worst mistake of his life. He couldn't get away from it. That one night ran over and over in his mind. That one extreme wrong plagued his life, his thoughts his dreams, his voice was filled with remorse as he spoke, Alice could hear it.
"So, the prostitute king does have feelings huh!" she said sarcastically through her anger as she put the car in gear!

//

Just outside of walkerton Keith pulled over. He was in Kinston. Kayla had been sleeping for atleast an hour now and Josh soon followed her suit leaning against the car window in the backseat with his mouth wide open and snores echoing through it. Keith was begging to feel the effects of the road. His eyes were trying to close and his mind was fighting not to succumb to sleep as the drone of the pavement under the tires

played its lullaby. Keith pulled over "Kayla?" He tapped her shoulder. "Baby wake up!"
"Huh?" she said with her eyes still closed.
"We're almost there!"
"Oh!"
"Where do we need to go first?"
"To a coffee shop!" she rubbed her eyes.
"I agree!, but I mean when we get to Walkerton!"
"Um……" she was trying to think through her still exhausted brain. "Let me call 411 and I'll get Colin's number, he'll know what to do!"
"Ok!" She pulled out her cell and dialed. Keith pulled back on the highway to find a coffee shop, coffee was definitely a necessity at this point. "But we need to call Pastor too! I didn't tell him much more than you did Jenn as we left last night and we need all the prayers we can get right now!"
"Definitely!" Kayla agreed. Keith was about ten miles outside of the Walkerton border. He couldn't go much further without risking Kayla or Josh being recognized. As it was they risked running into someone who worked outside the town borders or who was just out shopping. A donut shop was coming up on the left, Keith pulled in, coffee was usually good at donut shops, plus the little could use a sugar rush to wake him.
"Residential…Colin Sherwin" Kayla spoke to the automated voice of a woman who answered the 411 call. "Rosewood Falls…..yes…. Say it!" She wrote down the number on her hand as the automated woman called back the number to her. Quickly she hung up and then flipped the phone open again and dialed the number on her hand.
"Hello?"
"Colin?" She said with caution in her voice.
"Yes!"
"Colin Sherwin?"
"Yes who's speaking?"
"It's Kayla! You might not remember…."
"Kayla! Kayla Holmes?"

"Yes!"
"How are you?"
"I'm ok but listen I need to talk to you! It's extremely important. It's about the baby!"
"You know what happened?"
"Yes!"
"Where are you?"
"Just outside of Walkerton at the coffee shop in Kinston."
"Ok give me twenty! I'll be there!"
"Colin!?"
"Yeah?"
"Don't tell anyone that I'm here!"
"Ten four!"
"Ok! Hurry!" She flipped the phone shut. "Ok half an hour and he'll be here!"
"Good I'll call Pastor you go in and get the coffee!"
"Would you like yours iced Mr. Summers?"
"Not this time!" He smiled at her. "I'll take the risk!"
"K!" She stepped out and went inside standing in the line and thinking about what to order for Josh who was still amazingly asleep in the backseat.

EIGHTEEN

Westbrooke pulled into his driveway. He had searched the town over twice and ignored five calls from his frantic wife. Every message he had listened to was about how he better answer or she would get the police involved. Yet still she had just kept calling him and not the force. He sat in the car for a wile until his wife stood in the doorway motioning him to come in. Apprehensively he got out and ascended the porch steps to his front door. She was already screaming something at him, but what was he gonna say. He got to the door and he walked in right past her.

"TOM!"

"Call go ahead!" He said.

"Tom!" She was desperate for answers. She was shaky in her voice and body from the lack of sleep and coffee. "Why? Please tell me why!"

"Call the police Marge!…. Just do it!"

"You know where he is don't you! Tell me Tom please tell me!" She was hysterical. "Why won't you tell me where my son is!"

"Because I don't know Marjorie! I don't know!" He yelled at her from the couch.

"Why did you wait so long Tom?" She put a fist to her mouth trying to hold back the anger she was feeling. "Our son could be … he could be…"

"Call Marge, call!"

"Our baby Tom!" She was crying now, she couldn't hold it back anymore. She was scared for her son, angry at her husband's seeming lack of concern and his secrecy about why the police weren't involved yet! Her emotions could take no more.

"I know Marge! I know!….. Please call!" He put his elbows on his knees and his hands over his face. He was tired, tormented and becoming livid at his wife's badgering. He was angry at himself that by association he might have killed his

son who might have snuck away to be with him… maybe. He wasn't sure anymore if that's what he thought happened, he was exhausted and he couldn't think straight.
"Oh Tom!" She said through tears. She wanted him to hold her. She ached so badly for her son and she needed her husband to hold her. She stepped to the arm of the couch and touched his back with her hand.

A Fallen One had been with Tom for awhile now. This one was practiced at creating and stirring up rage. He was familiar with the part of the brain that generated anger. He pulled out his sword and pushed it into the son of man's brain. His breath poured out of his mouth in waves of black smoke as he talked to the human. "Tell her Tom! Admit to her what you did! MURDERER!…. MURDERER!" He said as he turned the sword causing the nerve signal's in Tom's brain to go erratic. Tom wanted her to leave him alone.
"Just call them Marge! Turn me in!" He said through gritted teeth as his face filled with blood and anger.
"WHAT?" She walked around to the front of him and crouched to see his face. "Why would I do that?"
"Because he's dead! Marge he's dead!" She gasped and put a hand to her mouth.
"Josh?"
"NO! THE BABY! THE BABY'S DEAD!" She looked into his eyes. Hatred filled them. She saw hatred in the eyes she needed comfort from. Only confusion and pain in the eyes of the man she loved. She didn't understand what he was trying to tell her.
"What baby Tom?" She said as calmly as possible but he just stood up and pushed her out of the way. He didn't know what he was feeling. It was a wide array of anger remorse hatred and fear. He paced in the living room.
"We killed him!" He said as he remained pacing. "Took him right out of her and cut off his supply to life!" Margorie stood up and stepped away from her husband. He wasn't himself he was possessed or something. He was rambling and she had no

idea about what.
“Tom?” She said with a shaky voice hoping to pull him out of his trance. “What are you talking about honey?”
“He’s dead and I let you kill him.” He wasn’t seeing reality anymore suddenly he was back in the room with Steele and Devin.
“Me?!”
“Yeah you! You Killed him Steele! I let you! Here in my business, you murdered him!” His insides ached for the child.
“Tom! It’s me, Marge!… Tom!” She was trying to knock him out of his trance with reality. She kept saying her name trying to make him realize who she was. It’s Marge Tom, it’s your wife!”
“NO! PUT HIM BACK!” He screamed at Marge but all he saw was Dr. Steele. “NOW!”
“TOM IT’S ME PLEASE! STOP!” She said hysterically. She was getting really scared, she had never seen anyone like this, never mind her own husband, she really should have called the police.
“Now Steele!” He lunged at her. She ran through the living room into the dining room. He wanted him to breathe into him, to make him live! Tom fell as he lunged at her and it only made him angrier. “Come here Steele!” He yelled as he picked himself up and chased her into the dining room where she was cornered by the table and the wall. “Fix him! Put him back! Steele this is your last warning”
“Stop Tom it’s me! It’s me!” She cried “It’s me!” He didn’t hear her only Steele and his resistance. The night was playing in his head this time the way he wanted it to. He wanted to have the Doctor fix it and to put him back inside where he could grow and live! He wanted that night to never have happened at all. Tom had Marge cornered into the wall behind the table. He pushed the table into her pinning her there with its force. It pressed in on her legs and she cried out from the pain. Tom climbed up on the table and over to her.
“TOM STOP!” She screamed out but he only saw Dr. Steele.

He only heard Dr. Steele telling him no. He grabbed her by her neck and squeezed.
"MURDERER!" He yelled as he squeezed harder and harder! "MURDERER!" He continued to say until the head fell limp in his hands. The Fallen One pulled his sword out and disappeared deep into the earth. His mission had been fulfilled and his lord would be proud. Tom's vision cleared of the altered reality and he saw what was really there. His wife's head lay limp in his hands and she wasn't breathing. He was atop their dining room table that had her pinned against the wall.
"Noooooo!" He screamed. "Nooooooooooo!" How could this have happened? " Marge! Marge!" He jumped off the table and tossed it to the side. Her body fell to the floor and he went to her side. He laid her on her back and began to breathe into her mouth. He did compressions on her chest and breathed into her once again. He had taken the CPR class when Joshua was born; he never imagined having to use it. After fifteen minuets of breathing and compressions he felt for a pulse, he watched her chest for breathing but there was nothing.... She was gone. He pulled her body to him and rocked back and forth holding her. He put his cheek to her's trying to savor what warmth was left in her body. "Oh God... What have I done...? What have I done?"..... He repeated over and over as he rocked back and forth.

//

The donut holes were satisfying Joshua for now. He was on his second chocolate milk carton and number ten of the donut holes. Kayla hoped he didn't throw up, but then again kids stomach's work differently than adults. Only kids can mix pizza, birthday cake, milk and soda and not vomit.

It felt like an eternity even when in reality only twenty five minuets had passed. Colin Arrived in his old dark green mustang and wearing street clothes. He stood tall and firm even out of uniform. Colin walked in and spotted the three. He

was surprised to see Joshua but he knew that whatever she had found out was going to be interesting. Very interesting, and he braced himself for the shock of whatever it was as he walked over to the table.
"Hello!" He held out a hand to Keith.
"Sir!" He said.
"Call me Colin please!"
"Ok Colin, I'm Keith!"
"Nice to meet you!.... Kayla!" He nodded in her direction. She stood up and hugged him.
"Thank you for coming!"
"No problem! Joshua what are you doing here? Where's your parents!" He didn't answer. He looked down at the floor and waved his feet back and forth under the table.
"I'll get to that Colin, please sit! Do you want a coffee?" Kayla asked.
"Sure that'd be great!" He said as he pulled out the empty chair and sat.
"Black, cream and sugar or iced?"
"Hot, cream, no sugar."
"Got it!" She returned a few minuets later with his coffee and had a seat.
"So what's going on?" He said trying to get to the point.
"Well I was hoping he could tell you!" She put a hand on Joshua's shoulder.
"Kayla!...Noooo!" He whined through his half chewed donut hole.
"Josh I know you want to protect him but what about Kaleb!"
"Yeah but he'll go to .... Jail!" He whispered to her hoping that Colin couldn't hear!
"Well someone please tell me!" Colin said. Josh shoved a whole donut hole in his mouth and smiled at Kayla like he was saying haha I can't talk.
"Well I wanted you to know what really happened the night Kaleb died and I wanted you to hear it from the source that I heard it from!" She looked at Josh again. "I only remember

bit's and pieces before and after but Josh here saw the whole thing!...I remember the guard with the scorpion tattoo carrying me down the hall. I remember the man in the mask drugging me and I remember waking up in the hospital. That's it.!.... Josh you wanna take it!" She looked at him again but the boy stared at the floor. For some reason he felt like less of a snitch telling Kayla than he did Lieutenant Williams. Colin leaned back in the chair he wasn't sure if he really was ready to hear this, from a child of all people. An innocent child who should be out playing ball somewhere with his friends.
"Kayla why did you leave! Why didn't you tell me!" Colin said.
"I just wanted it to be over! I wanted to be rid of my mistakes and to try and run from Kaleb's memory!" As she spoke Josh ran off into the men's room and Keith followed him.
"So where does he fit in?" Colin eyeballed the boy as he ran.
"He has Kaleb!"

//

Alice and Devin would be about two and a half hours away from Walkerton by now if this teenie bopper in the convertible hadn't taken her eyes off the road to text message.
"Well that's it!" Alice ranted. "I'm cursed! How can one person be hit this many times and in a rental no less!" She lifted her arms up past her shoulders and let them drop freely. The blonde haired blue eyed teenager tried to talk her way out of the situation a few feet away and Alice rolled her eyes. She had already pulled the crying card and now that the officer was demanding her father's number she was down to just excuses and her looks, neither were working for her. Alice couldn't make out all she was saying but she could tell by the cops face that he wasn't impressed with her or her mouth!
"This is gonna take all day!" Devin piped in.
"Yup!" She agreed with irritation as they both leaned against their backs against the rental and crossed their arms over their chest's. Alice wondered if any car rental company had ever

heard a story like this or if the extra insurance she purchased would cover two accidents and not just one of them!

//

"Ok!… so you mean he has the baby?" Colin said.
"Yup!"
"ALIVE?"
"No. He buried him and gave him a funeral."
"Oh!"
"How?" I want you to hear it from him, it's just…. Unbelievable and I don't want you to think I changed his story one bit or that we made it up and forced him to tell you!"
"Kayla!…I wouldn't…."
"Trust me! You want to hear it from him!"
"Ok! I'll wait!" he leaned back in his seat and stretched his legs out.

//

Inside the men's room Joshua lost his breakfast. All eleven donut holes and two cartons of chocolate milk. How could he rat out his daddy to the police? How could he turn him in and know that he would go to jail because of him. He also knew that if he didn't tell Kayla or Keith would. They would have to turn in the bad people who killed her baby! "I can't do it Keith!" Josh looked up at his new found friend. Keith squatted down to his level and looked him in the eye.
"I can't make you tell buddy but you came all this way to tell us what happened, you must have thought what they did was really bad! Huh?"
"Yeah! They hurt her insides and killed the baby!"
"So don't you think you should tell Colin?"
"but!"
"But don't you think the men who hurt Kayla should get in trouble?"
"Yeah!" He was sad. He knew his daddy was a bad man, but he still didn't want him to go to jail. He wanted him home to

play ball with him and read him bedtime stories.
"Common let's go I'll help you talk to Colin!" Joshua nodded sadly as he took Keith's hand and they walked out of the bathroom. At the table Keith took his seat and Josh sat on one of his knees. "Ready?" Keith asked.
"Yeah!" Josh said.
"So what happened little man?" Colin asked as sympetiecly as possible. Josh stared at a spec on the table the whole time he spoke. He told everything from what he saw to how he buried the baby to how he got here with Kayla and Keith. He spoke without stopping or any sentence structure but Colin heard every word. He was in shock from the words that came out the the mouth of this child.
He wanted to take it all away from him. How awful for a child to see such things. To hear such things and how amazing that he chose to what was right. "Oh my holy Lord." He said. Colin reached a hand across the table and took one of Joshua's. "You're a good boy! You did what was right by telling Kayla and me!" He held the boy's hand till he looked up at him. He looked into his eyes and reassured him again. "You're a very good boy!"
"Please don't kill my daddy!" He said looking down again.
"Oh.... Honey! We won't kill him!"
"Really!"
"We might have to keep in jail a long time though!"
"I know!" He agreed. "Can I visit him?"
"Yeah! You can visit!"
"Ok!....... I'm hungry again!" All the adult's laughed! Only a kid could bounce back like that!

//

Westbrooke got up from the floor. What had he done now? His wife was dead, his son was lost, and a baby was dead, all because of him. All that blood was on his hands. He picked up Marjorie fireman's style and carried her to their room. Tonight when there were no workers around he would take her in for cremation. They had talked about it many times; he knew it was what she wanted. She wanted to be spread over the nearest ocean and swim with the dolphins. Something she never got to do wile she was alive, though they had planned many times to go, each time something came up. He never got to grant her wish and now he had killed her. He remembered carrying her the way he did now the night they married. He swept her off her feet and over the threshold. Crazy to think that their son was conceived that very night! They so weren't ready, but she was a perfect mother from the start. He was so afraid of the kind of father he might be but it all just melted away when they placed him in his arms. The instinct came to both of them as they held their son. He remembered how much his love deepened for his bride as he watched her work and fight through labor to start their family and then as he watched in awe as she nursed him and helped him grow. Now he killed that very person, and that son was missing, maybe dead somewhere in a place he might never find!

//

Wesley flew above Walkerton and found Oren. "They have been delayed sir!" He reported.
"But not harmed!" Oren asked.
"Correct!"
"Marvelous! Good work, Praise the Almighty!"
"Praise the Almighty!" He responded.
"Praise the Almighty!" The Angels near to him echoed. Then the one's in their earshot all across the formation the Angels shouted praise. The Fallen One's felt uneasy as they knew the Host's were here. A few of the smaller deamons had already tried to fly into the places they felt the Host's but were struck out of the sky and had fallen to the ground to dissinegrate. The stronger ones were smarter they were waiting till they revealed themselves. Though the glory around them blinded their eyes atleast they had something to aim at!

//

The road she once saw in her rearview was now in front of her. Everything she'd left behind was now here for her to face again. Colin followed behind her in his mustang and Joshua directed Kayla to where she could park so they would be close to the burial site. They had to dig him up so forensics could prove not only that he was Kayla's but so they could prove once and for all how he really died. If the boys explanation was correct than that part would be obvious from the moment they examined him. As soon as they flipped him over they would see the damage done by the Doctor who killed him. Once they parked Colin called the station and alerted them to have squad cars in place at the residences of Dr. Steele, Mr. Westbrooke and Devin Copeland. He said as soon as they had the proof in hand that he would call in the order for them to make the arrests. Then forensics would have fourty eight hours to get the evidence in writing.

//

Alice and Devin finally got the accident report. Alice snatched it out of the officer's hand. "Thanks!" She said sarcastically.
"Drive safe madam!" He said in just the same tone as she had given him.
"It's not me you have to worry about officer!" She said as she eyeballed the teenager who had caused her such delay.
"Yes mam!" He agreed as politely as possible, just hoping she would leave. "Have a good rest of your day!" Alice smiled at him and then climbed into her car. Devin walked around and followed her lead by getting inside. She floored it and sped away! The cop didn't care he only wanted the old spinster out of his hair! What a thorn in someone's side she must be he thought!

//

An on duty officer met Colin at the edge of the woods. As instructed he brought along a shovel. They all followed Josh who had the advantage of height on his side. He was sweeping under branches and ducking under the brush with ease. “Wait up!” everyone called after him.
“Common!” He’d say as he stopped and waived them on. “Faster it’s just a bit more!” He called back. They began to hear the stream and knew they were close because of Joshua’s descriptive story of the grave site. Josh darted again excited to finally be keeping his promise to the infant. He was finally bringing his mom to him. The brush broke into a clearing and they all saw the grave. Just as he had described. At the bottom of an oak tree next to the stream.
It was a beautiful spot. They weren’t sure why but they all stopped for a moment. Like they were in reverence of the place the child had been laid to rest by the act of another child. It was serene and Kayla was touched by what Josh had done once again and her eyes flooded with tears. She walked over to Josh and hugged him tightly! “Thank you!” She said as she tried to stop her tears.
“Thanks! But your squishing me!” He said with strain in his voice. She let him go and let out a tiny chuckle.
“Sorry honey!” She said. Colin began to dig after removing the wood with Raccoon carved into it. The first ten minutes or so were a breeze but Colin was beginning to tire out. He was about two and a half feet down.
“Man kid how far did you burry him?”
“Six feet!” He said matter of factly.
“You sure about that?”
“Yup one foot over my head and I‘m five feet!” They all broke out in a laugh. This kid was something else. So smart and honest.
“You’re a smart kid you know that!” He said. Keith took over for the next stretch of digging. Kayla watched him. He was strong and handsome. She was so attracted to him, he was like a potion to her the perfect mix of strength kindness. After

about ten more minutes of digging he struck something. He tossed the shovel up to ground level and cleared off the box with his hands.

"Here you go! You sure you can handle this honey?" He stood up and looked at her till she gave a reassuring nod. Then he pulled up on the lid and inside laid everything the boy had promised. Inside laid an infant covered in a fleece blanket, inside lay Kaleb. Everyone froze at the site. Keith stood above the box in horror. He believed the boy before but now actually seeing the infant inside this homemade wooden box he just wanted to... cry. He didn't but he wanted to, for Kaleb, for Kayla and for Brooke. Atleast Kayla was getting to see her son; he talked himself out of his trance. Atleast this will bring some justice! He leaned over and picked the child up. His body was cold and as Josh had said the back of his skull had a gaping hole at the bottom. He could feel the hole as his hand supported his head. The smell of rotting flesh filled the air. Everyone gagged a little. He passed him up into Colin's hands and crawled out of the grave. Kayla had her back turned. This was harder than she thought it would be. There wasn't anything she wouldn't do to put life back inside that child. Her heart ached for him. She knew he was gone and in the arms of the Father, but still she wanted her son. She wanted to hold him and feel his warmth in her arms. She wanted to hear him cry and to be the one to calm his tears. Her heart ached in places she hadn't ever felt.

Colin looked the infant over. Everything Josh had told him added up. The mark's in the skin where he had injected the formalin, the gaping hole in his head where the doctor had put the scissors. Everything matched up, it turned his stomach. How could anyone do this? "Kayla?... Do you want to hold your son?" She turned to him. She wasn't sure she could but she wanted to. She reached her arms out and he placed the infant in her arms. Her son, finally she was holding her son. He had her nose, and his grandpa's ear shape. He was shriveled some but with imagination she could see what he would he have looked like. Tears welled in her eyes and poured down her cheeks. Her Kaleb!

In the realm the Comforter, the Holy Spirit came to her. He surrounded her heart and wrapped himself around her soul. He spoke to her. He is with me. Kaleb is growing and is healthy in heaven with me! We are preparing a place for you and him to live together one day! Oren loved watching the promises of the Almighty coming to work in the lives of the children of men. "Praise the God who comforts!" He shouted. Kayla looked at the infant in her arms, and though she knew he was hers, she felt like he wasn't. This isn't Kaleb, she thought. This is only the shell he once lived in. Keith stood by her side as she began to slightly smile.

"You ok baby?" He said quietly.

"Yeah!" She said lightly. "Yeah!" She said again more loudly. "Kaleb is ok, he's with God! This is just his body." She said as the revelation hit her mind. She handed the infant back to Colin and hugged Keith. It was really going to be ok! Colin gave the word over the officer's walkie and everything was underway.

NINETEEN

Tom laid his bride on their bed. Her lifeless body went wherever he commanded. He placed her Bible on her chest and put her hands crossed over the top of it. The bruises on her neck were more prominent in this dark room lit only by the overcast sky. His stomach turned inside him and he ran into the bathroom. He vomited all over the floor. He was disgusted with himself, with his murderous, tormented self. He was beginning to think he was some kind of bi polar lunatic. Like the life that filled the child now possessed him and the life of his wife was payment for what he had done. It was exactly what Lucifer wanted him to believe. Tom couldn't look anymore at his wife's bruised and battered dead body. He shut the bedroom door just in time. The Police banged on the door. "Walkerton police department open up!" An officer yelled as he banged his fist against the door. Tom wanted to be put behind bars. It was where he deserved to be. With all the other murderer's, thief's and abusers. He opened the door and let the police inside.
"Tom Westbrooke?"
"Yes!"
"You're under arrest for the kidnapping of Kayla homes and the unlawful removal of her unborn child." Without a fight Tom turned around and put his hands behind his back. He didn't want to fight it, didn't want to deny it, he only wanted to pay for what he had done. He deserved whatever they gave him. The officer pulled out his cuff's and began to place them over his wrists. " You have the right to remain silent, anything you say can and will be used against you in a court of law. You have the right to an attorney, if you cannot afford an attorney one will be provided for you." Tom chose to remain silent.

//

Dr. Steele placed his doplar device onto the gel that lay in

a glop on the woman's belly. Her and her husband listened with awe as the heartbeat became clear through the speaker. The woman smiled wide as she heard her daughter's heartbeat. The husband was in shock. He just couldn't believe that after two years of trying there really was an infant inside his wife's belly, and that in two months he would be meeting his daughter. Dr. Steele removed the device and wiped the woman's belly clean of the gel. "Her heart sounds great, you're measuring just right in uterus size, and I'd say that everything is just perfect!.... Do you have any questions for me?"
"No were just glad she's ok!" The husband said.
"Yes sir she's fine!"
"Thank you sir!" He reached out and shook his hand.
"My pleasure!" He responded as he stepped out of the room. As he did he ran right into a police officer. Two of them stood in the way of his passing in the hall. Quickly he shut the exam room door. "What is this all about?" He demanded.
"Are you Dr. Robert Steele?" The office questioned.
"Yes!"
"You are under arrest for the kidnapping of Kayla Holmes and the unlawful removal of her unborn child!" He didn't know what to say he just backed up against the wall and dropped the woman's file he clutched in his arm. Papers flew out of the file as it fell to the ground. No one went to pick them up instead all eyes were on the Doctor. The nurse at the triage station and her patient stared at him, the receptionist behind the window stared at him and the secretary that stood at the end of the hall sorting files stared at him all waiting for his response to such an accusation.
"Please turn around Dr." the officer asked. He did as he was asked to do. The steel cuffs felt cold against his skin and his chest muscles pulled as his arms were held behind his back with the cuffs. None of it hurt as much as the looks he was receiving from his staff. "You have the right to remain silent........" the officer read him his rights as they walked

down the hall and outside to an awaiting car.

//

Two officers ascended the steps to Devin's house. After two knock's a very scantily clad woman answered the door. "Hello officers!" She said in a seductive tone. "How can I help you?" Both officers kept their eyes straight ahead and remained steadfast in their business like stance.
"We need to speak to Devin Copeland please!"
"I'm sorry he isn't here, can I help you with anything?" She said striking a pose against the door jamb.
"No mam! We have no other business here other than seeing Mr. Copeland."
"Well like I said he isn't here!" Her tone was now of offense and she slammed the door their face. One officer ran around back to see if the suspect was trying to escape and the other radio'd in for a warrant and backup.
"I'll get the DA on the warrant; backup is on its way!" An officer reported over the speaker of the walkie. Each officer held their position around the house, waiting.... watching and hoping to get their guy and leave.

//

Colin laid the infant back inside his box and relidded it. Without a word he picked it up turned around and began walking out of the woods. He couldn't believe this was happening at all never mind in his town right under his nose. Everyone followed his lead and walked slowly out of the woods. Each with their own thoughts about what they had all seen, each with their own feelings of what should happen to bring justice to this horrible situation. "Kayla?" Colin finally spoke about five minutes into the stroll.
"Yeah?"
"What we need to do next is get some DNA samples from you and the ba.... I mean Kaleb."
"Ok!"

“Then you can have him back so you can give him a proper funeral!”
“Alright!”
“I’m gonna recommend a sample be sent to three different labs, each performing their own cross matching of your DNA and Kaleb’s, that way there will be no question as to the validity of the results when it comes time to have the trial!” She heard every word he said and it cut her deep. She didn’t want to be here that long. To wait around for test results and have to be in a court room feet away from the men who did this to her and her son. She felt once again like she did the day she left. Like she wanted to run, for it to just be over and everything be righted already. Well, at least righted as much as it ever could be. “Kayla?”
“Yeah I heard you!” she said.
“Ok! I know this is hard!” Colin stopped and looked at her. She knew he was, as always, being genuine. She tried to smile, it didn’t work she just grimaced and insisted they keep going. Keith rubbed her back as they walked unsure if he was helping.

//

Finally the welcome to Walkerton sign passed by Alice and Devin. They were here. Devin thought that maybe one of his girls may have heard something and so they headed to his house. The town seemed quiet enough, nothing out of the ordinary, but maybe just maybe wile they were out on the streets or traveling to a client’s house, maybe they saw something suspicious. It was nice to have a horde of spies, Devin thought. Alice pulled onto Devin’s road. She hated being in this part of town, hated being associated with the man who had turned it into the slum and brought it the bad name’s it carried. The home of the prostitute king, the hoe’s hole, pleasure road, Alice could think of many names this place had been branded by and she wanted to be out of here. The road

was quiet. How odd? Devin thought. Usually cars drove down here and pulled into his driveway. Usually there atleast a few cars parked along the side of the road and none of the above were present today. "Alice! Don't pull in!"
"What?"
"Don't pull in, drive past!"
"Why?"
"Something's not right!"
"Ok!" Alice agreed. She didn't want anymore trouble than she already had. Trees blocked his view down driveway, a few seconds passed and the trees cleared out of his way, and there they were, his suspicions confirmed in front of his eyes. Two police cars parked outside the front of the house and officers on the porch. Devin ducked in his seat as they passed by, hoping the tint to the windows was enough to hide his identity.
"Now what?" Alice piped in, this was getting ridiculous.
"Take the next left and it will lead to main,.... I have to call and see if they got everyone else!"
"Oh great secrets again!!"
"Alice!" Devin said in a harsh agitated tone.
"What?"
"Please just let me handle this!"
"Yeah, cause you've done such a great job so far!"
"Please!"
"DEVIN! If my life is in danger!"
"Your life is only in danger if you know! If we get caught then you can say honestly you don't know anything! Trust me the less you know the better!"
"Whatever!" She rolled her eyes and took a deep breath letting it out in a sigh. Devin pulled out his cell and dialed the first number he could think of, Dr. Steele's office.
RIIIINNNNGGGG..... RRIIIIIIINNNNGGG... "Hello! You've reached Dr. Steele's office. We will be closed until further notice. All appointments have been forwarded to Dr. Konk in Kinston. Please call his office for more information at

215-7889. We are sorry for any inconvenience."
bbbbbeeeeppppppp.
"@&^$&"* Devin cursed. He slammed his phone shut and rubbed his forehead.
"Where am I supposed to go Devin?" Alice protested as she sat at the stop sign.
"Just park somewhere!" Devin dialed another number as he tried to brush off the old woman. He listened to the other end ring over and over until finally the answering machine came on and Westbrooke's voice echoed through the earpiece, explaining how he was unable to come to the phone. Devin cursed again as he hung up and Alice pulled into the old Gas station on main street.
"Stop!" She shouted! "Stop!….. All that cursing isn't gonna get us anywhere!" Devin slunk down in his seat and leaned against the window. "Look we can't go to your house and I definitely can't take you to the seniors home with me so we need to get a plan, and fast!" Devin ignored her. "And!" She turned in her seat facing him. "I need to know what the heck is going on!" He continued to ignore her. "Now Devin!"
"No!"
"Get out!"
"What?"
"Tell me or get out!" Devin was exasperated. He didn't know what to say, if he got out he'd more than like ly be spotted and picked up by the police, if he told Alice she'd probably throw him out anyway, but maybe she'd be happy. She seemed to hate Kayla and maybe she'd be glad to hear of her pains.
"Um!"
"Well, what's it gonna be?"
"Ok, ok ill tell you!" He held his hands up in surrender. Alice leaned her back against the car door and crossed her arms, this is gonna be good, she thought.
"Well I…. it started when I helped Kayla out of her prearranged marriage. I told her she could come live with me and that I'd get her a job."

"Really!" She said in a sarcastic tone.
"So I had to, you know, break her in for the job!"
"You mean…."
"Yeah that's exactly what I mean!"
"So what that's exactly what id expect from you, but what about Westbrooke?"
"Well she got pregnant…." He could see it in front of his eyes again. The night that haunted him. The night he helped murder his son.
"And…" Alice interjected. She didn't get how this was all connected. Devin faced foreward in his seat. He put his hands over his face and leaned his elbows on his knees.
"We all killed him!" There he said it.
"Who?"
"The baby! My son! We killed him!" Devin looked her in the face. His eyes welled with tears. She was flabbergasted. How???… She thought. Her eyes met his.
"We kidnapped her, put her to sleep and took my son out of her! I watched as the Doctor shoved scissors into his skull and murdered my son!" Devin spoke through a lump in his throat, and as tears ran down his cheeks. Alice put her hand to her mouth and gasped. She forgot to breathe for a moment, she had never heard of such a hanus thing. Devin looked back at the floor and began to ramble.
"He told me he was just a blob of flesh but you didn't see him! My son had fingers and toes. He had eyes and eyelashes and my nose…. I let him kill my son," He hadn't allowed himself to feel anything about that night, he had just pushed it down further and further each night as he drank it away and filled the void with the women he laid with. "He looked like Kayla! I stole him from her! I watched that man kill a piece of my soul and then as Westbrooke walked away with his limp body in his arms!" He didn't realize it until now but he loved Kayla for carrying his son, for growing him inside her.

Alice felt a small ounce of sympathy crawling into her soul for this girl. This girl that her son had chosen, but still, she thought he deserved better. He deserved more than damaged baggage. Right? She didn't know.

//

"Open!" The lab tech informed Kayla. He placed a swab inside her mouth. "Hold it to the inside of your cheek for a minute." The swab was in the shape of a square. "What we can do then is cut it into three pieces and put one with each lab order" she nodded as the tech explained everything to her. The swab tasted funny and she fought to keep her mouth closed over the stick. "Fifteen more seconds" The tech informed her and she began counting in her head. Fourteen, thirteen, twelve......

The tech took samples from Kaleb a few feet away. He pulled three hairs from his head and placed them each inside its own little baggie. He placed one on each lab order form. One for each lab they would be sending the samples to. "Ok open!" He said again. She did as commanded and he pulled out the square swab. Quickly with sterile scissors he sliced the square into three's and placed the strips into baggies as well, one going with each hair sample. Kayla rolled her tounge around inside her mouth. The swab had left a salty taste on the inside of her cheek. The tech was absorbed in his work but without looking away he let Kayla know where a water fountain was and that she was good to go.

"Can I watch?"

"Sure, but this is really the boring part!" He said.

"I don't think so!" She insisted as she stepped to his side and watched him separate the samples and put them into the bags for shipment. Each had like five seals on it, each one needing a signature on it. "What happens if you mess up a seal?"

"Um then we have to start all over!"

"Oh!" She said. Colin watched the sealing process as did another tech and they both had to sign off on the validity of the samples and their proper handling. Each sample went into a

box and was sealed with security tape that read 'secure' until it was cut or ripped open at the lab. If the tape was tampered with it broke into pieces and the specimens would no longer be considered valid.
"Ok!" The tech said. "What will we be doing with the remains?" that comment stung in Kayla's chest but she let it go.
"Kaleb is coming with us!" She said.
"Sorry mam!" He said genuinely. "I'll get Kaleb wrapped back up for you!"
"Thanks." Kayla sat down and looked up at Colin. She wasn't sure why but she all of a sudden felt like a little kid. She wanted her daddy. She wanted him to forgive her, to welcome her back like the prodigal son, and she wanted him… and only him, to bury her son. "Colin?"
"Yeah?"
"Will you come with me to see my dad?"
"Kayla?"
"What?"
"You don't have to do that! You don't have to see him!"
"Yes I do! I want him to bury Kaleb!"
"You sure!" He squatted in front of her chair and looked her in the eyes. She nodded.
"I want him to bury my son!"
"Ok I'll go, but Kayla, honey… Please don't get your hopes up!"
"I won't!" She looked at the clock and then back at him. "It's Wednesday isn't it?"
"Yeah!"
"Well we can go get dinner and then show up at church?"
"Church?"
"Yeah that's where my dad will be! And…. He's less likely to make a scene in front of the whole congregation!"
"Alright!" Colin was hesitant but as soon as they had the ok to leave they headed straight to dinner without any objection from Keith and Josh who had been in the waiting room

starved for the last hour.

TWENTY

"Get out!"
"What?"
"Get out!" Alice made up her mind. She didn't want anything to do with this.
"But I told you…."
"You told me just how sick you are and I don't want anything to do with this!" Devin stared at her wide eyed with hatred in his eyes. He told her his darkest secret and now she was throwing him out like the trash. He did as she said reaching for the handle and stepping out. She didn't even wait for him to shut the door before she sped off, she let the force of her pulling away slam it shut for him. She knew he had a reason now to kill her but she refused to be part of whatever he was gonna do. She had to find Keith; she had to risk him rejecting her to let him know the truth. That he was in danger and so was his love.

Devin stood still in the parking lot as the shock wore off. There in front of him was his plan sitting at a red light. He could see in the windows of the vehicle, there she was. Kayla, two men and a kid he thought! He watched as they drove up one light and turned into Shelly's Diner. This would be easy now, all he needed was a car, forget that old hag! He thought.

//

"What should I say?" Kayla asked before she sipped her sweet tea.
"Honey Stop!" Keith kissed her cheek. "You'll know what to say when you see him! It will come to you!"
"But?"
"But nothing! Everything will be fine!" He met her gaze and kissed her.
"Yuck!" Josh said.
"Yeah! Yuck guys!" Colin jokingly added.

"Sorry!" Kayla said as she pulled away from his kiss.
"Oh don't worry about it squirt here will kiss girls someday too!" Colin said.
"No way! Girls have cooties!" Josh said twisting his face and shaking his head wildly to ensure everyone knew of his objection.
"Whatever buddy you will!, Now lets order so were not late!" Keith said.

//

The old gas station had been deserted years ago and left to rot. The owner left town and no one had ever been able to get in touch with him so the station sat as it was to wither away. Teenagers had broken in soon after the owner ran out and stolen what was left of the drinks and snacks but Devin wasn't after drinks and snacks. He rummaged around looking for anything that he could use to kidnap her. So far he had found some old twine a half used roll of duct tape and some matches. He wasn't sure yet how exactly he would pull this off or how he would get away with this but he was confidant that he would. In the back where the owners office was a half full gas can sat in the corner Devin decided he needed it, since he didn't have a plan the more resources the better. A honk sounded outside and now it was time to go. It was just him and the security guard that hadn't been caught yet so once again now they teamed up. Devin's mind raced with possibilities. What if he kidnapped her and took her out of town. Maybe they could try again. Maybe they could have a son together after all, he just had to get her away from this Keith character. He had to make it right with her, she had to be his, to have his child just the way it was meant to be! They sat along the curb near the restaurant and waited. They plotted they planned and waited for their prize to exit.

//

Kayla had only eaten three bites and everyone else

was done. She just couldn't she was so nervous. "Honey I can't! I think I might hurl if I eat another bite!"
"Alright!" He said putting an arm around her and chuckling. She was so precious, he thought. "I'll get the check."
"No let me!" Colin said.
"No! Colin you've done so much already! You came out to Kinston on your day off. You found Kaleb, you saved Kayla when her father was gonna leave her battered and bruised.... No I won't let you pay for dinner!"
"Fine! Well thank you!" Colin agreed. "But I did what I did out of a need to do what is right not for a free dinner!" He said smiling.
Kayla held Josh's hand on the way out. She smiled at the thought that one day on a street made of gold she would walk and hold her son's hand.

The church was close now and Kayla took deep breaths in and let them out slowly. She sat in the backseat with Josh and held his hand tightly. "Honey! Your gonna hyperventilate!" Keith looked back from the front seat.
"and I can't feel my hand Kayla!" Josh said. She let him go and tried to breathe normal.
"I'm sorry sweety! I am just nervoeous about seeing my dad!"
"Me too!" Josh agreed. He knew one day he would have to see him and he would find out that he was the one who turned him in. "but I can't wait to see my mom! I miss her!"
"Yeah!"
"But you got hurt your daddy shouldn't be mad at you!"
"Well he doesn't know I got hurt!
"Oh!" Josh said as they both realized they were here! Kayla looked up at the cross on the steeple and prayed. "Please be with me!" She said.

//

Oren and an army of Hosts flew around the church. The sky was filled with them all in formation ready to battle with the Fallen Ones for the sake of this girl. Oren now commanded a

regimen of Host's "The servants of Lucifer we will be battling are of great skill but the Almighty will stand with us! The Fallen will fight fiercely and with out mercy but we have the Lord on our side! Battle for the child of man with everything you have! Praise him name!"
"Praise his name!" resounded all across the sky! Oren blew the rams horn "Host's!" He called out! "Prepare for battle!" He blew the horn three times and the Host began to ready themselves. They all formed rings starting in the middle with Oren and then four surrounded him, and then a circle around them and on and on it went to form an impenetrable force field above the church. Each ring flew opposite of the other and created a whirlwind of protection over the place the battle would begin.

//

Devin and the guard remained behind a hedge of trees just a couple of feet from the church parking lot. Devin could from where he sat see them as they walked in. "Ok!" He said. When they shut the door behind them. "Pull around back and park!"
"What are you gonna do?"
"I don't know!"
"Devin I can't go to jail… I know what happens to people in jail!"
"I've got this! Just pull around back!" Devin said, but truthfully he wasn't sure he had this under control. He had gone here as a child before his mom and dad split up and both of them gave up on religion. He use to, back then, sneak out the back door and play in the woods during Sunday school and then when he heard the church bell he'd sneak back in and meet his mom in the sanctuary for service. He knew the pastor still came in and out this way and he hoped he still left it unlocked. The guard pulled around, Devin took the twine and balled it up. He shoved it in his pocket and got out of the car. "I'll be out soon ok! Be ready to gun it and have the doors unlocked, all of them!"

"Ok!" He nodded his heart was pounding he couldn't go to jail, he just couldn't. "Hurry!" He called after him. Devin remembered the church well. The halls went into a u shape behind the sanctuary. On one side was the classroom's on the other was the bathrooms and at the bottom of the u was pastor's study. He would come in at the bottom left of the u and be about ten paces from the study. Just ahead of him would be the hall with the bathroom's and at the end of that hall would be a large ficas tree. Ok he thought I'll go in hide behind the tree and wait for her. She'll have to go sometime and when she does I'll grab her and we'll be gone before anyone know's it.

//

Jacob still remained seated on the first seat of the pew and the choir was singing. He never looked behind him before he went to preach. Either the large crowd would make him nervous or the small crowds make him sad, so he tried especially here recently just to focus on the Lord. He felt God with him as he prayed. He needed so much help to learn to forgive, to let go of what his daughter had done. She was out there somewhere and he still loved her. He listened to the song as the choir sang "Forgive us our trespasses as we forgive…." The Lords prayer. How hard he had found it to follow that simple prayer, but he was trying. He was praying and hoping for power to forgive. All his life it had been right and wrong and now he needed to focus on forgiveness.

//

Kayla could feel each muscle move and contract as she walked into the sanctuary. She was tense, worried about how he would react to her presence. They all took a seat in the back and joined in as the choir sang the last verse of the song. They were four of only about fifteen in attendance minus the choir, but maybe that was a good thing. If her father was going to get angry and scream at her then the less people the better.

The choir finished their song and they filed out into the crowd. Jacob stood and took the pulpit, still not looking behind him.
He paced the three steps to the top of the stage and looked down as he put his Bible on the pulpit and then finally looked up. At Oren's order Wesley stayed at Jacob's side and spoke to him one word. "Forgiveness!" He said. He waited a few seconds and spoke to him again. "Forgiveness!" As Jacob looked at his daughter all the hate he had felt ran down his flesh and into the demon that followed the Pastor the past few months. The Fallen One descended into the earth with defeat, burdened by his new weight. Jacob's mind just kept hearing the word forgiveness, like an old hymn in his mind.
"Forgiveness!" He said loudly from the pulpit. It startled the whole congregation. Kayla especially jolted a little in her seat, not only from the volume of the word but from the word itself. Keith held her hand tightly.
"Forgiveness! That is one thing I haven't spoke on enough. The Bible is filled with right and wrong and do this not that but here recently I'm realizing just how much it is also filled with love and forgiveness….. That is what Jesus came for is it not! He knew we would sin…" Jacob looked directly at his daughter and hoped she would understand what he was trying to say. "He knew we would fall so he came to be our sacrifice. Our middle guy. The one we can go to and say forgive me and the one who will always say yes." Jacob felt like he was hearing this all over again for himself. Like he was teaching himself and not only his congregation. "Why would he come if he didn't intend to forgive us of all the wrongs he knew we'd commit?" He phrased it as a question like he was asking himself, why would he. " Forgive us our trespasses as WE forgive those who trespass against us! Church, I'm not perfect and tonight I have something's to confess and some things I have to forgive in others. If you have some of those things in your life please come pray with me!" Jacob stepped down from the stage and knelt at the steps of the altar. Kayla sighed

in her seat, it was gonna be ok, it really was gonna be ok. He was gonna forgive her! He practically did already! The pianist began to play a quiet lullaby and a few people went to the altar and a few shuffled out. Kayla had never seen this side of her father, it was God, he had answered her prayers. She let go of Keith's hand and walked up to the altar. She stood a few feet behind her father still nervous that it was a show. That it was someone else he had to forgive. She stood there behind him as he sat up and opened his eyes. He could feel someone behind him, close behind him. He turned to look and there she was, his baby girl who looked so much more like his late wife every day. He didn't know what say!
"Daddy?" She said in a hesitant voice! "I'm sorry!" The words came out as a whisper.
"No!" He reached his arms out for her to come to him for her to hug him. "No it was my fault! I never should have tried to make you get married."
"No, I ran, I did wrong!"
"We both did!" He looked into her eyes. "Forgive me?"
"Forgive me?" She replied as she nodded her head yes. Jacob hugged his Daughter again, he had a lot of hugs to make up for.
"Dad?" Kayla said as they embraced.
"Yeah?"
"We need to talk!" He pulled away from the hug and looked in his daughters eyes. They told a multitude of stories in their silence.
"Ok, Give me a minuet." Jacob stood up and ended the service for the few left in the congregation. He prayed and dismissed the service. Finally alone with just her father, the man she loves, the man who saved her life and the little boy who told her the truth, she sat down and told her father what he needed to hear.
"He raped me!" She didn't know how else to start.
"Who?"
"Devin!….. You were right, I didn't know him!" Kayla

studied the burgundy carpet as she spoke. "He told me I was defiled, that you'd never want me after what he did."
"Kayla!, Honey!"
"No dad please just let me get this out!"
"Alright!" Keith sat next to Kayla on the pew.
Jacob sat on the pew in front of them turned around in the seat facing them. Colin and Josh remained in the back of the church to give them space.
"So I stayed. He made me do horrible things, made me sell pieces of me to men I didn't even know. I wanted so badly to be back with you having to marry someone I didn't know, atleast it would have been just one man I didn't know taking my soul away!..... I ....I was pregnant the day he beat me up and dropped me on your front door." She took a deep breath and looked in her fathers eyes. He was taken aback, he was disgusted with himself for turning her away.
"I'm ...So sorry Kayla I....."
"Dad please, I'm not done." Jacob wasn't sure how much more there could be. This was awful enough but he silenced himself and listened. " When I was in the hospital I got to see him, Kaleb, your grandson...well I had to go to jail for atleast fourty eight hours ....I was almost out, a few more hours and I would have been free..." Kayla was having trouble telling this now. She was letting tears flow freely down her cheeks but her breaths were unsteady from her nerves and the pain the memories stirred. " They stole me. They took Kaleb from me!..... They killed him!"
"Who?"
"Ask Josh!" She said. It was all she could get out, she leaned into Keith and he held her.
"Josh!" Jacob called. "Come here!" Jacob was fighting anger at this point, at himself, at these people who hurt his baby girl.

//

Devin was becoming impatient in the hall. The ficas tree was tickling his cheeks and poking his eyes. He could hear

voices still but not once had anyone come into the hall to use the restroom. He snuck from behind the tree to the door way leading into the sanctuary. Slowly he turned the knob and inched the door just enough to see through the crack. All of them were sitting together.
He could see Kayla resting her head on the sholder of Keith, it disgusted him. He decided to go to plan B. One by one each of the things he had picked up from the gas station appeared in his head and he knew what he was going to do. He came up with a devious plan. If he couldn't have Kayla then no one could! He creped back down the hall and out the door. The car was gone but all the supplies were left on the grass, apparently the guard had too much time think. Doesn't matter Devin thought, I've got what I need. Devin picked up the matches and put them in his pocket.

TWENTY-ONE

"Are you sure!" Jacob interjected as Josh described once again the horrible events of the night Kaleb was murdered.
"Yes! I was there, we have Kaleb in the car!"
"What?"
"Yes Jacob! The boy's story does add up. We have the baby." Colin said. Jacob was silent as all this information sunk in. He was a grandfather. His grandson, was not only dead but murdered by a man he knew and trusted!

//

Devin picked up the gas can and began to drizzle some all over the back door. He was lenient with it for now since he only had half a can. He contined to drizzle as he walked around the side. As he neared the front he paused, looking around the corner for cars or stragglers talking in the parking lot. It was clear so he continued his plan. As he got to the steps he was more liberal with the gas pouring it in sloshes on the steps and over the front door. Once again he went around the other side and drizzled a bit here and there along the sides of the building. When the can was empty he ran back to the front and pulled the matches out of his pocket. Only for a second did he hesitate. Only for a second did he think this might be wrong… only for a second. His anger compelled him. The thought of Kayla with that man teased his mind and he lit the match tossing it onto the front steps. He watched as the gasoline ignited and the front door caught on fire.

//

Oren flew to Kayla's side, one Angel covered the cross and others flew to the sides of Keith, Colin, Josh and Jacob. Their mission was to protect them.

The battle began in the realm. Angels flew sword first into the Fallen Ones. Their glory blinding them and giving the Host's the advantage of the Almighty on their side.

From the ground dark forces filed in and breathed on the flames accelerating them with their sulfurous breath. Sparks flew as swords hit, flashes of light came from all over the realm as the Demons were sliced in half and exited the realm.

//

Devin ran around back and barricaded the door with the trash can. He tossed a lit match into it and it ignited. The fire from the trash can caught the back door on fire as the gasoline felt the pressure of the flames. A Demon blew on the can and door accelerating the action only for a second before a Host sliced off his head. The wood along the foundation had been weakened from termites and the holes let in enough air for the wood to drink in the flames.

//

The door ignited into flames as the group talked. It was quickly engulfed. The stained glass windows didn't open and each had atleast a ten foot drop. Everyone's adrenaline rushed through their veins. They all were filled with fear as they ran to the back door, and they watched in horror as it too was engulfed in orange flames. The gasoline drank up the flames and ignited fast all along the sides of the church. Each window and wall leading to the outside was covered in orange flames. "Bathrooms!" Kayla called out. "Exhaust fans!" Everyone ran into the ladies room. The fan was pulling up the smoke and for now at least they could breathe. The Angel's surrounded the bathroom spreading out their sets of wings. Each Angel alternated between their sets of wings pushing the smoke and fire away with the force of the flapping. One angel pushed the air with the top set of wings, the one next to him pushed with the bottom and then they switched providing a consistent flow of air pushing away the smoke and flames. The resting wings controlled the heat of the walls preventing them from igniting.

"Keith do you have your cell?"

“Yeah!” He frantically pulled it out and dialed 911.
“911 emergency how can I help you?” A woman’s voice came thru the speaker.
“ We’re stuck in a church that’s on fire!”
“What church sir?”
“Um.. Kayla what church is this?” He said. She took the phone from him.
“Were at Walkerton community church at 189 main street!”
“Ok mam rescue squads and fire department are alerted and on their way. Where in the building are you.”
“We’re in the bathroom where the only exhaust fan is. The flames are surrounding us.”
“How many people are inside?” The woman asked clearly and calmly.
“Five!”
“Adult’s?”
“One child!” Kayla responded.
“Ok do you have a jacket or top layer of clothing?”
“Um, I do!” Anyone else?” She looked at the group for a second only to realize they hadn’t heard the question. She focused her attention again on the 911 operator.
“Ok mam take off that layer and soak it in the sink.”
“Ok hold on!” Kayla handed the phone to Keith and took off her over shirt. She tossed it in the sink and ran the water over it. Taking the phone back from Keith she informed the lady that the shirt was soaked.
“Ok mam, now I want you to breath through the shirt. The water will cut the smoke and then after a minuet, pass it along let the child breathe through it and so on. Instead each person took off their suit jackets or tee shirts and each followed Kayla’s actions.
“Ok mam, you may also want to wet down any exposed skin, arms legs and hair, anything that will catch fire quickly” She did as she was told and the group followed her lead. Everyone looked like a wet rat when they were done. The sirens began to sound down the road and were getting closer.

"I hear the sirens!" Kayla said.
"Good. Stay on the line with me until they find you!"
"Ok!" Silence filled the room as everyone waited to hear the rescue crew break through. They listened for what seemed like forever and finally they began to hear footsteps and voices over walkie's.
"I hear them!" She shouted taking the shirt away from her mouth.
"Ok tell me how to get to where you are from the front of the church!"
"To the right at the front is a door. We're in the first doorway on the left once you're in the hallway!"
"Ok remain on the line I will inform the fireman!" They listened and heard the footsteps coming closer. Everyone began shouting.
"WERE IN HERE! HELP! IN HERE!"
"We hear them!" Kayla said to the operator. Keith watched as his love handled the situation with grace and dripping wet hair. He loved her!
"When you see them mam you can hang up!"
"Ok" They waited

//

The battle continued to rage. Angel feathers fell to the ground, pieces of Demons flashed out of the realm as they were separated from the Fallen Ones bodies. Host's departed into glory as they were sliced by the swords of the Fallen but by leaps and bounds the Host's were winning. Every second thousands of flashes shone all over the realm as Demons departed and were defeated in their mission of taking this daughter of man with them.

Inside the church the Angels still surrounded the bathroom, accomplished in holding off the flames and smoke from those inside. Faster, their wings went faster now but never out of rhythm with the next, constant and unwavering in their quest! Top wing, bottom wing, and top again they went.

//

Kayla could hear the footsteps coming closer. The whoosh of the breathing fireman's mask was becoming clear as well. "Were here! She called out.
"HHHHEEEELLLPPP! Josh called out as loud as his little body would let him. He missed his mom so bad and just wanted to hug her right now. Three times the fireman banged on the door and then warned them to get back. Within seconds the door was kicked in and a fireman rushed to their side. All held their shirts over their faces and had water still dripping from their hair. They followed the fireman's lead out of the building. They stepped over and jumped through walls of fire. Above them the roof crackled and dropped ash. The walls around them raged with flames and the floor beneath was weakening. They were all coughing now as the smoke filtered through the shirts but they were nearing the exit. A loud crack sounded above them and a rafter fell from the ceiling at an angle in front of the doorway. It was burning red hot, the fireman ran to it. He knew time was running out, the roof was unstable and any minuet it could cave in on them. He pulled on the rafter with all his might to no avail. Quickly he retrieved his walkie and called for backup. Two fireman arrived at the door and started pushing as the other pulled. Slowly inch by inch it began to budge from its wedged state angled over the exit. Oren and three other Hosts' flew to the rafter and pulled. It fell flat on the ground now and the group could jump over it. The steps were still intact for escape since they were made of cement and not wood. Josh went first as the fireman lifted him over the rafter and onto the steps. Down he ran to safety. Kayla next jumped over followed by Keith, Colin, Jacob and then finally the fireman. Everyone's out he radioed and the effort to put out the fire began. Water hoses turned to full blast and showers of water fell onto the flames. Keith ran to Kayla and scooped her up in his arms. "Oooh I love you!" He said as he let out a deep sigh of relief.

"I love you too!" She hugged him back just as deeply. Josh went to Kayla's side and hugged her leg. Each was covered in in ash but they had made it, once again they had made it.

TWENTY-TWO

Devin watched from the woods. He could see just barely as the five exited the church. He cursed. All five had made it and now Kayla and that man were hugging….deeply. He wrapped his arms all the way around her and pulled her close. He cursed again. He still had the twine and he twisted it in his fingers. He followed the woods to the edge as far as it would go. He figured there was about a twenty yard dash between him and Kayla. He surveyed the area, fireman were paying attention to the fire, rescue teams were assessing the little boy and Pastor for injury and Keith who had released his grip on Kayla was talking with Colin. Now or never he thought as he charged from the woods. He had the twine pulled in a straight line between his hands, he paced the distance beautifully and resisted the urge to scream like an Indian warrior. Before she knew what was happening a rope was flung over her head and pulled at her neck. It was taking her breath away and she couldn't scream. He pulled her with the rope towards the woods, all he had to do was get her there and she was his once again. Kayla reached for the rope at her neck trying to pull it away but she couldn't. Oren flew to her side and put his hand in between the rope and her neck. She could breathe now a little. "Host's!" He shouted. "Get their attention!" All in unison they called out.

"Keith!" They shouted breaking the barrier between the realms. Keith heard a strange echo of his name and turned around. It felt like slow motion as he saw his love being pulled away and as he reacted running in her direction. Colin saw it too now and ran to her as well, followed by Jacob and a fireman. "Let her go!" They called. Devin pulled harder but Kayla had found a new strength and she pulled against him more and though it choked her she refused to go with him. She would never be his slave again.

"No!" He said through gritted teeth. "Your mine!" Keith was gaining on them, Devin tried to pull faster but Kayla became

like a pillar. Oren flew in the opposite direction pulling the rope away from her neck. Devin didn't understand why he was loosing grip. Finally when Keith was seconds away from them he let the rope go and ran into the woods. Keith went to Kayla's side and Colin ran after Devin, determined not to let him get away!
"Baby!" Keith held her once again. Not one of them believing this whole night. It had to be a nightmare.
"Don't let me go!" She said desperate for the security of his embrace. "Please!"
"I won't!.... I won't!" He said.
"Mam?" An EMT asked from behind them.
"Yeah?" She said as she still held onto Keith for dear life.
"Are you ok?"
"Yeah!"
"Are you dizzy? Can you swallow or do you feel like your throat is swollen?" Kayla released her death grip on Keith and he followed her lead. She felt her neck and took a few deep breath's followed by a swallow.
Um,... I'm fine! He wasn't holding the rope that tight"
"Alright! But the next day or so if you feel dizzy or out of the ordinary please go and see a Doctor!"
"I'm sure he'll make me if I need to go!" She smiled up at Keith.
"I sure will!" He looked back down at her leaning in for a kiss. She was beautiful. Ash all in her hair and smudged into her face. She was all he needed he knew it. He pulled away from their kiss and took her face in his hands. "I love you Kayla Marie Holmes... Will you marry me?" He looked in her eyes, she felt the blush run into her cheeks as she heard the question over and over in her head. She looked at him, ash falling out of his hair and smudge marks on his face, his strong arms that had saved her more than once. He was all she ever dreamed of.
"Yes! Yes! I'll be your wife!" They kissed deeply and from all around them clap's and cheer's sounded. Kayla vaguely heard

them, she was engulfed by the roller coaster of emotion's she had been put through today. Fear, happiness, horror, courage and now finally this one. The best feeling she ever felt! Surrender. It wasn't how she had planned it to be but it was everything she had ever hoped for. They pulled out of their kiss and looked at each other once again. Kayla's cheeks filled with blush again, he could look right through her into her soul. Keith slid his hand down her arm and grabbed her hand.
"Common, let's go talk to your Dad! I need his permission you know!"
"Ooh old fashioned!" She said giggling alittle.
"Very!" He replied.
"Good!

//

Leaves brushed Colin's face as he chased Devin. As hard as he tried to push the branches and brush away the dark defeated him by hiding another. He could feel his face bleeding as the warm blood trickled down his cheeks cooled by the night air. Darkness seeped into the tree's and the spaces between them, Colin ran after Devin following only sound. The leaves crunching under Devin's feet gave him his map guiding him ever closer to his prey. He knew at any moment a root or stump could be lurking in the darkness awaiting his demise and the end of this chase. Just as he was thinking it he hard Devin yell and then a thud. He tried to slow down but as he did he found out what Devin had screamed about. His right foot mid swing caught on a root and he toppled onto Devin. Oren sent warriors to Colin's aid. In order to keep Kayla safe Devin needed to be detained. Before he knew what hit him Colin felt a punch to his face and it flung his head to his right side. Instinctively he balled up a fist and punched back. Devin lifted up his right leg and pushed it hard against the ground giving him leverage to roll. Suddenly Colin was the one on the ground. His face took two more punches until he grabbed both of Devin's wrists. He tried to flip him off of him but Devin had the advantage of gravity working on his side. Colin however had an ever stronger force on his. Devin pushed against Colin's grip, his hold made his hands immobile. Devin got on the balls of his feet and put all his weight on Colin's arms, they were giving into the weight but Laurence flew into the space between them. He held Devin's wrist the same way as Colin, Devin felt Colin's grip almost double and before he knew it he was on the ground again, face down. Colin's knee was in his shoulder blades and his wrist's felt the cold of handcuffs. He tried to push up but he was immobilized by Colin's knee. Once he was cuffed he pulled Devin up to his feet and pushed him along back out of the woods.

//

Jacob had his arms crossed over his chest as Kayla walked over to him with her fiancé in hand. Before they even had the chance to say anything Jacob piped up. "Now you know I'll have to hear the story of how you two met before I give my blessing!" He started to crack a smile. Kayla threw her arms around his neck!

"Thank you!" Jacob hugged his all grown up little girl and all his anger with her was gone by the grace of God. All the horrible thought's he had towards her faded away like paper in a flame.

"I never gave you a chance! I never had faith in how I raised you!"

"Daddy!"

"I'm sorry!" He said hugging her alittle tighter and then releasing her. "Now tell me about this man you have chosen!"

"Dad! This is Keith!" They played through the introduction a second time.

"Hello sir!" Keith held out his hand and Jacob took the offer.

"Thank you for taking care of my little girl!"

"No problem!" They smiled at one another and then at Kayla who was beaming. She never thought all the ugly in her life would turn out so beautifully. That all the bad things could have set her up and put her on this road to happiness.

//

Colin finally emerged from the last bit of foliage and into the open. Both he and Devin were covered in dirt, cuts and some emerging bruises, but Devin was in custody! Kayla didn't understand why but sympathy washed over her. As they came closer she could see his face and she truly felt sorry for him. She watched as they came closer and then as they passed.

"Wait!" She called after them. They stopped and she ran up to them. Colin held tightly to the cuffs as he paused.

"Thank you!" She said as she looked at Devin. He was flabbergasted, what could she have to thank him for? "You hurt me, gave me life, then stole it. You beat me and then threw me out like the evening trash, but you set me up on the road to find my life, my love, my best friend's memory and my son who I can now bury! Only my God could turn all you did into something beautiful, one day I hope you can learn to know him!" She almost walked away but she quickly tuned back around. "Oh and just so you'll never wonder, I do forgive you!" She looked at him one second longer and then turned to walk away.

"Did you say you found our son?"

"Yeah! Josh saved him from being cremated! He buried him for me, for us, and his name is Kaleb!" Silence filled the distance between them and Colin pushed him foreward again towards the cop car. All these things ran through his head as he was put in the backseat. She forgive's me! My son, his name is Kaleb. She forgive's me, how? She should hate me! She should want me dead! Who is this God she serves, how does he work? The door slammed shut and suddenly he was alone with all these questions, with all these things he needed to say. He banged his head against the window trying to get attention. He had to tell her something. His head hit the cold glass and it ached but he needed to talk to her one more time! Finally the officer Colin had assigned Devin to got into the

front seat.
"Hey! Can I talk to her one more time please?"
"Who?"
"Kayla!"
"Hold on!" He huffed stepping back out of the car and calling her over. "Make it quick!" He said sticking his head in the car again and looking at Devin. Kayla came and she sat backwards in the front seat. She viewed Devin through the steel mesh in between them.
"What is it?"
"I wanted to tell you something! He… he looked like you. Ive been haunted by him ever since I watched him be taken out of you. Ever since I didn't hear him cry. Ever since I couldn't fix what I did! I murdered our son and I'm sorry!" He looked down in his shame and Kayla was silent for a moment. Hearing it from him made it more real than Josh telling it, made it more real than finding Kaleb. He really did do what Josh had said he had done to her and Kaleb, but once again she found it somewhere deep in soul.
"I … I still forgive you!" She met his gaze as he looked up. "And thank you!" She said as she stepped out of the car and went to her fiancé's side ready to start her new life.

Colin let the officer on duty take Devin to town and he decided it was time now to go home to his bride. To hug her and give their kids a kiss goodnight. He took the box holding Kaleb out of his trunk and gave it to Kayla.
"Thanks Colin! Youv'e been wonderful!"
"No problem but I'm going home now to my wife who is probably worried sick!"
"Good idea!"

The fire was dwindling down and Kaleb was safe in the trunk of Jacob's car after a few sob's and I'm sorry's. Jacob was sure that if it wasn't for him Kaleb would be here but Kayla was coming to understand there's a reason for everything. That God can turn around all the ugly, all the consequences of people's free will on others and make it

beautiful. Something was wrong however. Kayla felt like something was missing. The fire trucks were being packed up, the ambulance's were gone and so was.... "JOSH!" Kayla blurted out. She hadn't seen him in awhile. "Has anyone seen Josh?" They all looked around the scene, nothing.
"No!" They responded. No one had seen him in atleast an hour.
"Where would he go?"
"Where did you last see him?"
"With the EMT'S" Keith piped in. They were all frantic once again on the roller coaster of emotion the night had put them on.
"Home!" Kayla said. "He kept saying he missed his mom in the car! He went home!"
"Well let's go! I'm not going home till I know he's safe!"
"Ok wait a sec." Kayla ran over to the fire truck and informed the fireman of the lost boy. The fireman responded without delay. He got on his cb radio.
"Dispatch... come in"
"This is dispatch go ahead!"
"This is fire Chief Nelson we have a missing child report!"
"Go ahead!"
"Name..." He paused and looked at Kayla.
"Joshua Westbrooke."
"Joshua westbrooke!... Age..."
"Ten or eleven I think!" Kayla said.
"Nine to twelve range!.... Eye and hair color,
"Brown!"
"Brown,...height, weight?"
"Um...." Kayla held her hand to the level where he would stand. "Maybe four eleven?" She said. "About eighty pounds."
"Average height and weight!" The fireman called into the speaker.
"Police will be notified, Ten Four!" The dispatcher called through the box.

"Ten Four!" He said. "Is there anywhere you think he may have gone?"
"Home!"
"Ok well have a police car head out there do you know the address?"
"No but it's the Westbrooke funeral home!"
"Easy enough head over there!"
"Ok!" She ran to the car along with Jacob and Keith. Within seconds they were on the road.

//

The last of the Demons retreated back into the abyss they came out of. They went cursing at the Host's as they did, wallowing in their defeat.
"Praise the Almighty!" An Angel said raising his sword high above him towards the sky!
"Praise the Almighty!" Resounded all across they sky as each Angel took place in the praise. The Fallen One's blocked their ears as they descended quicker and quicker into the darkness beneath the earth. Oren shouted praise once more and then blew the rams horn four times. A signal of victory to the Host's. They had won their battle and Kayla was the Lord's. Burst's of light shone all across the realm as the Angel's returned to the places they had come from, awaiting another battle, awaiting to once again defend his name!

TWENTY-THREE

The house seemed quiet enough. Only a few lights were on. Kayla walked up the drive and pressed the doorbell. No answer. She knocked loudly three times. Nothing. Finally she tried the knob. It turned easily and opened. "Hello?" She called out. "Mrs. Westbrooke?" No answer came. From the other room she could hear sobbing. A child sobbing. Josh's sobbing. She followed it through the house and into the master bedroom. She flicked on the light and she wished she hadn't. The sight made her stomach twist into knots and her breathing cease for at least five seconds. "Oh God!" She said in a loud whisper. Joshua lay next to his mother's dead body. She was bruised around the neck and she layed limp with her Bible on her chest. Like she was laid that way by her assailant. Josh had his face pushed into her side and his arm wrapped around her midsection. He sobbed and breathed in gasps as his little body shook. Kayla remembered feeling that same way the day her mother was buried, when she threw herself onto the casket and begged them not to kill her.

"Use the past Kayla!" Oren spoke to her. "Use your experiences to help him!" She went to his side and lay next to him. Maybe this was another way God could use her. She could help him because she knew exactly what it was like, what he felt she had gone through. She put her body right up against his and her arm around him. She hummed a random tune, she remembered it was all she wanted after her mother died, to be held and comforted but then Granny died too and she had no one to fill that desire of warmth! Of safety. She felt like she could at least try to be that for Josh.

"Kayla!" A voice called from down the hall.

"In here!" She called still not moving an inch away from him. Keith rounded the corner and came into the doorway. Like Kayla he froze. The site was horrible and filled with sadness.

"Call the police again, let them know we found him and….!" Kayla whispered. "His Mom!"

“NNNOOOOO!” Josh held tighter to his mother’s frame. “They’ll take her away!” Kayla didn’t say another word she just nodded in Keith’s direction he understood her, someone had to call the police, he didn’t know why they weren’t there already. Kayla remained at Joshua’s side, he was to a point now that he couldn’t cry anymore he just shook and breathed in air in quick gasp’s. She hated this for him but she was doing all that she knew how to and he seemed to accept it, to want her to hold him. To make up for the warmth that was missing in his mother’s body!

Keith and Jacob had taken seats in the living room. The sirens began to become audible. Closer and closer they came until they were right outside and there was a knock at the door. The flashing blue and red lights could be seen through the windows and they cast prisms of dancing light all over the walls. Jacob let the officer’s in and they started their investigation. First thing’s first they needed to see the body and that meant removing Joshua from it. Kayla stood up and tried to pry him away from his mother’s side. He held on tightly, he was moving her from the position she was laid in. Kayla knew she needed to remain the way she was for investigation but she didn’t know what else to do, he wouldn’t let go.

“Josh honey… you have to let go!”

“NO! I WON’T!”

“Sweetie! They need to see your mommy you have to let go, come here I’ll hold you!” He fought only a few more minuets and then he let Kayla pick him up. He wrapped his arms around her neck and his legs around her torso each with a death grip. This was so much for him, she thought. First what he saw happen to her then the fire now his mom’s gone. *oh lord please show me what to do, show me how to help him.* She prayed in her head as she walked out of the room. She sat on a couch in the living room and rocked from side to side as Joshua let himself fall into sleep. There was chaos all around them. A police photographer snapped photo’s of the wall that she had been slammed into and of the other item's that seemed strewn out of place. Other's dusted for fingerprints and other's prepared the body to be moved to the medical examiner's office.

Not long after Josh fell asleep a woman walked into the house. She reeked of drama. She had the typical suit and pumps on that you'd see on any working woman in the city. Her hair was cut at her jawine and fell in straight lines, all perfect. She was at a glance an A type personality. "Hello?" She said from about ten feet and closing. "I'm Nancy Drake!" She went right up to Kayla's side and sat on the couch next to her. "Is this the child in question?"

"This is Joshua and he is fine!"

"Well that's my job honey! I'm with the department of social services, I understand you aren't a relative!"

"No mam, we are friend's of the family, they attended our church!"

"Oh! Well that's nice! Have any of his family member's been notified?"

"Not yet mam!" Kayla was irritated by her. She was pushy and nosy.

"Well you do know they have a right to request custody!"

"Yes mam I'm just here right now to help him! He wanted me here!"

"As I can see! His affection for you is obvious! Will you remain here on the premises until tomorrow?"

"We can!"

"I would like you to. Tomorrow I will meet you here to discuss the child's future!"

"Alright! Tomorrow we can discuss Joshua's future" Kayla was irritated by her uncaring business like nature. Joshua wasn't someone's property he was a child, someone, a person.

After a few more hours the crowd's cleared out and everyone settled in for sleep. They found blanket's in the hall closet and they each took a piece of furniture and turned it into a bed. Around three am Kayla began to hear a whisper.

“Hey” it called. She listened “Hey!” There it went again.
“Yeah?” She called back in a whisper.
“It’s me! Keith!”
“What is it?”
“Come here!”
“Ok!” She slunk along the floor and went to his side sitting on the carpet. “What is it?” They continued to whisper.
“I want Josh!”
“What?”
“I want to adopt him!”
“Really!”
“Yeah!”
“Good! Me too!”
“Ok it’s settled then if his family doesn’t claim him he’s our son!”
“Yeah! It’s settled.”
“Ok! Goodnight!”
“Goodnight!” She crawled back to her spot and tried to go back to sleep. Dreams of fire filled her mind. They separated her from Mrs. Westbrooke. She didn’t know why but visions of how she might have died filled her mind. The day had taken a lot out of her but she just couldn’t sleep. The street lamps cast only a dim light into the house. She had to find a bathroom but she didn’t want to wake anyone. She felt along the wall feeling for a molding or a doorknob. She felt picture frames and open wall but no doors. At at the end of the hall she felt a door and pushed it open. It definitely wasn’t a bathroom. In the corner’s of the hallways in front of her were dim security light’s. One hall went straight ahead and one went parallel. This is the funeral home, she thought. She had never been here before, atleast not when she was awake but for some reason these hall’s felt familiar. These creepy hall’s felt like some kind of dejavu. She stepped over the threshold and followed instinct. Apparently her instinct knew where it was. As she followed the dimly lit hallway to the right she began to hear audio memories. “Go left at the end of the hall!”

A man's voice said in a loud whisper. She did. There was something strangely familiar about the smell of this place, was she dreaming? "Next door on the right!" There it was again a man's voice that sounded extremely familiar.

Joshua sat up on the couch. He heard Keith's snoring but he didn't see or feel Kayla next to him. He could see the dim light filtering in from down the hall, he followed it.

Kayla placed her hand on the knob and hesitated, why was this place so familiar? She took a deep breath and let it out slowly as she turned the knob.

"That's the room!" A voice came from behind her. She jumped around and saw the boy. Joshua had followed her.

"Oh Josh you scared me!"

"Sorry! I saw the light from the hallway, you left the door open."

"I was looking for the bathroom!"

"Well your way off!" He said.

"Oh"

"Go in! I'll show you!" She wasn't sure she wanted to but she opened the door and she stepped in. The voices continued in her mind. The room was tiled on the floor. Simple white tile. Along the wall to her right was a long counter top made of green marble that held a large stainless steel sink. Above and below the counter top was a long row of cabinet's. Directly to her left was the cabinet Joshua must have been hiding in. In the middle of the room was a stainless steel slab on top of a wooden base, next to it sat a stainless steel surgical tray. The room was clean and smelled like a Doctor's office. "Over there!" She heard the voice call out.

"On the table!" It said. Kayla walked over to the table and ran her fingers along the steel.

"That's where they put you!" Josh said. The voices continued.

"She's waking up Doctor!"

"I'll handle it!" Another voice called out and then they stopped altogether. She must have been waking up that whole time.

“That’s where they took him out of you!” Josh said.
“Josh!” She walked over to him. “You shouldn’t have seen all that!… But you are so brave to have come and told me!”
“I know!” He said with as much asureity as a boy who just lost his mother could have. Kayla looked around the room and imagined what it must have looked like, three grown men standing over her violating her rights as a human, violating the rights of her son to be safe and grow inside her. How much pain did they inflict on him as they punctured his skull and his brain. It made her sick! How could…. No! She decided. She wasn’t going to let it get to her, She was going to move on; to live the life God had blessed her with. To marry Keith and raise Josh, if the state let her and to go on each day one breath at a time. “Ok little man where’s the bathroom?”
“Follow me!” He ran out of the room and down the hall.

//

Oren assigned Laurence to Joshua. He would now be his guard. Joshua’s battle was just beginning. A legion of dark forces would be trying to attack his unstable heart and soul. The Fallen Ones love to prey on the weak and the venerable. Keith and Kayla would be the key to his healing. The initial battle had been waged and won but countless battles were still in the cards. Everyday the Lord of the Fallen looks for a slot, a way into the life of each child of man. Lurking, seeking whose open, who’s unguarded and free for him to devour.

//

No one could sleep now. Kayla and Josh getting back under the cover’s on the couch woke up Keith and soon after the whispering between the three woke up Jacob. Everyone took turns showering and changing.

The meeting with Nancy went favorable. The family wasn’t responding to her phone calls and for now Kayla was a good placement for Joshua, Nancy agreed. He was stable and seemed to be comfortable with her. Nancy recommended

Kayla for temporary guardianship as long as she remained in town. Josh moved in with Jacob and Kayla, wile Keith took up temporary residence at Colin's. Kayla gave Josh her old room and she slept in the study on a blow up mattress. She didn't mind, she got to keep Josh at least a little longer. She knew she could help him. Somehow she could use her past and all her pain to help this child with his.

TWENTY-FOUR

The memory of this place hadn't changed a bit since she was little. Everything still seemed black and white. Even the sky seemed to be tinted a shade of gray. The crowd today was much smaller than the one she remembered from her mother's funeral, it's strange, she thought, how vivid the memories of that day were still in her mind. She could remember looking down at her shoe's and could even remember the pattern that was on her white leotards. The emotions even were as strong as they were then. She really thought they were going to bury her mom alive. She didn't understand death then and now she wished she didn't.

Kaleb's tiny casket sat above the hole dug for him right next to her mom's grave. There was a spot for her father on the other side, and one for her and all of her family in this graveyard owned by the church, by her father. The tiny cherry wood box was covered in white carnations and yellow gerber daisies. Her emotion's rose in her throat and tears in her eyes. She knew that only Kaleb's body lay in the box and his soul was with God but she still wanted her son to be alive and in her arm's. As the final prayer was said and everyone started back to their car's Kayla got a vision of Kaleb in heaven. He had probably met her mom and Granny and one day they would have a family reunion on the streets of gold. It made her soul quiet and her emotion's settle some. Somehow it made it better to think that they would be taking care of him in her absence.

Jenn and Pastor Blake had arrived from Rosewood this morning just before the service. She was surprised to see them, Keith hadn't told her they were coming. She was grateful and needed all the support and friendship she could find right now.

The quarter sandwiches and cheese cubes were all laid out. The veggie tray and dip were set up on the table. Keith stood in the corner with Jacob and Pastor Blake talking about who know's what. People went around the table with the small paper plates picking little pieces of the appetizer's and Kayla sat with Jenn. The next few days would be rough. Kayla had to help plan the funeral for Josh's mother and see if the court would let him see his father. She doubted they would because of the testimony Josh would need to give in court against him, but she thought it would help them both to talk to one another. Josh still didn't know that his father had confessed to the muder of his mom, Kayla didn't know how to tell him. She figured it would be best to maybe let Mr. Westbrooke confess it in person. Truthfully in a situation like this she didn't know what was best. She had heard that Mr. Westbrooke was pleading insanity instead of guilty in the case of the murder and that complicated things even more. She didn't know what kind of judge would let a child into jail to see his insane father. Still she felt like it would help Josh to see him, if not now than someday in the future. Her only fear was that by then, all the feelings would fester and seep deep down inside to places forgivness could only find with the help of God.

Keith could see his future now. He knew what his plan was and that he was ready for it. He waived Jenn over from where she sat next to Kayla and filled her in on the plan. He and Jacob had been discussing the future of the church. Jacob wasn't sure he wanted to continue being Pastor. He needed time to find himself again. To find God and get to know him in a way he hadn't in the past. The way he should have all along. Keith saw an opportunity. To build a church and a youth center behind it. To move here, to marry his beautiful fiancé and to raise the child God had blessed them with. The plan was to call back home and get the realtor to put Keith's home in Rosewood up for sale. Keith and Jacob would be going around town trying to find a house here, one Kayla would love. Jacob knew from things she said growing up what kind of things she wanted in her future home. Things like a window seat where she could read. A large bathroom with a tub where she could take bubble baths. Jenn was on waiting duty. The next few days. She needed to be ready to take Kayla out and find her a dress. To get her hair done in a "practice" run for the wedding and then to bring her to the instructed place all dressed up and ready for the biggest surprize ever. Keith told Kayla that he was going to sell the house and that he just wanted to marry her so they had planned to go to the magistrate in the next week or so as soon as they had a plan they both agreed to. They were both ready to be together. To be married and live under the same roof and to adopt Josh. As far as Kayla knew Keith was planning to find an apartment, Keith could hardly keep quiet with his secret, he wanted to make her happy and he knew a surprize like this would be the best thing to do it. He could tell she was sad about having to marry at the magistrate's office. She had always dreamed of a real wedding day and he was gonna give her one.

//

Keith needed to find his mom. He needed to get a birth certificate and quick. He knew she must have one. The car sat parked in front of the Walkerton minimal assistance home and Keith sat inside. What would he say to her? After all she had done with Brooke and now with Kayla. He didn't know if she just didn't want him to be happy or if she was trying to get back at him for not coming home after boarding school. Well... he thought, I'm about to find out.

The place smelled of food, medicine and bleach. He hated the way these places smelled and he wondered why she had moved in here to begin with. He walked up to the desk and rang the bell for service as instructed by the sign.

"Can I help you son?" A woman in all white nursing attire came up behind him.

"Um, I'm looking for my mom!"

"What's her name?"

"Alice Cartwright?" A moments pause fell between them.

"I'm sorry did you say Alice Cartwright?" The woman looked

confused.
"Yes?" Keith looked at her strangely.
"Um…. Let me get her for you?" The woman went down the hall. Keith was really confused. Why had the nurse acted that way? Didn't they know she had a son? Didn't she get visitors? A few minuet's passed and the nurse returned to Keith's side. "Please come with me!" She said. He followed her down the hall and into Alice's room. She stood in the middle of the room and watched as her son walked in. Her son. Her son was here to see her. Silence filled the air between them as the nurse stepped out and shut the door. She had given up on ever seeing him. Given up on trying to mend things with her only living relative and now he stood before her and maybe just maybe she wouldn't die holding onto her secrets. Her reasons why she did what she did to Brooke and ultimately her son.
"Mom!" Keith said in a low tone.
"Keith!" She answered loudly. "You… yo.."
"I came to see you!" She was speechless. "We need to talk!" He went over to the chair she had by the window and sat down. He didn't face her he just talked. "I need to know why!…. Why you did all this. Why Brooke?,…. Why Kayla?…. Or is it me? Do you not want me to be happy?….." There he had said it but silence still filled the room. Alice went to the closet and pulled out her box. The box that held all the thing's she made for her dead grandson. The one she mourned in secret for the past year and lied about to all her friends. She walked over to Keith and handed him the box.
"I just didn't know what to do! You wouldn't come home."
"What!?"
"You wouldn't come home, you were all I had left and you wouldn't come home! Brooke was…. Well I didn't know that you were with Brooke till it was too late. I didn't know I was gonna have a grandson till I tried to come see you and you were burying the both of them!"
"Then why! Why her?" He yelled not understanding why his mom would have anything to do with Brooke if it wasn't

because of him and their relationship.
"I ....can't....I"
"and Kayla mom? Why her too!"
"She's a prostitute son!"
"She was forced to be a prostitute! What she is, is a wonderful woman!" Keith said with force in his voice.
"I thought you deserved better!"
"Like boarding school?"
"Exactly!" She said with every ounce of herself.
" Do you know how bad I just wanted to be here with you? With Dad! To have family dinners and to play board games. To have YOU!!! Help me with my homework and not some stranger who was paid to help me!" Keith looked down at the box and all that was in it.
"I'm....I'm sorry!" Alice sat on her bed and looked at the floor. "I made all the wrong choices and all wanted was the best for you!"
"Why didn't you just ask me what I wanted?" Keith struck a chord inside of Alice. She didn't realize all this time that she should have. She never, not once had asked her son what he had wanted, but how could she have let him come home from that school when so much was going on? How could she have explained it all to him, how could she explain it all now? She thought.
"Ok fine! What do you want son?" She said genuinely. Why was he here? Why did he come? Today...At all? She wondered.
"I want to know where I can get my birth certificate so I can marry my fiancé!"
"Fiancé?" She questioned.
"Yes mom. I'm marrying Kayla!" She didn't know what to say. Instead she grabbed her keys and instructed Keith to follow her.

The ride to the bank was quiet, neither knowing what to say or how to express what they had felt the last twenty years or so. The bitterness they felt or the remorse. Alice never wanted to hurt Keith she had wanted a better life for him. It's what she thought she was giving him by sending him away. She pondered on that thought as she drove. Keith sat next to her in the passenger seat and wondered why even after boarding school was done she had to mess with his life and in the aftermath make him loose more of the things he loved. He tried to focus on what good had come out of loosing Brooke and his son but today more than yesterday it hurt to think of her. To think of what might have been, to think of ….. He didn't want to think about it because of Kayla. Because he loved her and what was in store for them. Still, losing Brooke and Kaleb had taken part of his soul it seemed.

Walkerton bank and trust was quiet today as the two were

Shone down the hall. In a small room with just a table and chair's inside it an associate went and pulled her deposit box and laid it in front of her on the table and stepped out. Inside was Keith's birth certificate and a copy of his social security card along with other papers and document's Alice had put away for safe keeping. She handed Keith his birth certificate and social security card. "I wish I could do more for you! I'm sorry I ruined your life!" She said.

"Mom!" Keith said. He didn't want her sympathy.

"I can give you some money for the wedding?"

"No! It's all covered!…. Look why don't you….. Come." Keith looked down at the table. If he was going to live here so close to this woman he knew as his mother then they needed to mend things.

"Can I?"

" I want you to! Come to my wedding, accept Kayla as my wife and your daughter in law!" He looked at his mom and turned to her, facing her in his seat. He took both of her hands in his and waited for her response. Alice pondered what that would mean. That she would have to get over all that Kayla had done. All that Jacob had told her about what Kayla had done to him and how she slept around. To accept all her baggage. Accept that she was going to have a baby, and that Devin had stolen that baby from her. That she was damaged and that her son loved her anyway. Accept that one day she would have to tell her son her secret. Alice was damaged herself, she knew she was but she could do this! She could have a daughter in law, and a son for the first time in her life. She could ponder about it a wile longer and figure out a way to tell her son her most sacred secret, the one that might turn him away again.

" I will!" She said and silence filled the room as they looked at each other wondering if this really could be possible. Could he and his mother get along?

"One more thing..."

"Ok!"

"Can you show me where Dad is buried?" Her mouth dropped she knew if she did that secret would have to come out sooner than later. Like today!

//

Keith's home had been on the eyes of a few couples in Rosewood Falls. The couple's had lived in rentals and apartment's the past few years and were ready to settle into a home, their own home. Within a week of the for sale sign going up two bidder's had called the realtor and were ready to view the property and hopefully settle.

In Walkerton the house Keith had his eyes on was a hundred and fourteen thousand, he needed at least that in an offer before he would sell. Both couple's were competing against each other. Starting at the asking price and moving up. The realtor kept Keith in the know as they battled.

Pastor Blake went home to pack up the house. The Thomas' and a few other families in the church were by his side loading up the moving van, and were ready and willing to help unpack it in Walkerton. They loved Keith as did their children but they understood that he felt a calling leading him away. They understood that the Lord has other plans for people than the one's they make for themselves sometimes.

//

Kayla went through the remnants of her things at her father's house. They were all in same places as the day she left. Clothes she had forgotten she had, jewelry, stuffed animals. All the things she walked away from waited right here for her to come and claim. Mr. Rumples the stuffed bull dog she loved as a child still lay on her pillow and the only picture she had of her mom was still hidden under her mattress. Her father hadn't wanted to see any of her pictures after she passed so she had to hide one. She didn't want to forget what she looked like. This picture was her favorite, it had her, her mom and Granny in it. She was just a toddler in the picture. She wore a puffy white lace dress and carried a parasol to match. Her mom and Granny wore the same classy blue silk blouse. Granny leaned in next to Kayla on her left and her mom leaned in on her right as she sat on the photographer's carpeted table. How she wished they were here to see her get married, even if it was only at the magistrate's, She thought.

Josh sat quietly at the end of the bed hugging a pillow. Kayla felt so sad for him. All he had done for her and now she didn't know how to help him. She knew in a few hours they would be going to the Johnson funeral home where they would be planning his mother's funeral. She wanted to make him smile to help him go into his future with hope! "Hey munchkin?.... Wanna go get some ice cream?"
"No!" He said still looking down at the floor and hugging the pillow at his chest. Kayla walked over to him and gently pulled the pillow away from him as she squatted to his eye level.
" Hey!..." She said in a low tone. " Come here!" He went into her arms and she hugged him tightly. " I know it's hard! I know!" She patted his back and looked up at the ceiling, at God and mouthed what am I supposed to do. She hoped her silent prayer would be answered. She wanted to... needed

to.... help this child desperately!
"The last time I saw her alive was the night I snuck away to find you. She was asleep and I kissed her goodbye!" Josh said as tears fell effortlessly from the inner corners of his eyes.
"She knew you loved her honey! She knew!" Kayla didn't know what else to say.

//

The graveyard was quiet. The sun warmed Keith's back as he followed his mom to the place his father was laid to rest. Birds chirped in the trees that formed a semicircle around the back of the graveyard and clouds passed by the sun blocking it's light for a few seconds and then letting it shine freely again. About ten rows into the graves his mom stopped and placed half of the flowers in her hand on a gravestone. It read, Michael Allen Summers, Beloved Husband and Father to my sons. Next to his stone marker was another with the name Summers on it. Sean Michael Summers. This stone only had one date on it. Keith glanced at both gravestones. First at his fathers making sure that he really did see a plural in the word sons. He had. Once again he looked over at the next stone, Sean Michael Summers. Slowly he let the idea sink in, a brother? Do I have a brother?

Alice still held half of the bouquet in her arms as she looked down at the second gravestone. "The same accident that took your father stole him too!" She didn't look at Keith as she said it or after she just placed the rest of the flowers on the grave and stared down at it. Silence filled the place, even the birds seemed to quiet as he heard what she said repete in his head a few times. "We had gone to a Christmas party at the Easton's. We were the first ones there and we could hear yelling and all this commotion from behind the door. Your dad knocked but no one came and the commotion we heard just kept getting louder. He opened the door.... It was unlocked. He followed the noise up the stairs and I foolishly at eight months pregnant followed him. We were gonna surprise you and bring you home after Sean was born." She changed the subject momentarily and looked at him. "I'm sorry!"…… Keith had no idea what to say and so Alice looked back at the headstone and continued her story. "Behind the second door down the upstairs hall was Mr. Easton beating his wife wile Brooke watched from a scared crumpled ball in the corner. "Jack!" your Dad called out to him. "Stop" He charged in and tried to pull him off of her. It fired back on him, Jack lunged at him sending him back out of the room's doorway and tossing him into me. I…. wasn't strong enough to stop him. We both fell into the hand rails and then through them as they cracked into pieces behind us. We were airborne and back onto the first floor before we could blink." Keith couldn't believe what he was hearing! "He would have lived if he hadn't of landed on the fireplace tools…. They went through him and punctured his organs. He was bleeding to death and they couldn't stop it. They couldn't stop it….. When they arrived he was already gone….And Sean, your brother, he didn't survive the impact of the fall! I tried to turn over in mid fall but I couldn't, I landed right on him, right on my stomach!" Tears started to fall down her cheeks now. She knew this would be the hardest part to admit, the hardest thing to tell her son. "I …. Wanted revenge. I wasn't strong enough to file charges and put him in jail! They, Jack and his wife, just reported that it was an accident. I was too shaken up to talk." Alice was silent for a moment and then she turned to look at Keith. "She watched as my husband and son died!… Years later when I heard that she was sending Brooke away I searched, I found out where she was and I told him. I told Jack,… that abusive sorry excuse of a man where she was! I didn't know! I didn't know she would be involed with you, that I would hurt my son, the only one I had left! I didn't make the connection, you were in Rosewood Falls and so was she, I was just blinded by my need for revenge!" Once again the word run repeated itself in Keith's head and his vision tunneled showing him the way to act on that word. Showing him what way to go. Instead he froze. He didn't move or blink. How could she? How could she care that little about someone else whether they were involved with him or not? How deep must her hatred be? To want revenge that bad for her to have helped an innocent person to suffer? To die? The look of disgust came over his face, how could she have wanted the little girl that was crumpled in a ball scared to death in the corner the night her husband died to suffer? Didn't she think that child suffered enough at the hand of the same man who killed the one's she was missing? Keith's mind raced with these thoughts. How could she have wanted another to die in vein? Finally without a word he turned and walked away! Alice fell to her knees in between her husband and son's grave's. Her actions had taken her only living relative away from her again.

//

"Joshua can you tell me what some of your mom's favorite things were?" The associate from the funeral home was trying to get some ideas for the casket and her ceremony. He knew it was going to be mostly planned by him and Kayla but he needed some insight as to how she would have wanted things. Joshua just shrugged his shoulders and looked down. This was so hard for him, Marge's mom was in a nursing home a few towns over and she couldn't make it to help or even be at the service. Marge was her only child and she didn't have her till late in life so she had no one else to come and help plan this, it was all left in Kayla's hands and she barely knew the woman.

"Hey!" Kayla whispered to the man. "Write down what you need to know and I can ask him in here alone, I think that will work better!"

"Ok" The man agreed and wrote down a list of questions then he stepped out. Kayla read over the list. She whished she could just answer them for him. That she could look into his brain and read the answers.

"Come here!" She held her arms out and he ran into them.

How could these people expect this child to do this? "I love you munchkin!" She squeezed him.
"I can't!"
"Ok! You don't have to!" She would figure this out somehow.

//

Keith leaned against the car and crossed his right leg over his left at the ankle. His arms were crossed over his chest and he stared at the gravel. Studying the little rocks and gray colored stones as he let all the information he was just fed sink in. He remembered the day the principle of the boarding school came and told him that his father passed away. The halls echoed as he spoke with his deep raspy voice. "He was in an accident son!" The sound of his voice reverberated over the tiles of the hallway and over and over in Keith's mind now. He was buried before Keith even knew about his death, he had forgotten about how much resentment he had towards her for not allowing him to say goodbye or be at the funeral. Now he knew why. She wasn't just burying his father; she was burying a son too. A brother he never knew he had. A sibling he had always wanted buried next to his father who died trying to save another. Trying to save the mother of the woman he would one day love. The mother of a woman who would one day carry his child, a woman who would die in vein, just like his father and his brother did! Kayla, what about her? He loved her, everything about her. Was Brooke's death really in vein or did she now understand that God's plan needed him to be free for her? She needed to heal and find God too, now that she was in heaven he wondered if God explained it all to her, or if she even knew what was going on down here? How could he know till he joined her? How could he do anything but see Kayla as a blessing? She made him face all his fears and all his Demon's. Everything they had been through together and everything that was ahead of him was a blessing. A church where he could build a youth center, a little boy to raise as his own and a woman who truly loved him. Maybe it all wasn't planned. Maybe it wasn't all in his plan to happen this way but he turned it all into something good. Maybe it was the choices all the people in the mix of this situation made that turned it into what it was today and God just took all the bad and found a way to fix it for his children. For him so he could be happy and have a purpose once again. For Kayla, so she would know what true love was and come into his plan once again and for Josh, so he could have a family.

Alice stood from her knees and walked over to the car, then around it and into it without a word. All her secrets and all her Demons were now out in the open and in the hands of the only person who could truly hurt her with them. To turn her away once again and disown her would be death to her heart, so she waited for the man who held her very heart in his hands to tell her his verdict.

//

Jenn went with Kayla to the Westbrooke's home wile Jacob watched Josh. " I just don't know what to do Jenn, he is so quiet and lifeless. I want to help him but don't know how?"

"You are helping him! Just being there is helping. I mean that's what me and Keith did when Brooke died. We leaned on each other, given it took Keith a lot longer to heal but he never let it all out till he met you! You helped him a lot you know?"

" Yeah I guess!" Kayla mumbled.

"No! There's no guess about it! He would still be in Rosewood denying her death and keeping that room shut up hoping they would walk through the door one day! Hoping to avoid his own house and dreams at all costs!"

"You think I helped him that much?"

"Absolutely! You know, I was mad about it at first, I wanted to help him but he needed you, just like Josh does. When he is ready to talk or cry or anything he will come to you, you just need to be there!" Jenn said.

“ I hope so…and I hope it’s not a year from now either!”
“I don’t think it will be, little boys aren’t as stubborn as their grown up counter versions!”
“We’ll see!” Kayla pulled into the driveway. She had given Jenn a copy of the list and they hoped there were some clues around the house that would give a hint to who this woman was and what she liked or didn’t! The list had things like favorite color, song and or scripture. Religious affiliation, dressing and hairstyle preferences. Kayla figured they needed a good picture then they can go with the outfit she wore in the picture, if they could find it and the hairstyle she wore as well. Joshua had taken her bible as a keepsake so she imagined the woman was of the Christian faith and well if they couldn’t find a cross stitched pillow with a scripture or song verse on it then they would just go with amazing grace and the verse in Corinthians saying oh death where is your victory.

//

Keith still leaned against the side of the car. He didn’t know how he was supposed to respond to this. Should he be angry that she never told him of the accident that killed his father and his brother that he never knew of? Or, should he be understanding that maybe it all would have been too much for his young mind to understand. Was it actually her doing better by him, by not telling him, by not bringing him home to a vengeful mother filled with anger and hate? Keith thought for a moment more and then he dug in his pocket for his cell phone. He needed Kayla right now. Quickly he dialed the seven numbers and waited for her to pick up.

//

The quick dings and chimes sounded. Kayla ran to her purse that she had laid on the couch. It rang again as she picked it up and found the green answer button. “Hello?” She answered.
“Baby?”

"Hey!"
"I need you!" Keith said in a monotone voice.
"Ok! What's going on?"
"Can you come get me at the Walkerton memorial cemetery?"
"Sure! Are you ok?" Concern filled her voice now.
"I'm fine! I just need you; I have to talk to someone that I can trust."
"Ok but Jenn is with me?"
"Good! Bring her too!"
"Were on our way babe!" Kayla hung up the phone and got Jenn up to speed as she ran out the door with Jenn now on her heels.

//

Kayla was nine minutes away at regular speed, however she made it in about four. She found Keith in his regular pose leaned up against a car with one leg crossed over the other at the ankle and arms crossed over his chest. He looked distraught and angry. She pulled her car up behind the vehicle he was leaning on and put it in park quickly unbuckling and jumping out as she did. "What's going on?" She called out as she ran to his side. He scooped her up in his arms without an answer. He let out a deep breath that he felt like he had been holding in for days and embraced her more tightly! Jenn came up behind them and stood back, allowing them space.
" I needed you!" Keith said into her neck.
"I'm here!.... I'm here!.... What's going on?" She pulled from his hold and looked into his eyes.
"Walk with me?"
"Ok?" Still confused she took his hand and followed his lead up the rows of graves and past headstone after headstone until he stopped in the middle of two with names Summers on them. Jenn let them go alone. She got back in the car and waited for them, just as Alice did. Alice wanted to pull out and squeal tires to make a scene but she didn't want to loose her son... again! Kayla read the inscriptions and looked over to

Keith. “I don’t understand, is this your Dad?”
“My Dad and my brother?” He put a balled fist to his mouth as he said it.
“Brother?”
“I…. didn’t know!” Kayla read the stones inscriptions again and realized the date of the father’s death was the only date on the child’s marker. They must have died together.
“What happened?”
“Brooke’s Dad killed them!!”
“What…. How”
“My dad tried to stop Jack from beating on his wife and he knocked my dad and mom over the second floor railing in their house. My mom was pregnant with him.” He pointed to Sean’s grave. “My Dad was killed by the fireplace tools impaling him and Sean died because of the impact of the fall.”
“Why didn’t he go to jail?” Kayla squatted down by the graves.
“My Mom didn’t, or couldn’t talk. She was shaken up and the Easton’s lied to the police.” Kayla was exasperated by the news. How everyone was all tangled up in this web. Everyone seemed to have apart in how or why people were dead.
“Kayla?”
“Yeah?” She looked up at him from her squatting position over the graves.
“She’s why!”
“Who? Why what?” Kayla stood up and placed a hand on Keith’s back.
“Why Brooke’s dead!….. My mom told Jack where she was!” Kayla’s mind took a moment for that to sink in, her best friend was dead because of the mother of the man she loved, but the man she loved was her’s because her best friend was dead! A web of death and deciet formed into the path of her finding her true love. She didn’t know how she should feel. “I don’t know how to feel, baby!” Keith said.
“Me neither!” She put her arms around his neck and tried to understand what he might be feeling. He just found out so

much. How his Father died, that he had a brother and that his Mom is the reason why his fiancé died, the reason he doesn't have a son. "All I know is that I am glad I have you!" She spoke in low sad tone hoping he still felt the same.
"I am too!" He put his arms around her and held her close, truly he was glad to have her. Glad that God had given him a second chance at love when the world took his first away. "I don't know what to do about my Mom!" He pulled her away from him and looked at her.
"Do what the Lord would! The one who lives inside of you, the one you lead me too!"
"Mmmmm!" He nodded at her and gently kissed her lips.
"Walk with me… I have someone to introduce you to!"

TWENTY-FIVE

The van was all packed up. Boxes of Keith's belonging's and his furniture were all ready to travel over the state line to its new home. One box sat next to Pastor on the passenger side seat floor. He didn't know if Keith was ready but since he wasn't going to be around anymore he needed to give it to him and let him decide if he was ready to see what was inside. Mr. Thomas was in the passenger seat hoping this little gesture could thank Keith for all he did for him.

//

All kinds of phone calls and faxes were going on between Keith and the realtor. He was trying desperately to get the money transfer from the sale in Rosewood so he could buy the house for him and his bride. So he could marry her and surprise her with the wedding of her dreams.

The final offer on his house was three thousand over the amount he needed to get the house here in Walkerton, three thousand would cover so much for the wedding. The tent and the lights and the food. All he needed was a dance floor and a magistrate to meet them there. Right now he needed to be there for his son. In an hour Josh would be burying his mom and he knew that strong brave little boy would need him there. He drove over and met his bride to be and his son and they were on their way.

The casket was closed per Kayla's request. She didn't think that Josh could handle it if he saw her lying there. She knew she wouldn't have been able to if she had seen her Mom dead in the casket when she was a child. A song was sung and the staff Pastor said a few words. Then the group of ten or so people were led by police car to the burial site. Another prayer and a few words later Josh let out the loudest cry. Through tears he screamed " Noooooo I don't want her to die!" Kayla remembered that feeling. The one that made her plunge herself onto the casket of her Mom as they lowered it into the earth. Kayla pulled him close to her even though he fought it she knew that's what he needed. Just like she did, she wanted in that moment to be scooped up by Granny and held till the pain was gone so she gave Josh what she never had a chance to receive. Granny died to quickly after her Mom passed to give her any of the love she needed, she just hoped she could give Josh what he needed.

The drone of the machine motor echoed as they lowered her into the earth and Kayla continued to hold tightly to Josh until he finally gave up into her embrace and she lifted him up into her lap. The few people that attended her funeral began to file out as Kayla remained in her metal fold up chair and held onto that little boy for dear life. Keith put an arm around Kayla's back and one around Josh. How were they gonna help this child? He wondered, knowing that the sooner he could get the house and the wedding set up the sooner they could try. The sooner they could make everything feel like a real family for him.

//

"Colin?" Keith said into the receiver.

"This is?"

"Hey it's Keith!"

"What's up?"

" I need your help, I need to know how I can get a magistrate to come out to a wedding site!"

"A magistrate?"

" Yeah see here's the thing, I'm going to surprize Kayla with a wedding so therefore we can't go and get our wedding license because she is expecting to get married at the office when we go!"

"Oh quite the romantic aren't we!"

"I just want her to be happy!"

"Ok well you'll need to first have a copy of both of your birth certificates and I think since the magistrate is a friend of mine that he'll make a house call."

"Really? Awesome!"

"Yeah but there's one condition!"
"What?"
"I have to be invited!"
"Of course!" Keith answered.
"Ok when is the date!"
"Um I'm not sure yet, I am waiting fot the final paperwork on the house."
"You've been a busy guy!"
"Yeah I am just ready to start our life together and with Josh."
"Ok well I'll give the magistrate a heads up and then you need to let me know the minuet you decide on a date and time!"
"I will! Thanks!"

//

Jacob rummaged through his closet searching for the box that Anna, his bride had put away with all of important paperwork in it. She had been so organized and he had just continued all these years to pile things in this space. He had pulled all of the boxes off of the shelves on the left side of the closet already and now was starting on the right side. As he pulled down the next box he felt his heart melt a little. The box was labeled simply, *HER*. He had put all of her favorite belongings in here along with her pictures the week after her funeral. He couldn't bear to look at them then. He wondered if even now he was ready to see her once again but he was going to find out. Relinquishing his search only for a few minutes he walked over to his bed with the box and started to pull at the tape the separated him from all he had left of her. It began to come off in little pieces and strips until finally he was able to get a big enough piece to pull all the way across. There it was, the only thing that separated him from his beautiful Anna's memory was pulled free.

Inside the first thing that his eyes went to was the picture of her he had placed on top, the one of her on their wedding day. He picked it up and ran his hand over the glass. "How

ashamed of me you would be!" He said. "You'd be proud our baby though! She's grown to into quite a woman, without any of my help!"
"Daddy?" A voice came from behind Jacob from his doorway.
"Kayla?" He looked up into his doorway.
"What are you doing?"
"Come here! You should see these things too!" Kayla sat on the edge of the bed and looked through the things with her father. Things he had kept hidden for all these years were bringing them closer. She loved learning about her Mom and who she was. Looking through her old yearbooks and photograph's filled her mind with pleasant memories and hopes.
"Here!" Jacob handed Kayla a small blue velvet box.
"What is it?"
"It was her's! She wore it on our wedding day! If you want you can wear them on your's!" She opened the box to reveal a delicate tear drop pearl set of earrings.
"Oh wow! Dad really? Can I have them?"
"Their yours, She would have wanted you to have them!"
"Even though I'm only getting married at the magistrate's office!"
"Even though!" He smiled her. If only she knew, he thought.

//

Everyone had turned in for the night. Josh had been sleeping in Kayla's old room and Kayla had resigned herself to a blowup mattress in the study. For now she sat in the old wingback chair even though she was exhausted sleep just wouldn't come yet. She was so amazed at what her life had become. At how this web that was weaved by Satan to be something awful had turned all around somehow by the grace of God and made good. Kayla looked around the room thinking she might turn in when something caught her eye. It was her old diary sitting on the second shelf of the bookcase in the corner. She remembered it well. Its teal silk cover and the pink embroidered flowers weaved into it. Quickly she retrieved it from the shelf and sat back down. She flipped through and memories leaped from the pages. A day with Granny and Mom she had written about, a day she had a tea party with Polka, Granny's cat and so many other's she had jotted down with bad handwriting and spelling. A few pages remained in the back and she snatched up a pen from the nearby desk.

Dear Diary,
It's been quite awhile since I last wrote. So long I fear that these few pages will not be enough to fill you in on the memories and horror's that have come and become my history so I will start with now. As of now I just buried my son Kaleb. Kaleb Lee Holmes. He was stolen from me. Taken out of my unwilling body by his father and then a miracle named Joshua hid him for me and risked his life to tell me where he was. I will always be amazed at his courage and bravery to do what is right at all costs.

I miss Kaleb and long to hear his cry so I can run to him and comfort him. I still long to hold him and feel him nursing at my chest knowing he is growing strong from something only I could give him. At night my dreams are of him. My fingers long to tickle his tummy and my eyes to see his smile. It seems every part of me somehow misses him. Every ounce of me loved him as he was being formed inside me by the hands of God and every ounce waits for the day those hands that formed him, hand him over to me in heaven. Even though I know Kaleb was gone way before his funeral it was at that moment I truly let go. At that moment my heart released Kaleb into the hands of God and laid his mortal shell inside the ground. Though I will always miss him today I choose to live. Today I choose to start. Today I choose God and all the plans he has for me! Sincerely,
Kayla Marie Holmes!

THE END

About the Author

Dianna Dixon was born in Massachusetts but spent most of her childhood along the coastline of the Carolina's where she still lives with her husband and son. Since she was a teen she has loved the written word and writing. Some of her poetry is published under her maiden name of Lowe on poetry.com and she continues to have a passion for searching the word of God for secrets to the mysteries of the supernatural. Keep looking for more thrilling novels to come!